SPIRITS IN THE DARK

ALSO BY H. NIGEL THOMAS

NOVELS

Behind the Face of Winter
Return to Arcadia
No Safeguards
Fate's Instruments
Easily Fooled

STORIES

How Loud Can the Village Cock Crow?
Lives: Whole & Otherwise
When the Bottom Falls Out and Other Stories

POETRY

Moving Through Darkness
The Voyage

LITERARY CRITICISM

*From Folklore to Fiction: Folk Heroes and
Rituals in the Black American Novel*
*Why We Write: Conversations with
African Canadian Poets and Novelists*

SPIRITS
in the
DARK

A NOVEL

H. Nigel Thomas

WITH AN INTRODUCTION BY KAIE KELLOUGH

ESPLANADE BOOKS

THE FICTION IMPRINT AT VÉHICULE PRESS

ESPLANADE BOOKS IS THE FICTION IMPRINT AT VÉHICULE PRESS

Published with the generous assistance of the Canada Council for the Arts, the Canada Book Fund of the Department of Canadian Heritage, and the Société de développement des entreprises culturelles du Québec (SODEC).

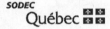

Canada Council   Conseil des arts
for the Arts   du Canada

Esplanade Books editor: Dimitri Nasrallah
Cover design: David Drummond
Typeset in Minion and MrsEaves
Printed by Marquis Printing Inc.

LIBRARY AND ARCHIVES CANADA CATALOGUING IN PUBLICATION

Title: Spirits in the dark : a novel / H. Nigel Thomas.
Names: Thomas, H. Nigel, 1947- author.
Description: 30th anniversary edition.
Identifiers: Canadiana 2023045822X | ISBN 9781550656336 (softcover)
Classification: LCC PS8589.H4578 S65 2023 | DDC C813/.54—dc23

Published by Véhicule Press, Montréal, Québec, Canada

Distribution in Canada by LitDistCo
www.litdistco.ca

Distributed in the U.S. by Independent Publishers Group
ipgbook.com

Printed in Canada on FSC*certified paper.

CONTENTS

7

The Voyage to the Other Side
A note of gratitude for the work of H. Nigel Thomas
Kaie Kellough

13
Spirits in the Dark

317
Afterword

The Voyage to the Other Side

A note of gratitude for the work of H. Nigel Thomas

I RAN INTO THE EDITOR of Esplanade Books, Dimitri Nasrallah, in Guadalajara late in 2022. We were both in the city for literary events related to the Feria Internacional del Libro de Guadalajara, and we found some time to share an espresso. Our conversation turned to books and music and quickly arrived at *Spirits in the Dark*. We both expressed strong appreciation of the book and agreed that it deserves a renewed reception. This moment may be good for a reintroduction, given the changing politics of the literary arts and the current interest in re-evaluating novels that break traditional form in order to tailor themselves to their subject and their unique cultural milieu.

Spirits in the Dark is an ambitious debut novel that borrows from several different genres. Part bildungsroman, one in which a young man's sexuality is of central concern, the novel draws upon Caribbean realism to present a portrait of urban and rural society on a fictional Caribbean island, Isabella Island. It also operates as a political novel by exposing the social and economic conditions that limit the lives of those on the island. At the same time, it focuses on the prejudices held by the islanders, examines the limited choices available to the central character, and connects those limitations to region, race, and sexuality. In addition, *Spirits* is a story of spiritual progress and, through that progress, of Afro-diasporic dislocation and attempts at reconnection.

The first half of the work is driven by realism and sharp humour, and it recalls the style of early works by Samuel Selvon and V.S. Naipaul. In this first section, Thomas's writing is nimble, and it deftly recreates scenes of life at school, in the country, and in the city. Characters are clearly delineated, and the story is animated by boyish insouciance. The first half also introduces us to the tensions and limitations that will later come to circumscribe the central character's life, and this is partly what makes the novel so successful. Just as the character reaches an age where we expect his life and opportunities to expand, they narrow, and he must exist within that narrowed scope for the rest of the novel. He must find his freedom and live his life within that narrowing.

Within that narrowing, right where characters' aspirations exceed their circumstances, we encounter an unforgiving humour. The writing targets minute details, like a broken zipper or a scuffed shoe, and amplifies them into larger humiliations. These details undercut pretense, and the humor to which they give rise is not gratuitous. It is a product of social circumstances, and it points to the cruelty to which we are all vulnerable in moments of aspiration or effort. It illustrates the smallness of our victories and the fragility of our hopes.

But if the first half of the novel moves like a flight, with wit and velocity, the second half slows to a pace that I can only describe as rooted or grounded. The humour dissolves, the pace slows, and yet, in this second half, the story achieves

8

spiritual elevation. One of the dominant themes is the need for a spiritual life. The central character, Jerome, who has been struggling with his sexuality, gradually comes to understand that if he remains on the island, he will never live publicly as a gay man without being subject to mockery, violence, and severely restricted opportunities. His agonizing choice is between a fugitive life or a life of enforced sexual suppression.

This question of how to exist is tied to spirituality, which is linked to history and ancestry. In order to be able to exist, to endure, Jerome must be able to commune with something that exceeds his daily life. He must understand why he is on the island, how he arrived, and where he comes from. He joins a religious sect, under the guidance of a gentle man named Pointer Francis. In his initiation, he enters the "mourning cave," for an extended period of isolation and meditation, away from the demands of the world. As Jerome progresses in his meditation, his suffering deepens, and yet he must persevere. He must see the spiritual journey through to its end. We realize that the character's gruelling progress is an echo of that earlier passage across from Africa to the Caribbean, and that if he is to know himself and find spiritual grounding in the world, he will have to complete the passage.

The way the book slows down as its subject shifts from coming of age to confronting life on the historical and spiritual levels, while still dwelling in the present, mirrors the sudden and brutal closing in of Jerome's horizons, and yet it reminds us that we are all, at some point, forced to confront who we are and to reckon with the life we are living.

Dimitri and I discussed the novel's spiritual power over the espresso at the bar in Guadalajara, and I reiterated that I would like to write this preface both as a reader and admirer of *Spirits in the Dark* and also as a friend of the author, who has been supportive of my writing and of the writing of other Black poets and novelists in Montreal. We are fortunate to have a writer of Nigel's stature in our community. We are fortunate to have encountered a writer of Nigel's experience, technical ability, and sensitivity, and we should all be grateful that he has given us *Spirits in the Dark*.

Kaie Kellough
Guadalajara, Mexico
December 2022

1

ON THURSDAY MORNING, just as the mountaintops began to be tinged with gold, he entered the consultation room of the mourning house. Pointer Francis was waiting for him, seated on one of the two basalt blocks that were the only furniture in the room.

Pointer Francis told him that the purpose of the journey was to get to know himself and renew himself and come out a different person. "No light going be in the cave. No vision must come from outside. All yo sight must turn inward, on yo soul. In the upcoming days, you going to discover yo strong points and yo weak points. You will meet a lot o stumbling block and you and you alone going ha to decide what to do bout them. If they don release you after you take different kinds o action, and you feel you not able to handle the situation anymo, all you ha for do is knock with the cane above yo head. I, or, if I ha to go on some emergency, Deputy Pointer Andro will come down right away and bring you up to the Sacred Room, if it call for, and let you cool out. But, before you do that, remember that life is trials and tribulations and that you down there to prove you can handle them. In the mourning cave, you going be practising how to overcome tribulations that powerful, so that them you meet in life going be easy fo handle. Remember that patience and common sense is always helpful."

Pointer Francis handed him the long black towel that had been resting on his lap and the long cane that had been lying on the ground beside him. "When you have to go to the kitchen or the toilet, this cane going be yo guide. I telling you again, while you making yo journey, no earthly light must interfere with the light in yo soul. That light in yo soul have to grow and keep on growing. Which is the same thing as saying more and more darkness will leave yo soul. So you must use this cloth to cover yo head and yo eyes every time you come up from the cave. Fold the cloth in three and bring it down almost past yo nose and tie it so that it won't come loose. I will practise with you a little bit before we go down and on yo own.

"A bed down there, but the first night you must not sleep on it. The reason for this is that you must love the earth. You must believe it good and helpful, a living thing with feelings. You must see and like it like yo own mother, and you must see it like God, and you must see yourself as a part of it. White people call it dirt. And they think it filthy. But for we it sacred cause it is what we make from and it is what keep we alive. So you will have for sleep at least one night on it, the way children lie down in the womb o their mother. Of course, if you want, you can sleep on it for the entire journey. But you can also use the bed.

"While the journey going on, you won't be able to bathe. Is a way of getting you to accept yourself in different ways. But each day you will get a fresh gown to put on. When you go down you will meet one on the bed down there. You will

14

change into it and give me yo clothes to bring back up. And every morning when you go to the toilet, you will meet the clean one hanging there. Take off the dirty one and hang it up where you take the clean one from.

"Since you cleaning out yo soul, it is a good thing for you to eat less. Mother Biddows and the others will come and cook for you three times a day. It up to you how much you eat. If you having hard visions that leaving you weak, it will be a good idea for keep yo strength up. But, if you have to fast for bring on the spirit, eat as little as possible. Drink a lot o water, beginning today. You will find a fresh goblet down there already, and every morning I will leave one next to the dais. When you take that one you must leave the empty goblet where you take the full one from.

"We can't risk you going outside on yo own, so you must use the pail in the toilet. If after I show you how to get around, you still not able for find the right door, just knock on any door three times like if you counting, and I or Deputy Pointer Andro will come and lead you to where you want to go and carry you back.

"Every once in a while, I will come down and check on you to see what progress you making. If you is in the middle o yo visions, I won't disturb you, and if you really in deep, you won't even hear when I come. And, if you find you making good progress—I will tell you if you is and I will tell you if you is not—you can come up to the sacred room and relax a little, as long as you keep the blindfold on."

They spent half an hour practising with the blindfold and the cane, following which he could find the doors to all three rooms, even without the cane, and could tie the blindfold so that no light entered. Then Pointer Francis stood beside the dais, slid it to one side, mounted the single step, and told him to follow. When they were on the steps leading down to the inside of the cave, Pointer Francis slid the dais back into place. "Don't forget to close it every time you go in and out. Come try it." He pushed it, and the dais moved easily.

The cave was dark. It felt like a weight upon him, and with each footstep, he felt as if he were stepping off into space.

Pointer Francis showed him where the bed was and then led him in the opposite direction, where there were two stone stools. Pointer Francis sat on one and he sat on the other. They sat there quietly for about half an hour.

"Anything else you want to know?" Pointer Francis asked him.

"No," he said, though he should have said yes. But the only way you knew what was at the other end of the road was to travel the road.

A short while later, he heard Pointer Francis's voice above him, now quite distorted from the effect of the cave, and he knew Pointer Francis had got up to leave. "The rest is in yo hands now. You will want to look at yo life—the mistakes you done make, and from them you will get a clearer idea o yo future. I leave you with three words that will come in useful: *I will endure*."

He heard the multiplying echoes of Pointer Francis's footsteps ascending the stairs, followed by the slide of the dais to open the entrance and the slide of the dais to close it.

Now he was on his own. He had watched when he heard the dais slide to see whether any light had entered the cave, but none had.

What next? he asked himself.

Nothing. Wait. "Meekly wait and murmur not."

Eventually he began to accept the darkness and to see the appropriateness of the whole setup. Light was only the absence of darkness and darkness the absence of light, and light was really energy, and where there was no external light energy, there had to be darkness, and if he wanted to lighten his own darkness, he had to generate his own light energy from within. This cave was exactly as his mother's womb would have been.

He spent several hours ruminating on such thoughts. He drank a few times from the goblet and gourd in the cave. He had to mount the stairs twice to get to the toilet. He had no trouble finding the toilet and using the slop pail and finding his way back into the cave again. He did not even have to use the cane: he remembered right and left turns and approximated angles. It was strictly a question of mathematics.

By what he guessed to be late evening, he began to be aware of the weight of time. He was not hungry. It was so different from the times he was in hospital.

2

THE LIBRARY WAS A small two-storey cement building rising off the weed-covered sidewalk, adjoining the abattoir that smelled of cattle dung and decaying blood. It fronted the hospital, behind which was the churning, angry, blue Atlantic. *Dragons.*

He was six then and had been to school for a year. The words *Public Library* frightened him. The woman's eyes were blue, just like the sea, her hair the colour of cane trash and her skin a little whiter than his mother's. A ray from the setting sun was on her face, showing all the tiny lines under her eyes.

"What you want, little boy?"

"A book." He stared at the ground and only half muttered the last word.

"A book? You can't even read."

"Me can read." This time he looked directly into her eyes. She was laughing, and tiny creases appeared under and outside her eyes.

"What book do you want?"

"The one bout Alibaba and the robbers them. Teacher tell we the story and me want for read it."

The woman stayed still, then told him to go home; he was

too young to join the library; he couldn't care for the books properly; when he was eight, he could come back with his mother. But he didn't move. He began to cry. She pushed him gently toward the door, but he resisted her.

After a long standoff, she walked over to one of the two bookcases that stretched all the way up to the ceiling, mounted a stool, and lifted down a huge book. Returning to her desk, which was just inside the front door, she said, "You see, you can't even carry it." She placed the book on her desk, was silent for a little while, then said, "If you come after school and during the day on Saturday, you could read in the library." She sat down. "Come and let me hear you read."

He moved toward her and stood looking at the still-closed book. She put an arm around his shoulder, took a handkerchief from her pocket, and said, "Blow." He did not even know his nose had been running. She opened the book.

He read, "'The Story of A-lad-din; or The Won-der-ful Lamp. In one of the largest and ri-rich-est ci-ties of China there once lived a poor tai-lor name Mmmus-tapa'—"

"'-Tafa,'" the woman corrected. "P-h is pronounced like *f*." She reached across her desk for a piece of paper and wrote *sulphur*. "Pronounce this."

"Sul-fa."

"You *are* a bright boy," she said, squeezing his shoulder.

"'It was only with the grea-test di-fi-cul-ty that, by his dai-ly la-bour, he was able to'"—he formed his lips cautiously, just like his teacher had told him to—"'maintain himself, his wife, and his son.' What *maintain* mean?"

"Feed them, buy clothes for them."

Maintain, maintain, he said over and over in his thoughts.

19

"*Maintain* mean the same ting as *mantain*?"

The woman—he couldn't remember when he learned the word *librarian*—laughed. "There's no such word as *mantain*. That is bad English. And you mustn't say *ting*; the proper word is *thing*." They spent the remaining ten minutes practising *th*'s.

While he walked the half mile home, he thought about bad English and good English and decided that he would speak good English, the English the librarian spoke. Not the English his mother spoke, for she said *mantain* and *ting*.

He and the librarian—her name was Millicent Logan—became good friends up to the time he was in high school, the time when she migrated to the United States. He had even taken Yaw to see her, and he hadn't thought of taking Yaw to see anyone else. For about five years after her going to the US, they had exchanged cards and notes at Christmas.

His father did not like all this reading. But his mother said it was good. "You want him for work in Mr. Manchester cane field like me and you?" she would ask his father whenever he started taking a set on him about his reading. His father would then sulk, or scratch his head, or go outside in the yard, which was what he always did when he did not have an answer. Now, if it had been Errol's stepfather, he would have slapped her. His father never understood why. But his father was always ordering his mother around... So after a while his father would say, "You and yo book them! You can't larn everything from book" or "Why the hell you don go and play with the other children?" And his mother, if she was around, would stare at his father, and he would stop talking.

And each time his father returned from the trip across "the Jordan," he would get angry with him. Only once did he say something—"All this blasted White man larning! It not everything, you know, and it not even the truth"—before returning to his angry silence, which he broke only when he wanted something done.

Sometimes his father was gone for two or three nights, and he would ask his mother where his daddy was, and she would say that adults had things to do that didn't concern little children. This was when he used to read about Jack and the Beanstalk. So he stopped asking her questions, but he still wondered about his father. Later he found out that men sometimes had several women, the one they lived with and the others where they spent their nights. But something—he did not know what—told him that his daddy lived only for him and his mother.

Slaying the dragon. Miss Gonsalves Bulldog. That was what they secretly called Miss Anderson on account of her pug nose. *She died at least twenty-five years ago.* Miss Anderson's breasts were like watermelons pushing out of her dress, the flesh from her arms hung and swayed like liquid in half-full sacks, their coal-black skin glistening from what must have been Vaseline. They called her legs mango stumps—from the calypso, "Woman, don't be a mango stump / Get up and jump! Jump! Jump!" *But Miss Anderson was too heavy to jump.* Her buttocks rippled when she walked. The flesh under her chin was like a coiled scarf. Her lips were always pouted, and she definitely had a snout, not as big as a pig's but nearly. They never said anything about her snout. A proverb said: "Pig ask he mudder why she mouth long so; he mudder answer, 'Wait, me pickney, is grow you growing; you gwine fin out when you

21

get big.'" Her hair was never any longer than a quarter of an inch and curled into little balls that resembled black pepper grains. When she straightened it and brushed it back, it looked like a husked coconut, and they said, "She got a man head."

The Bulldog came "all the way from capital, thirty very long miles," to teach them. The education officer introduced her as "a very accomplished woman who has studied overseas," and it was "from the goodness of her heart that she assented to teach you." He hoped that they "would diligently reward the assiduous and unflagging devotion with which Miss Anderson executes her task." After this speech they sang "Land of Our Birth, We Pledge to Thee."

On Tuesday morning Miss Anderson was executing, her eyes glowing and her nostrils dilating like an asthmatic cow's. She swung a thick leather strap while she blocked the front door, waiting for the late arrivals. The bell rang exactly at nine, and they quickly lined up and entered the building. While her assistant conducted prayers, Miss Anderson closed the doors and began beating the latecomers on their bare legs. It was January, and many of the students had to take their fathers' breakfasts to whichever cane fields they were working in, some of them as far away as three miles. All principals knew this and gave them an extra thirty minutes during the cane and arrowroot harvests. They tried to explain, but the blows muted their words and deafened Miss Anderson.

On Wednesday morning there were no late arrivals. Miss Anderson's nostrils flared just the same, with obvious displeasure. But the school was half empty. On Thursday she beat them for "unjustified absence."

As headmistress, Bulldog was responsible for his class,

standard seven, the cream of the school's most senior students. She taught them square roots the first thing Thursday morning. She gave them the first problem, and only Gwendolyn, Albert, Percy, and he got it right. She called the unsuccessful students to the front of the room and gave them two straps each, the boys on their buttocks, the girls on their legs. She wrote the second problem on the blackboard and then went to the office. Everyone got that one right.

She shook her head, looking a little like a pawing bull. "You all think I was born big." She gave a third problem and remained in the class. Everyone got it wrong. This time she beat them all without bothering to count the lashes. But they noticed that the blackest and smallest students got the most.

Just after she got through, they heard a loud voice saying, "Show me where the fucker is." It was a cane-cutter with bits of burnt sugar cane talks sticking out of his hedgehog hair. There were tiny runnels in the black cane dust that covered his face. He barged into the classroom. "That is the fucking bitch?" he asked the little girl accompanying him.

"Get out!" Miss Anderson ordered, her hands on her hips.

"You ever swallow yo teeth?" he asked her.

Miss Anderson was quiet and her arms were now hanging.

The cane-cutter bent down and pointed to the girl's left leg, which looked satiny and was almost twice the size of the right one. "You call this teaching?" he asked Miss Anderson, thrusting a finger in her face. "You fucking well call this teaching?"

Miss Anderson began to tremble and back away from him. "Don move!"

Miss Anderson stood still.

23

"I don ever have to beat this child. She is the obedientest child there is. You don ever put yo fucking hands on she again. If you do, so help me God, I will knock every fucking teeth outta yo head! What you trying to prove? You don know is the cane crop? You don know the children have for carry their parents' food? How the fuck you think we feed and clothes them?" He stopped and wrinkled his brow. "Ain't yo mother name Melda?"

Miss Anderson gasped. The cane-cutter laughed and shook his head. He spat on the ground in front of her.

"You is as common as dirt. You is nobody. Miss Anderson! Huh! You better find out who yo father is." He became silent, then pulled his daughter's sleeve and turned to leave. Then he stopped at the door. "I sure didn want for hurt yo feelings, but I hope you preciate that we have fo earn we living, that the children have for bring we food." He left.

Miss Anderson's assistant, Mr. Jones, took over the class for the rest of the day. But they certainly speculated about Miss Anderson after that. After that, she never flogged them for coming late.

Standard seven. Dreams started and died there. Parents began to brag when their children got to standard seven. Those who didn't get there took it for granted that they would spend their lives working in white men's fields. It was the only niche the British gave them. A few of them, if they were good Methodists or Anglicans, got hired as teaching assistants. Some got into the police force, a few into nursing school, and the best student in the class got chosen to write the scholarship exam for the Expatriates Academy, if the head teacher recommended him

24

and if he passed the standard seven exam, which was set in England and asked many questions about England. And there were few passes.

During the first week, Miss Anderson hung a poster of the royal family at the back of the class where she could stare at it constantly. There was never a singing session when they did not sing "Rule Britannia, Britannia, rule the waves, Britons never, never shall be slaves." Thursday afternoon was usually reserved for singing. A lot of it was spent learning the words to "God Save Our Gracious Queen," "Land of Hope and Glory," and "Land of Our Birth, We Pledge to Thee." *Miss Anderson definitely thought she was an Englishwoman.*

One afternoon she read to them from the history text by a fellow called Daniel how Hawkins had "cleverly" tricked Africans onto his ship, pretending to offer them food, and after he had got them drunk, sailed away with them. "British wisdom is a good thing," she added. "We should be proud to be part of the British Empire. Wherever you travel, all you have to show is a British passport and people will respect you." *Where had Miss Anderson travelled to? She was only doing the job she was paid to do and priming them for what they should write on the exam. He did not know that then. And Hawkins had never tricked anybody. That part was invented to make them think that Africans were stupid, easily outsmarted by the British. Hawkins had to bargain with African slave traders for the slaves he got. At least that's what he read in Davidson.*

"Miss Anderson, what's so clever about tricking Black people?" He asked the question thinking that his father would want him to.

"Jerome Quashee," her breasts rose and fell like the Atlantic breakers, "You outta your place. Don ask me no foolish questions. When country pickney learn for read and write them think them ka-ka smell sweet. Lord, country corbeaux love for show them feathers. Get outta this class! This very minute!" Her nostrils flared more than ever and her lungs hissed.

It was only a few years ago that he heard the story about a principal who had been dismissed and never reinstated because someone had anonymously reported that he'd said, "Every day bucket go to the well, one day the bottom will drop out." This had been in the 1950s, when there was the campaign for universal suffrage. Her reaction, he realized now, had been far more calculated than he could have ever imagined at the time.

That afternoon and for a few days afterward, over a hundred students gathered to watch Maurice do a takeoff on Miss Anderson. They clapped and laughed because, on the second day, Miss Anderson had given the school a lecture on why it was wrong to speak dialect. She had ended by saying, "Respectable people don't speak dialect." "Boy, Miss Anderson don play she respectable, no." After that they added Respectable to the names they called her.

In November, when the scholarship results were announced, Jerome Quashee was not one of the names. His parents were hurt and started asking questions, and they found out about the question he had asked Miss Anderson, and his father said he was stupid. *He couldn't tell him he had asked the question thinking his father would be proud of him.* He was twelve at the time, and his father asked his mother to buy him a hoe—but his mother had stared at his father and said, "You don think Jerome done pay enough for this?"

In January he returned to school, his short pants too tight, his voice already cracking, and discovered that he had indeed placed among the scholarship winners. But Miss Anderson had left, had been sent to a school nearer the capital. There had been four other passes in the scholarship elimination exams. Betty, whose mother was Mr. Manchester's cook, got accepted into nursing school. (She was big, with huge breasts, and was already fifteen; her mother had lied about her age when she went to school.) Maurice and Fred became police cadets and later police officers. *Fred went to England and qualified as a lawyer. Imagine. If that business with Peter had worked out, he too would have been something.* And Albert became a pupil teacher.

Mr. Edwards was the new teacher. He joked with them sometimes and used the strap only if they were rude. They asked him a lot of questions about Miss Anderson, but he only laughed. At the end of the year, Jerome got his scholarship.

"Don get no swell head now," his father said. "People begin plenty things they don finish." "Pussevere! Pussevere! You must pussevere," his mother said. "I still remember the first day you came to the library," Miss Logan said. "You is the first one from Compton for go to secondary school," his father's friend Beatty Baptiste said, "and you have for show Mr. Manchester that he can hold back some but he caan hold back all."

Many times he wondered how different his life would have been if he had been like Errol. *He did not want to think about Errol. At twelve, Errol quit school to work in the field. Years later, he loaded and unloaded a truck. That Sunday, when he came out of his haze, Errol was the first of the villagers he saw in the hospital, even before his mother. And he dreamt about him when he had his first wet dream. Peter was the only other guy that happened with.*

Errol lived in the first shack after you crossed the canal bridge. They were all squatters, living in thatched mud houses on the edge of the cane fields where most of them worked. Errol was light skinned, oval faced, and had semi-straight hair. His mother was half Indian, and his father, whom Errol did not know, was said to have been half Portuguese. From the time Errol was nine, he would interrupt school in November, when the arrowroot season started, and would come back in January. Errol was smart in mathematics and memory subjects but had trouble with composition.

At nights during the August holidays from high school that first year, he sometimes stood behind the hibiscus hedge to listen to Errol and the other boys bantering. There was an open extension to their hut, where the man who lived with Errol's mother kept his donkey. In front of it was a pile of stones where his mother bleached her clothes. Errol and his friends sat there, especially on moonlit evenings, and talked and talked. One night while he listened, Pinchman was saying, "Man, me drop me trousers and she see what curl out, and she bawl, 'Murder, haul back on yo trousers!'"

"So what you do?" Errol asked.

"Man, me hit she pon she backside, and me say, 'Shut up!' and me push she down and me open she leg and me shove it in and she double up under me."

They all laughed, even he.

"Man, you hear this guy?" Errol said. "Is only in he head he do that, you know. You just like Jerome. You don even know what woman stay like."

"I swear to God that is what happen."

"You hear how he blaspheming!" Bertie said. "And talking bout snake! All o we does bathe together naked. You forget that, Pinchman?"

"But serious now, wha wrong with Jerome?" Pinchman asked.

"He not got nothing in his trousers," Errol said. "I hear that when you read too much book, it does shrivel up and break off."

Mullet said, "Pamela say she pull him down pon she one time, and he get up and run and bawl for his mother."

A lie!

"Why Pamela don try that with me? She going keep coming back," Errol said.

"But serious, Errol, you and Jerome used for be good friends—he even used for invite you for read under his mother bed."

Loud laugher.

"Why you don't tell him that, if he don do nothing, all that water going fly up in his head?" Pinchman advised.

"Man, you don know what he doing in town. They say town girl hot, you know, man," Errol replied.

"Well, if they so hot, I sure is run. Jerome running from them cause he fraid them going burn him," Mullet added.

They talked on for hours about everything, most of it fanciful. It was that night he dreamt about Errol.

3

GOING TO HIGH SCHOOL meant that he had to live in the capital. The buses that went to town returned long before school was out. It was a distance of thirty miles, and during the rainy season mudslides sometimes blocked the road. He had been to town a few times before that. The first time must have been when he was four. His second trip was when he was seven. It was around the time that the police had come to their house to question his father about the whereabouts of Butler, a man the government wanted. Old Mr. Manchester came with the police. His father and other people said Butler was for poor people. He was fighting so that everybody, not just those who owned plenty of land, could vote. They said the government put Butler in jail, in a wet cell, because they wanted him to catch consumption and die. *Butler did not die. He became prime minister.*

When he and his mother got to town, they saw a man dressed in a gown that looked like it was made of animal hair. The man was talking to a large crowd. His mother pulled him away from the crowd, but he resisted her long enough to see the man pull at something that released a tail bearing a flyer. It read, "England, kiss this monkey's black arse." The crowd clapped. His mother pulled at him more fiercely and half dragged him away. A little way down, they met about thirty policemen heading toward the crowd with their clubs swinging. A few days later, he heard his father and the other men talking about what the police had done to Boysie. Boysie, he later found out, had been trying to organize workers' unions on the large plantations.

He thought he had seen Boysie a few years ago, dressed in the colours of the Ethiopian flag, selling African trinkets to passersby near the post office building. But that was probably another of the illusions and hallucinations he had been having off and on during the first two years of his insanity.

He boarded with an acquaintance of his father's family. Miss Dellimore was about forty-five. She lived in a three-room shack on a hill overlooking Hanovertown. Her four children lived with her. The oldest, a woman of twenty-eight, shared a bedroom with her mother. The second, Alfred, a man of twenty-five, worked sporadically on a road-mending gang. Alfred and his mother were always quarrelling. She accused him of spending "alla o yo morney pon poussey," and he countered, "You only jehlous cause no man spending nurtting pon a dustbag like you." She threatened constantly to put his clothes in the street, and he dared her to so he could knock out what remained of her teeth, but neither ever got around to carrying out the threat. He shared a bedroom with this fellow. The other two children, boys fifteen and twenty, slept on mattresses in the general room: kitchen, sitting room, storeroom, and at night, bedroom.

He paid Miss Dellimore fifty of seventy-five dollars he

received monthly, and each week, his mother sent her bags of ground provisions and baskets of fruit. But Miss Dellimore still complained. His mother would laugh and say, "Town people will dig out yo eye if you let them." Miss Dellimore always wanted to know what the neighbours were telling him and would conclude her questioning with, "I don't trust those blasted people; town people will thief bread out o them own pickney mouth."

It was a new experience. Instead of the large plains of sugar cane, sometimes green, sometimes brown, he now looked at the buildings crowded upon one another. Most times the people's faces seemed as blank as the asphalt streets on which they were standing or walking. The sea, too, was so calm, almost like water in a tub. Not like the Atlantic, where he came from—it shouted, it pounded the shore, it made you know it was there. The people here did not speak to anyone they did not know, and they didn't seem to have feelings. It was the first time he heard the expression "nothing for nothing."

He used the public library a lot and usually stayed there until it closed at eight. He did his homework there. He read books other than his textbooks and copies of *Time*, *Newsweek*, and the *Manchester Guardian* that the principal, Mr. Bunyan, loaned him. When he finished at the library, he sometimes walked to various points in town. The first night, he came upon the sidewalk beggars, not yet asleep, quarrelling with one another over their favourite politicians—their unwashed bodies and festering sores blending with the odours of stale fish and rotting fruit rinds. Occasionally he walked onto the jetty and surprised someone shitting in the sea, or he walked into the sheds where bananas were piled before being shipped to England. People made love there on the days they weren't used. He liked when he got home to find the Dellimore family asleep.

It was shortly after he moved to town that he began to think a lot about the relationships between men and women. He noticed the number of Black men in the capital who had White wives. He heard people say that all Black doctors and lawyers liked "milk in their coffee."

People told all sorts of stories about these marriages. You couldn't hang around the market women for very long without hearing one. One White woman was said to have given her husband strict orders not to talk to Black women, but she had missed a little detail: he was interested mostly in Black men. They clapped whenever they told that one.

These relationships forced him to think about the people in Compton. One night when he was seated near the lily pond in the Botanic Gardens, images of barefooted people walking on hot asphalt, the stinking beggars quarrelling with one another, naked children with snot running over their lips, women bent from too many pregnancies, men beating their women, preoccupied him. Why?

His father did not beat his mother and he brought his wages home. One time his mother worked in the fields. One day Mrs. Manchester saw her and told her a woman of her colour shouldn't be out in the sun like that and promised to take her on to nurse her daughter. His father forbade it. He heard then the story of his maternal grandmother, who used to be a housekeeper with the Montagues. Mr. Montague slept with the household help. He hired them himself and with his sexual tastes in mind. That was why his mother looked

33

almost White. Many of the children around were the sons and daughters of the White plantation owners. So his father had stopped his mother from working completely.

He had never heard his father say please to his mother. "Get me a basin o water!" "Press my blue shirt!" "Bring my dinner outside." She stopped whatever she was doing to do whatever he'd asked—whether she was kneading flour, mending a dress, or washing her feet. She said so many pleases whenever she asked him for anything and would stand there like a child expecting him to say no. When he said yes, she was full of gratitude. Sometimes he wanted to scream at her. One day he started to say to her, "Aren't you tired of being a towel for Daddy to dry his hands with?" But he thought better of it. She bragged to the neighbours that "Henry never once raise his hand for hit me." *He realized now that that was a part of his mother's strategy for handling his father. Unquestionably she was the stronger of the two—and she probably knew it, too. But he did not understand it then.*

He preferred Roly-Poly Richard. On Sundays in Compton, he used to watch him, his fat belly hanging over his trousers and his Indian hair falling onto his shoulders, rocking from side to side along the canal road, his three youngest sons, his grandson, and his wife—a fat brown-skinned woman— accompanying him. One of the boys would be carrying a pingwing basket with food. They picnicked and bathed at Bellevue River. He would have liked his father and mother to do the same thing. Roly-Poly taught his boys to wrestle, and they lived like brothers. The men said Roly-Poly was soft in the head, that he spoiled his children, and that his wife wore the pants.

Roly-Poly died while he was home recovering from his first breakdown. He went to the funeral. There were hundreds of people. An ordinary person didn't bring out that many people. Secretly, they must have admired him.

Barslow was another case altogether. He was String's father. String was sixteen but looked twelve. The older boys joked that, in elementary school, they used to tease String that they would use him for fish bait. String's father left his mother because she would not drop a case against him. Jerome was around ten when it happened. He had seen only part of it but had constructed the story from various bits his mother and others recounted.

Barslow had stopped giving Eunice money. One morning she asked him for some, and he told her she should try whoring. At lunchtime, when he came in expecting food, there was none.

After he finished beating her, an ambulance took her to the hospital and she aborted a pregnancy on account of it. A group of women from Hanovertown urged her to take Barslow to courts. The villagers advised her against it. The townswomen promised to take care of her, and she prosecuted him. The judge found him guilty but let him go unpunished because he had a clean record. The townswomen were outraged but soon forgot about Eunice, and Barslow never again gave her a penny. Eventually she began wasting away from consumption, and String had to leave school to work in the fields to take care of the two of them.

On Sunday morning, when it wasn't raining, he walked to the edge of the promontory a little distance out to the coast to watch the sunrise. He still had the scrapbook in which he'd written a description of it.

He stared long enough to see the sea become its usual royal blue, the land green, and the mountains grey.

The sea had always fascinated him. Since he was around eight, he'd often climb the hill a hundred yards outside his village to look at its corrugated blue, white-flecked surface. When it pounded the shore on windy nights, it left him with a vague, haunting fear. In August, when it was calmest, he would go into the shallow parts because there were whirlpools just outside the shore and bury his body in it and enjoy the sac-like feeling of the water around him.

The farthest he had ever got when he ran away from the hospital was the Olgay beach. He did not have time to take off his johnny shirt because the police had been chasing him. He'd only wanted to get that feeling of the water. They were sure he'd gone there to commit suicide and had afterward put him in seclusion and on heavy medication.

He never quite saw the full effect of a sunset because the sun always set over the mountains. True, it was lovely to look at, with the ridges standing there like walls blocking a flaming sky, but he would have liked to see the sunset from the mountaintop, watch the sun dip into the sea. But it would have meant walking at least five miles up into the mountains, and to have to walk back alone in the dark did not appeal to him. *A few years later, when he and Peter were friends, he had thought of asking him to go with him. But, after he'd had his dream about Peter, he became a little afraid each time he was alone with him.*

By the time he got to the Coastal Highway, which fronted Miss Dellimore's house, the country buses would be already streaming into town with food and shoppers. There were, too, the women laden with huge bamboo baskets ringed and crowned with vegetables. They'd already walked six or seven miles, had already lifted down their baskets, sold from them, and repacked them many times. A dozen or so shoppers waited for specific vendors. There were friendships between the vendors and shoppers. Occasionally a vendor brought a gift for a shopper and vice versa, and during the transaction they spoke of children and illnesses and brothers and sisters and relatives overseas. Then the baskets would be hoisted onto the cloth pads that cushioned the scalp, the arms would again plop down to the women's sides, and the trek would resume down to the valley floor, where the capital lay in as yet unheated asphalt and concrete.

Later, when he got down to the market, which occupied the quadrangle in the commercial heart of the city, the women would be seated like queens on wooden crates, surveying their heaps of tannias, dasheens, yams, sweet peppers, carrots, string beans…and the potential customers. They served several customers all at once, never closing a transaction without trying to convince the buyer that she needed something else: "No tannias for the Sunday soup? Smell this thyme. You must want lettuce! Them sweet peppers! Ain't they juicy?" Often the contradictions were glaring. But they broke off when they saw another potential customer or when the shopper, usually smiling, left. The plaid heads, fat arms in short-sleeve dresses protected by dungaree aprons with arm-deep pockets—where wads of dollar bills lay, coming out only to engulf other dollar bills—created a carnival of colour. He loved to meander among them, hear their enticing talk, and picture their lives at home.

The open-air market was flanked by the indoor markets— grey barrack-like structures with iron grids for windows. In one of them, everything except fish and meat was sold. There, the professional market women, who bought wholesale from growers, reigned, sometimes cursing, sometimes fearing, sometimes threatening to poison, their competitors. Country lore abounded with tales of them, of the sorcery spells they'd put on other market women, causing them to go crazy or produce deformed babies. He knew an albino child who was said to be the product of such *maljeu*.

They boasted about their children in secondary schools, overseas, in nursing school, in the civil service. They were proud their children didn't speak "bad." That was why they slaved day in and day out to make a better life for them. "Is only them what don got ambition what going foller in we footsteps." Over the years, as he understood what was going on, he found it funnier and funnier that these women spoke dialect and their children replied in standard English—were expected to reply in standard English. He wondered how they felt about their parents. He knew how the parents felt about them.

The rear wall of the fish and meat market was in contact with the sea. It had an external extension, an enclosure of chicken wire with a floor of beach sand—it was actually an enclosed part of the beach—littered with candy wrappings and fruit rinds. Here the fishermen sold their catch, first to the indoor vendors, and the leavings to the outdoor ones. Some outdoor buyers, depending on the season, bought a hundredweight bamboo basket of fish and sat on the street outside the wire mesh and sold to the passersby. Outside the mesh, at a spot where the sea lapped the land, little boys scaled, gutted, and salted the fish of the customers for a small fee.

On slow days, the outdoor vendors put the baskets on their

heads, slung conch shells over their shoulders, and leaving an odour that ought to have discouraged buyers, wandered into the suburban communities, announcing their presence with the shells. On the slowest of days, they hired taxis and took the fish all the way into the country, where on arrival it stank and the price tripled.

People in the villages didn't have that kind of pluck. They took orders. He liked the market women. They owned some of the biggest houses on Isabella Island. The villagers called them robbers.

The food vendors intrigued him most. They operated from the sidewalk beside the fish and meat market, very close to the public latrines. He had heard numerous stories about them. The first time he began observing them, they were talking about some market woman's son who had done well in school, was employed in the civil service, and had the gall to want to marry into an establishment family.

"He want for hang he hat too high."

"Education must be turn him stupit."

"Them say the old man come out with a gun and tell him for scatter. Jesus Christ! He knock the flowers off the steps and run through the flowers garden and over the hedge. Lawd, the servant gal say she laugh till she piss her drawers."

"Good for him. He class not good enough for him."

"Missah Blizzard should o shoot him."

Most of the food was contained in four-gallon biscuit tins. Invariably there were pots of fish in a thick brown sauce; rice and peas; and sliced provisions, plantain, and breadfruit. It was all covered with sauce-stained towels to discourage the swarms of buzzing flies.

Country people looked down on people who ate this food. "Is town food what got you so." They liked to pick on one or two of the vendors who, they were sure, put shit in the sauce to bewitch the eaters. How else could people in their "right head" return to buy food from them? "You don see is Obeah!" Others, they were convinced, spat in the food. (A woman who sold coconut-sugar cakes under the gallery of a bookstore made them from coconut her children had chewed.) "Town people, them nasty anyhow. They don wash they pot." Convinced of their stories, they would spit in disgust.

One Saturday, Jerome bought food from one of the women, after looking around to make sure that no one he knew was in sight. The lady served him sitting on a wooden crate hunched over the biscuit tins. She ladled a scoop of rice and peas onto a tin plate. To that she added a slice of tannia, a slice of plantain, and a slice of breadfruit; onto that she put a slice of fish and a full ladle of sauce. He ate it and liked it. The lady asked him how it was, and he said good, and she smiled, pleased.

She came to him in the hospital, opened her thighs and tried to swallow him, mixed food with her feces, opened his mouth and forced it down his throat, quacking like a duck all the while and changing faces—his mother's, Miss Anderson's, Miss Dellimore's, Olivia's, Hetty's, but mostly keeping her own—and left him only after he had swallowed it all.

The food vendors quarrelled frequently among themselves. Among the six women was a man whom the buyers and non-buyers said was the biggest woman of the lot. They called him Sprat. He had an enormous frame and was over six feet tall. He was not fat. His face was broad and the colour of fresh asphalt. His huge, red, bulbous lips resembled Sambo's. He arched forward slightly, was pigeon-toed, and had a big, projecting backside.

He got more customers than the women. While Jerome was eating, a customer approached one of the female vendors, began to order from her, but changed her mind and bought from Sprat. The disappointed woman pouted and fidgeted with her headtie and cut her eye at Sprat.

"Melia is not me fault if me cooking sweeter than yos," he told her, laughing.

"Go long, woman, yo pussy bigger than mines," she shot back.

"Is yo husband that tell you so."

"Me husband don sleep with man."

"But you does sleep with oman."

The other women paid no attention.

Another customer came, renewing the competitive spirit and ending the row.

He bought food from them on numerous occasions. One day he was around when Sprat loaned Melia ten dollars to buy some ground provisions somebody was selling at a bargain. Another time, a big-hipped, big-breasted food vendor had it out with a thin light-skinned one. He did not know what had started it.

The big-hipped one said, "This oman without no drawers always taking way me customers."

The light-skinned one lifted her dress to disprove the accusation and told the big-hipped one to do the same.

This time everyone laughed.

"Anyway," the light-skinned one continued, "is flour-bag drawers you does wear."

Eventually they got around to whose nightgown had a red rooster on the front, from a popular brand of flour. One was unable to keep a man because she never cleaned herself. The other kept one only because she'd given him something to drink that turned him *dotish*. One had eaten some of her children and was therefore a cemetery; the other, who had none, was a mule. One was a whore by day, the other by night.

It wasn't ten minutes after they'd stopped quarrelling when the big-hipped woman discovered she was out of pepper sauce and the light-skinned one gave her some.

On another occasion when he went, Sprat wasn't there. While he ate, people came and asked for him. Sprat had the flu, and three of the women had been to see him. One said he would be out the next week and she was buying supplies for him that day.

When he returned to Compton that first July-August vacation, he found that it was not the same village. The cane fields, in full growth then, even the mountains in the distance, didn't give the serenity they'd previously given. Neither the booming billows of the Atlantic nor its occasional flat surface stirred him. He could no longer imagine the monsters of the deep, changing their shapes like the waves. Or shipwrecked sailors crying for help, their powerful arms threshing the billows—as he had done in earlier times.

Now he was aware of history. The fields reminded him of the whips during slavery. He fancied he could still hear the lashes and cries in the wind sweeping through the cane blades. The low pay of the villagers and their fear of White people told him that slavery hadn't quite ended.

Several years after he had joined the civil service, he'd reflected on how unhappy he was, although he did not have to worry about the basic things that bothered the majority of Isabellans, and he'd written in his journal that "all emancipation ends in slavery / too subtle for the emancipated to see."

A great deal was festering there. Butler had been chief minister for some time, and some of the estates had unions; many, probably most, of the union organizers were in jail or in hiding. The police were under the control of the British administrator. Six policemen were on permanent duty in Compton, with orders to arrest anyone who came around to talk union activity. The administrator had been quoted in the *Isabellan* saying he agreed with the planters that, where the workers were squatters, the union organizers were trespassers. A few of the villagers had gone to public meetings Butler's men organized and had been fired by Mr. Manchester and ordered to remove their shacks from his land.

A lot had changed in the thirty years! In the last election, Butler's party lost every seat. They found out that he had two houses in New York and a fat bank account in Switzerland. His finance minister fled to England of all places the day after the election. The British did not extradite him for the trial. Beggars on horseback flogging beggars on foot. The beggars change places but the lash goes on. Butler was crippled now. His cronies didn't even visit him, it was said. At least they named the trans-island highway after him. The workers he fought so hard for in the early days when he wanted to hold on to power were still struggling. Very few earned a living or even half a living on the estate now. Much of it had been turned into a golf course, and very little was cultivated elsewhere. It was the party of the middle class that had passed the law giving squatters on the estates title to the land their shacks were on. Immediately they'd begun tearing down the shacks to build small wooden and concrete houses. Not enough land though. Their two-bedroom house was surrounded on three sides. Three feet from the back wall of their house was the front door to their neighbour's house. He had seen his mother stretch across a window and hand something to Millicent over in her house.

He did well in school that first year. Except for algebra and science, he got the highest marks in his classes. He was a year older than the other boys. They decided to let him skip a form because of his performance. His mother insisted he take his report to show his elementary school teachers. That embarrassed him. He was no six-year-old showing off the toy he had got for Christmas.

One evening his father was sitting on the steps. He had just come in from the fields. He looked at Jerome and shook his head. "Don think cause yo head getting full o what White man know, you better than we. I sure o one thing: White man not teaching you the most important things what you supposed to know." He wanted him to talk on, but his father was a one-sentence man.

4

IN THE SECOND YEAR of high school, their composition teacher was a White American from Arkansas. The civil rights campaign in the United States was in full swing. The radio stations carried it. He read about it in *Time*, *Newsweek*, and even the *Manchester Guardian*. They all took turns on Miss Hunt's accent, especially her "yalls." One time she said, "Yous guys over there doing nutten but talkin, yous the ones I mean." Another time it was, "Yall think it's easy teaching yall? Come evenen, Ah feel like Ah been drug through dirt."

"And not even as good," Randolph said under his breath.

Peter renamed her Miss Blunt, although he needn't have: her name rhymed well in the obscene poem he'd composed about her.

Miss Hunt frightened him because of Little Rock. He and the other students asked her about it. She said she had studied English, not politics.

"You could have saved yourself the trouble," Peter whispered.

What was he to make of this White teacher from a town in America where Black and White children couldn't go to school together? *During his grandmother's time, they couldn't on Isabella Island either, and before that, Blacks weren't allowed in school at all.* He was uncomfortable even with Mr. Bunyan, though he felt the English weren't as bad as the Americans.

She taught composition to the first five forms. Bunyan taught form VI English, the only course he taught. Miss Hunt taught the same thing to everyone. "A little grammar never hurt nobody," she said in her singsong way when they asked her why they were doing the same work as form I. "Miss Blunt's grammar *hurt* everybody. Ya gotta unlearn it."

One day she told them that the semicolon could be used instead of the comma. Jerome looked at the Indian boy, Rajan, who sat next to him.

"Rajan, ask her if you can use semicolons instead of commas in this sentence." He scribbled in Rajan's notebook: "When the clouds had completely drifted away and the moon came out, the forest became alive with hopping opossums, hunting snakes, flying bats, and other nocturnal creatures."

Rajan read it and passed it on to Peter. Miss Hunt had put all three of them to sit right in front of her because Peter got them in trouble constantly.

"Miss," Peter shouted, "suppose we have this sentence?" He started to read it.

"Put it on the blackboard."

Peter wrote: "...the forest became alive with hoping opossums, hunting snakes, flying, bats, and other nocturnal creatures." Peter was bigger than all of them, even several inches taller than Miss Hunt. A thin bronze glaze covered his pink skin; his firefly eyes were ablaze; the only other time they glowed like that was at assembly when he sang his own words to

"A Mighty Fortress Is Our God" or "Awake! Awake! To Love and Work," making it difficult for them not to laugh. "Now, Miss," Peter said, sounding like a born-again preacher, "can we put semicolons where these commas are?"

Kenneth asked, "Shouldn't the comma be before flying?"

Miss Hunt looked at Peter, who was still standing. "Did ya mean hunting snakes that fly?"

The class laughed. The recess bell saved her that morning.

During lunch the Eurafricans and several of the Whites were angry. Harold insisted they draft a petition and present it to Bunyan. He amassed everyone who was available and they drafted the petition. Jerome didn't take part. His grandma, dead since he was ten, used to say, "White people always leave Black people for put out the fire what them done set together." About half of them signed it. But the next morning they all said they wanted their names off. "Make a new one," they told Harold. He tore up the old one and made a new one. But none of them signed it.

She created a lot more drama with gerunds and past participles, holding forth that she was right in spite of the textbook. They were interested in her mistakes. Whenever she taught them seriously, they passed notes to one another or made signs about Peter, who was always working up an erection every time Miss Blunt stretched to write on the board, here miniskirt sliding even higher up her thighs. In a light moment they'd suggest she stand on a chair to write.

When she didn't feel like teaching (or didn't know the topic well enough to teach it), she made them recite poetry. On one such occasion she told them that the word *gyre* meant kite.

"Kite!" Rajan exclaimed. "It don't make sense."

"Doesn't," Kenneth corrected in his pseudo-British accent that always annoyed Jerome.

"Rajan Singh, you are out of order! Ya questionin ma competence? Ma BA's from Ballahoo University—"

The class exploded. They switched to dialect.

"Is Ballahoo University she come from."

"It plain as ever. Is a windbag that!"

She turned pink as a plumrose, began to cry, and walked out of class.

No one came to replace her for the rest of that period. And they never heard anything more about it. But after that they joked about who was going to study at Ballahoo University. Sometimes they told Bullock there was where he'd end up, because Bullock had the notion that he was going to university.

One afternoon in late June, Mr. Bunyan sent for him. When he got to his office, Bunyan was writing and motioned for him to sit in a chair that gave a view of the harbour. Through the louvred windows he watched the roofs of the buildings that sloped down the valley to the business district, the harbour, and the smoky shapes of the islands rising out of the sea.

Bunyan looked up from his writing and pushed the sheet of paper aside. "I sent for you because at the beginning of August six students from Ghana will be visiting us. They're coming as part of the Ghanaian government's attempt to develop an understanding between Africans and Negroes in other parts of the world. I think those were the exact words." Bunyan took a handkerchief from his breast pocket and blew his nose. "I need to assign these youngsters to six reliable

48

students. In point of fact, I have already assigned five of them to boys in the fifth and sixth forms. I wish to assign the sixth to you." He paused for about thirty seconds. "Do you think you can handle it?"

Can't let anyone stay at Miss Dellimore's, he thought. He could never ask a guest to pay. But Miss Dellimore would. Where would the Ghanaian sleep or bathe? He himself bathed at the public baths two hundred yards from where Miss Dellimore lived…sometimes the water was turned off…most times you waited twenty minutes for an available tap. "I would love to, sir, but…"

Bunyan waited, a wily look in his eyes, his lips visibly contracted, his hair multicoloured: grey at the roots, blond at the tips.

"I can't put him up, sir."

"That most certainly would not be a problem. They will be housed in the girls' pavilion and have sleeping bags, and the domestic sciences teacher will supervise their meals." While speaking he pulled open a desk drawer and removed a pipe and a tin of tobacco. He filled and lit his pipe and began puffing away. "Well? What say we? Do we or do we not?"

"It's possible, but…I mean, I would like to."

"One more thing." He paused and took three puffs in rapid succession, his grey eyes alight; he even looked pleasant. "You will have to take your charge on excursions around the island." He paused again. "How are you going to disburse these?"

Jerome was silent. His neck muscles were stiffening.

"Well, I have made provision for that. I'm most certainly aware that you are a lad of modest means. The other chaps are from wealthy families—at one time or another their

49

parents have entertained me. The school's personnel will be on vacation, but I shall leave you a handsome weekly stipend to defray your costs. You will merely have to present yourself at the Education Department and ask to see a Mrs. Granger. How's that?" He winked, his eyes still glowing.

Jerome nodded in relief.

"By the way, please understand that this comes out of my own pocket."

He felt the intensity of Bunyan's stare. "Thanks," he said, his voice quavering.

While walking back to class, he felt uneasy. He should have been elated to be the one Black chosen. But he thought of Mrs. Manchester and the shilling she sent each Saturday to Martha, her childhood nanny, now bedridden. "What a shilling can buy?" his mother, who prepared a meal for Martha, used to ask, speaking to herself. "And pon top of all this, she going round the place telling people how she taking care o Martha, like if shilling a week can feed, clothes, and house a grown somebody!"

The first Friday morning in August, Yaw and his five compatriots arrived. Two of the boys had half-moon scars on their faces. They were all very black. One had a straight nose, though.

By noon the next day, they were ready to go off with their charges. The parents of the other boys owned cars. Jerome watched them drive off while he and Yaw crossed Main Street, which led to the centre of town. They had already decided to sightsee around Hanovertown. Yaw had opted for the Botanic Gardens first. Jerome proposed they go in a taxi. Yaw asked how far. When he found out it was a twenty-minute walk, he suggested they walk.

As they crossed the market area, Yaw stood a while looking at the market women. "They wear the same sort of headdress as African women. They can't drive hard bargains, though. Only Ashanti women know how to do that." He was smiling.

"How does the headdress resemble the African women's?"

"You'll see from our film."

He would be careful what he said to Yaw. Africans. He had seen many fights in elementary school between boys, girls, and even boys and girls because one had called the other African. Cross, a big, dunce, big-foot, red-skinned, and very long-lipped girl from Campden, had scratched him in the face and spit on him for precisely that reason. In Compton, whenever women were cursing, the first one who got a chance to called the other a Zulu woman. The *hurt* woman would invite her opponent into the street. "Come out in the road and lemme rip off every piece of the hand-me-down clothes you wearing off yo skin what you does take off of a night when you go round sucking people blood. You sow mouth! You *Jablesse*! Fancy you, black like the ace-a-spades and smelling like cattle dung, calling me, a respectable oman, Zulu oman! You wouldn say so if you wasn hiding behind yo door! Imagine, oman don wash sheself ovva night and calling me Zulu oman!"

If other women were present, and they usually were, they'd say, "But you say that the last time they call you Zulu oman. Is high time you change the tune."

At the Botanic Gardens, Yaw began to examine shrubs and trees with a frenzy. He had a frantic way about him, like someone staying up all night to study because he was afraid of failing an exam. This was a—*No way he could remember the names now. Shit, that was twenty-five...no...more like thirty*

51

years ago. Only to discover that it wasn't quite the same tree, but almost, anyway. Some he correctly identified and gave their African names. He pointed out some weeds that he said were medicinal.

"Do your people use herb medicines?"

Jerome nodded.

"When my mother was a young girl, she lived with her aunt, and one time my mother became very sick. Her eyes got yellow like the sun and she couldn't stand up. They took her to the White doctor thirty miles away, but the sickness was stronger than his medicines. They tried different herb doctors and African priests, but the sickness was stronger than their medicines too. So they said the ancestors were calling for Akosufa.

"But, one night, my dead grandmother came into the hut where my mother was, holding the leaves of a certain tree in her hand. She gave the leaves to my mother and left.

"And my aunt, she made tea with the leaves and gave the tea to my mother, and in two days my mother got better."

Jerome told him that he knew similar stories. His grandmother was given a cure for his mother's marasmus by her dead mother—but it had happened in a dream.

They slapped palms and Jerome began to feel relaxed in his presence.

When they got to the summit of the gardens and were facing the spur of the valley where the tombstones sloped all the way uphill, Yaw asked, "Is that a White cemetery?"

"No, it's for everybody. Few Whites are buried in it."

"The White man built many cemeteries in Africa too. My father says they turned Africa into a cemetery. But we like for

52

our dead to be buried in the family clan. That way they are not angry with us and protect us. Even our people when they move away from the village come back home to die."

Probably all people who live in close-knit communities feel that way. Just two weeks ago he read a poem by the Chinese poet Shirley—Gosh, what was her last name?—that asked the Chinese living in America who would feed them when they were dead.

"What do you do for your dead?"

"What do you mean?" He was nervous about people who deal with the dead. They had evil powers.

"I mean what you do to show the dead that you love them and want them to be around? How you get them to send messages to you?"

His hands began to perspire. "I don't know what you mean." He knew many stories about people who roused the spirits of the dead and got them to torment others. There was a girl in the village across the stream from Compton who sometimes crowed like a rooster and spoke in several languages though she only knew the dialect. Sometimes her voice was a man's, sometimes it was a middle-aged woman's, other times it was a baby's. When the spirit got her out of control, they used to beat her to calm her down. *He knew nothing about autism then. That girl really did put people on a trip. She used to name villagers she said were tormenting her. People who weren't getting along with her parents. Harriet Buntyn ran away to Trinidad because of her. Her parents sold all their cattle to pay the Obeah man for cures. She used to name dead people, too, saying they were in the room or sitting on other people's heads or what have you. They said the spirit haunting her was Alfred Jones's, who died before the girl was born. The spirit had been sent for her mother but because of some mix-up had entered the girl.*

He was both scared and intrigued. "Tell me more about your dead." Here was the "dark continent," but he mustn't laugh.

"Let me look for examples to explain this," Yaw said, looking out over the valley. "Would you like for your mother and father to put you to sleep out in the wind and rain?"

Jerome shook his head and waited.

"People that don't feed their dead and look after them live in wind and rain." He paused. "The body is where the gods must live. When the body dies, what is to happen to the gods before they come again in the young? And if you don't take the right care of them, they would want vengeance when they come back."

What was he talking about?

"If we don't take care of the gods, they might even leave us, and our enemies will conquer us. You know the English proverb 'A chain is as strong as its weakest link'?"

He nodded. *That proverb's been used to force people to do a lot of things their conscience wouldn't otherwise let them do. Group tyranny!*

"Every ancestral spirit is a link."

"I understand," he lied.

Yaw pulled at his chin. They resumed walking aimlessly until they got to the stump of a tree with tiny sprouts at its base. The ground around it was worn from people sitting on it. He and Yaw sat down, almost touching.

"You did not answer my question."

"What question?"

"What sort of ceremonies you hold for your dead?"

"None. We bury them. If you don't, they stink, you know."

"Yes, I know!"

"Well, actually, on the third night following the death, some people hold a kind of service for them. On the ninth night there is a feast. On the fortieth night there is another service. Once a year we go to the cemetery to put candles on their graves. Some people go twice. Well, not everybody does. Those who belong to the Christian churches frown on it. Most of them break the rules for this. But it's mostly the workers on the plantations, the people who can't read, that really take these things seriously." He'd already read somewhere that such practices were superstitions.

"The ones who can't read," Yaw said as if he were interrogating the statement itself. He smiled broadly.

He was laughing at him. He wasn't laughing in jail now, unless at his own nonsense. Bwanda took care of that brashness. Freddy showed him the article in The Nation *shortly after Yaw had been arrested. Somebody should arrest Bwanda? But that was another matter.*

Later they walked from the other gate of the Botanic Gardens, crossed the cemetery, and took the road leading up to the other promontory, which together with the one he visited on Saturday mornings formed the outer edges of the horseshoe of Hanovertown harbour. A fort was up there, started by the French and completed by the British after they had been *given* Isabella Island in the Treaty of Paris.

At the top Yaw tapped the stones with his knuckles and gazed at the heavy cannons pointing out to sea, shaking his head all the while. "I wonder how many Africans they killed here.

"Their forts are all over. Everywhere the leeches went. All along our coast. I went into one at Elmina. They would be at Kumasi too if we weren't strong."

He knew where that was. The *Isabellan* had carried an article about a book by a writer named Richard Wright. The article was titled "American Negro Revolted by What He Saw in Ghana." The book was among five on the shelf labelled "Africa." The rest of the shelf was empty. One book was by Albert Schweitzer, one by Joyce Cary called *Mister Johnson*, something or the other on David Livingstone, and he couldn't remember the fifth. Wright's book said that African women's breasts were so long they slung them over their shoulders after they finished nursing their children. He had a lot of trouble imagining how they looked, certainly not like Miss Anderson's. There was something, too, about a black stool that got its colour from dried human blood. The chief told Wright it was sheep's blood, and Wright told the chief that he was lying, that it was the blood of people they'd killed for that purpose.

"What tribe are you from? Are you Ga?" Wright's chauffeur had been a Ga. He didn't get along with the other tribes.

"We don't want to use anymore the world *tribe* in Africa. Don't ask me what tribe I'm from."

"Sorry."

Silence.

"We say *nation*. I'm from the Ashanti nation."

"Are all of you here Ashantis?"

"No, we belong to different groups. My nation extends into Togo. Do you know where that is?"

Jerome shook his head.

"I'll show you on a map sometime back at the school."

He was caught between not making Yaw feel that he was totally ignorant and wanting to see whether Yaw was lying about his country. He was dying to ask Yaw about cannibals in Africa. There was a calypso that everybody was singing at the time that talked about cannibals in the Congo. *The whole thing was really supposed to be a satire on men who performed cunnilingus. But the calypsonian, in using African cannibalism as his metaphor, actually reinforced what Europeans had taught West Indians about Africa. What a relief when he saw Basil Davidson, a White historian, on television saying, "No White person ever ended up in the African's pot."*

"I read somewhere," he told Yaw, "that when the Ashanti king dies they kill his favourite wife and several people to accompany him in the next life. That's terrible!"

"No, it's not. Those were our customs, which the British had no right ending."

"Well, I find that horrifying."

"White people want us to feel ashamed of our past, that's what my father says, and we mustn't make them succeed. Hitler was a White man. You know the terrible things he did."

Jerome nodded. "My history text says that Africans sold slaves to White slave traders. It mentions the Ashantis specifically. You all exchanged us for guns. You even had the Dutch working for you, training your slave-catching units."

"That's an outright lie. My people have been too intelligent for that. Ashantis would never practise slavery. Never! White people wrote that book." He pulled at his chin.

"Well, my text says that when you all went to wars you used to kill the men and make the women and children slaves. It says that when the Europeans came, they persuaded you folks to sell them the people you'd otherwise kill. After a while you all got to liking it so you went out hunting specifically for slaves and you even started to sell women and children."

"That's another lie. Lies! Lies! A pack of White people's lies." His hand was on his chin.

"According to my book, the Efficks were some of the worst slave catchers."

"I'm not Effick. I'm Ashanti. Get your geography right! The Efficks are in Nigeria." This time his hand fell from his chin.

The sun was setting. They were to return to the girls' pavilion at six, and already they were late. So they started descending back into town. White history brags about how many people they murdered and how many countries they stole, Yaw told him. *Other people's histories, he had thought many times, were litanies of the atrocities others had committed against them, which they hadn't been able to commit against others because of numbers, geography, lack of resources, and so on and so forth.*

"Ashanti is a great nation. All sorts of people lived under our rule and paid us tribute. Nobody can insult an Ashanti and not pay for it. We are born rulers."

What then distinguished their history from White history?

Three days later, they were on the lawn that separated the boys' and girls' pavilions, leaning against one of the frangipani trees. They had just returned from the commercial district. It was near suppertime, but they continued their conversation. "We go back to the country at every opportunity we get. We live in Accra because my father teaches at the university just outside Accra and my mother lectures in a nearby teachers' college. My father is the headman of a secret society, and he has to go home a few times a year to fulfill his office in the important ceremonies. And I and my brother have to have Ashanti culture planted in us.

"Why? Because my roots are Ashanti and everything I will bear must be Ashanti."

"Can't you learn that culture in school?"

"No, it is not put down in books. Anything that's put down can be stolen."

Silence.

"What I learn we don't want White people to know. It's like taking a clean piece of cloth. It gets dirty after many hands touch it. We keep it for the Ashanti hand only."

"Where would that get you people?"

"It would keep us from rolling to the bottom. After the British came, our culture started to die. If we learn it, we would stop it from dying."

"I really thought you folks wanted to get civilized."

"Civilized! What you mean, civilized? You call White people civilized? You shouldn't let my father hear you. People who burn people in ovens? You know the Belgians killed three million people in the Congo because they couldn't collect rubber fast enough for King Leopold's needs?"

Where did the circle end? They said Hitler was one of Idi Amin's idols. So much hogshit. If you weren't a member of some tribes, it was as if you weren't human. Yaw really laid it heavy on him. If Yaw had descended from Ashanti slaves, he wouldn't have talked like that; he wouldn't have heard about Isabella, let alone visited it. Histories of Africa omitted all references to the thriving civilizations Europeans found there. Apparently the Spanish Inquisition forbade historians of the New World from writing that the Spanish met colonies of Blacks living there. The French, too, met Blacks on Isabella Island. They were sure the only way they could have got there was because a slave ship had sunk with them somewhere off the coast and they had swum ashore. They hadn't bothered to see that the mixture in the population was the result of several centuries. Why would they? Africans were savages and savages did not have the technology to cross the Atlantic.

"Richard Wright wrote a letter to Nkrumah telling him he should use the Ghanaian army to stamp out those things you go back to the bush to learn. He said those things are holding back progress in Ghana."

"I said *my village*. Richard Wright can write whatever comes in his mind. Those things he wants us to kill were what kept our soul from drying up. When Ashantis became Christians, the missionaries used to lock them up in compounds to keep them from going back to Ashanti ways. So the converts used to take the Ashanti ways and christen them and practise them, and the missionaries loved it. They didn't know any better… You know about Cecil Rhodes?"

Jerome shook his head.

"Your mind is like a clean piece of paper. You don't know anything about your past."

But he'd been lying. UDI was very much in the air then. It was just that he was tired of the conversation.

"What's going on in Rhodesia now, Cecil Rhodes started it. But everywhere in Africa where White people are in power, they do as they please. They did the same thing in Ghana, Kenya, everywhere. When Africa gets its complete freedom, we'll pour poison into their stomachs."

"But if Africa is so this and that, why you all never drove the Europeans out?" *He wanted to hear him say that some Africans were traitors, just as how there had been a man spying for Mr. Manchester and the plantation owners. They found his decaying body in one of the cane fields that had already turned sour because of the long strike. The police arrested Pointer Dublin, Pointer Francis (he wasn't pointer yet), Henry, and three other men. They kept them a week in jail to try to beat information out of them. When they released them, over a thousand people came from the surrounding villages to greet them. Nearly a hundred police officers armed with shotguns were stationed outside the canal bridge, but there was no trouble. People said that it was a police officer that told Pointer Dublin that Pucker was carrying news to Mr. Manchester.*

"They're just so much stronger than we. But, you see, we Ghanaians were the first to become independent of Europeans and one of the last to be conquered too!"

"Albert Schweitzer thinks Africans are children."

"Albert Schweitzer can think Africa is a ghost. It makes no change to me. My father says that when a swarm of killer bees lands on you, you freeze until they fly off. Let Schweitzer think what he likes. One day we will drive every last one of them off the continent. We might even conquer England. The Arabs controlled Spain once. Arabs are African. And they don't forgive their enemies. They're like Ashantis. When an outsider kills one of us, it's war unless they send us a victim and pay damages."

Or unless he's more powerful than you.

"You people forgive too much. That is why you remained slaves for so long."

Jerome smiled. "For how long?"

"I don't know."

Jerome laughed this time. "On Saturday you said something about everybody serving his community. Suppose a person doesn't want to?"

"He leaves the community. Some of our people working for White people in Accra or freeze-drying up in England feel like that. Now they're too afraid to return. They broke the initiation oath."

"What's that?"

"You won't understand.

"My mother tells a story about a herd of buffalo in which a mother buffalo gave birth to a special calf. From the time that calf was little he showed special gifts. He showed the herd that they could use their horns better if they rooted at a different angle. He made up a set of exercises for the young buffalo to strengthen their neck muscles and triple their butting force. He showed them how to put their feet so they could double their speed. He could smell leopards and lions from miles off.

"After he became leader of the herd, they never lost a member and they wounded and killed many leopards and lions. The leopards and lions met and voted to leave them alone.

"One day that buffalo started to think: 'It's my intelligence that makes this herd feared and respected. What have I got for it? Head buffalo? Pssh! That's only because they want my protection. I'm leaving. They can get eaten for all I care. I would work less taking care of myself.'

"So he walked off and left the herd.

"So one day, about a month later, after he finished dinner, he made sure that the trap beside his sleeping place was well disguised with dry leaves and lay down to sleep. A loud crash woke him up. A lioness had fallen into the trap. He gored another with his sharp horns. But three others were at his flanks, and two others bit open his throat.

"'It's the buffalo chief,' they shouted in a chorus, surprised. And his meat was sweet because of all the frustration he had caused them."

"That's a good story," Yaw told him as they rose to go in for supper.

After a week, he had shown Yaw all the places worth seeing in Hanovertown and the surrounding areas. They'd swum a few times at the beach near the capital. "I haven't met your parents yet," Yaw told him, staring directly into his eyes.

"They live way out in the country."

"That's why I'll like to meet them. I want to see how your people live."

"Its difficult to get there. The buses leave early and they make only one trip."

"I would still like to meet your parents."

He would have never invited his classmates to his home. It would have embarrassed him and his parents. *This was long before his parents had even thought of building a cement house. They lived in a two-room mud shack and had a pit latrine. Some didn't even have a latrine. They just dropped it in the canal. They used to bring water from a standpipe Mr. Manchester let them use. It was almost a mile away. It used to be his duty to bring water from it on mornings to fill the drum they kept covered beside the hut they used for a kitchen. In the dry season his mother used to wake him at four o'clock, before the sun came*

63

up and the water dried up. Their huts were just below the canal bank, and when the canal silted up or there were heavy rains it sometimes overflowed into their yard, washing away the earth from the stones they had put there to prevent erosion. When the estate was sold, the sugar factory closed, and the canal was emptied around the time people started building wooden and cement houses on the land.

The year before, his father had stopped working for Mr. Manchester. He had taken over the cultivation of a twenty-acre farm from a mixed-race woman, Mrs. Bensie, who had inherited it from a White half-brother. Her husband was dead, and she was old and couldn't cultivate it anymore. So, when Jerome went home the next day to discuss Yaw's visit, he found that they were at the farm. He walked the two miles, over the low hills down to the valley on the other side, because he was eager to hear what his parents thought. Henry thought for a while and said he would like to meet the African. Cosmie said nothing. That was Tuesday. He arranged to arrive the next day.

5

JUST AS YAW AND HE got off the bus, Pongy, their neighbour, and his entire family crossed the canal bridge laden with bitter cassava. Yaw's attention was taken up by them. Not too long after that, the landscape began to glow with moonlight covering the thousands of acres of growing canes stretching to the foothills of the mountains, and crickets, owls, bullfrogs in the canal, and dogs began the noises of the night. Pongy and his wife, the children, and even the semi-feeble grandmother had begun to attack the cassava: the grandmother and the two older girls scraping; the father, son, and mother grating; and the twins toting water from the canal to wash the scraped cassava.

Jerome saw Yaw join them. He heard him ask for a grater. Jerome could not see their faces in the moonlight, but he was sure they laughed and were embarrassed. A year before, he'd overheard Millicent telling his mother how she was ashamed when Pongy's sister Ursula, who was visiting from the States, had decided to stay over one night. "Comsie, me feel wrong side out. The oman custom to toilet inside she house. Me couldn't let she go outside cause me fraid red ants bite she batty and you know what else. Me had for give she the tensil. And me really feel topsy-turvy. Then wha for give she for eat in the morning when she get up? Me send Pongy all the way over Brenchy go buy bread, cause that morning is roast breadfruit we did plan for have, and we was going eat it without saltfish. Then me had for trust saltfish from the shopkeeper for make a *bulljow* give she, cause me couldn let she eat just the dry bread. Lucky thing the bus leave just after we eat else it would o be another rackle-brain for find what for give she for lunch.

"Me tell Pongy for tell her next time she must stop by she relatives them what got big wall house in town, sewerage, and everything. Oversea people is more botheration than me can take. Them come neck and hand heavy down with gold, shoes ten-inch off the ground, and when them walk the silk just-a-talk. No, oversea people is just plain botheration."

The only visitors they got were White American missionaries, who came in search of their souls.

They refused Yaw a grater. He stood there. Later he took a bucket and helped the twins tote water. By this time everyone was chuckling. Henry and Comsie had come into the yard to look at him. Yaw stayed with the family until they'd finished. He'd managed to scrape, wring, to do whatever had to be done to the cassava. Strange thing, Jerome had thought then; he'd have only done that if his parents forced him to. He sometimes helped the neighbours write their letters, read their receipts, or calculate the value of produce they were selling, at those rare times when they had produce to sell. This Yaw was really something special.

His parents gave Yaw their bed. He refused at first, but they insisted.

The following morning Yaw was up to see Pongy and his

wife baking the cassava cakes. They sent a dozen to Comsie. The villagers lined up to buy, and they were all treated to the story of the African who stayed up and helped them prepare the cassava.

After breakfast, Henry picked up his cutlass and was about to head for the farm. Yaw looked frowningly at Jerome. "Aren't we all going to the farm?" *It was one of those questions that haunted him for a long time. Even when he was in the insane asylum. His father and mother rarely ever quarrelled. But they had done so over him the Christmas holiday before. His father had wanted him to go to the lands with him. He was burning coals at the time. Jerome hadn't wanted to. His mother had sided with him. "Henry, that is yo work. Jerome ha for concentrate pon his books. We, all o we, got we own work for do. Yours is fo burn coals; Jerome own is for read books." His father screamed, "Comsie, go fuck yoself!"—the first time Jerome had heard him swear—and stormed out the hut. He did not go to help his father, although his mother had pestered him to do so for an hour after his father left. Wesi liked that sort of thing. Wesi liked everything Jerome didn't like, except reading; and he read books on science— not novels.*

They all went to the farm that day. Yaw helped his father cut yam poles while Jerome helped his mother cook. While they ate, Yaw told them that they were farming exactly as his people in Ghana farmed. *It was only when he read Davidson's book a few years ago that he realized that tropical agriculture was mastered by Africans and brought to the New World by them. It was one of the reasons that African slaves were so prized—for their knowledge of mining too, especially in Brazil.*

Yaw said that in Ghana everyone went to the farm when

the children weren't in school. The women and girls did the light work, like preparing the meals, weeding, and harvesting, and the men and older boys did the ploughing.

"Jerome, you listening?" Henry asked.

Reflecting on this over the years, he concluded that Yaw and Henry didn't realize that the Ashantis were never forced to work other people's lands as slaves, for other people's benefits. Selling people into slavery, that they did. He doubted whether, even if he had thought it then, he'd have had the courage to say it. Besides, people who had money didn't put their hands in the earth; they paid others a pittance to do so, or got others to do it on shares, for a pittance too, while they reaped the benefits, as Mrs. Bensie did to his father.

In the village, around dusk, Yaw stood looking at the steelband players. *The shed was still there, on the seaward side of the canal bridge, visible from their living room window; it had been repaired many times and now had a corrugated steel roof.* Then it was a thatched-roof structure, open on all sides. Yaw scrutinized the players, muttering to himself and fluttering his arms like a conductor. The players, who already knew who he was, looked at him, smiling benignly. Occasionally they looked at Jerome stiffly, then back at Yaw. Jerome despised them and they knew it. *"Respectable" people flogged their children for associating with steelbandsmen. Mr. Branch, who was headmaster of a nearby primary school, had beaten his son badly, causing him to crack up, because the youngster didn't stay away from the steelband. You'd have been denied a job as a teacher or a civil servant if the authorities knew you were a steelbandman. After several years he understood that the steelband frightened the British, who must have associated it with the African drums and neo-African sects that they had banned from the beginning of slavery and even long after slavery. It frightened the Black Anglo-Saxons even more. His father did not play but was often at the shed when they were practising, and he told Comsie that he wanted the steelband to accompany him to his burial.*

Yaw was closely observing how the players used their sticks. He never quite figured out how Yaw spotted the band-leader, because there was nothing that marked him out. He asked to try out the pans. Everyone stopped playing, and the lead panman handed Yaw his batons. He tapped each of the marked zones to identify the notes. Within five minutes he was hesitantly playing what must have been an African tune. And within ten he played it as though he'd been playing pans all his life. When he handed back the batons to the leading panman, the bandsmen embraced him, slapped their thighs and shouted, "Coo-yah, is not rassclart fust-class panman dat!"

"Give Jerome the stick-them," Bundy said to the lead pan-man. Everyone, panmen and onlookers, laughed. He stared at them. Thereafter they ignored him.

The villagers began to gather. The drummer handed his batons to Yaw and motioned to him to take his place. Then the fireworks began. The strange melody brought the people running. Some with babies at their breasts, some with babies on their hips, some with babies in their wombs, some with bits of dough clinging to their fingers, men with one foot washed and the other unwashed, people still in their field clothes, children of every age and every shade from black to beige—they surrounded the panhouse. A few of the panmen at first, then later all of them, joined in and improvised around the drumming, and the onlookers began to dance.

It was bright moonlight when Comsie came, pulled at Yaw's sleeve, and said, "Come, put something in yo stomach. Empty bag can't stand up." She took the drumsticks out of his hands and gave them to the bandleader.

After they had eaten, people began to gather in their yard. The first to arrive was Pointer Dublin. Pointer Dublin took Yaw aside and talked with him for about ten minutes. The yard kept filling up. People were bringing fruit. Beulah Quammie, who was high up in his father's religion, came wearing her mauve religious headdress—they called her "mother" or something. She said to him, "Boy, you come for claim yo own. Is what you have for teach we? We done forget most everything." She groaned a deep groan, and his father and Pointer Dublin responded with something that was gibberish to Jerome.

"Which part o Africa you hail from?" Beulah asked him.

"Ghana. Ashanti. You know Anansi."

"Sure, me know bout Nansi—and Toucouma too."

"Good. Ntikima and Anansi and I are from the same place. You know about Nyame?"

There was silence, which was eventually broken by Pointer Dublin. "Perhaps, but not by the same name. Anyhow it not safe to talk bout these things in the open like this."

Nyame wasn't one of the gods they'd kept. But they had kept the folk tales of the Akan. He read somewhere that Ogun and Shango of the Yoruba were an important part of the Shango cult in Trinidad. The Haitians still clung to a lot of them in their Voudou: Ogun, Shango, Damballah, Legba, and countless others. Pointer Francis hadn't yet told him about any such names, so maybe they'd simply disappeared with so much else they'd dropped or that had been beaten out of them.

By then the moon was high in the sky and the children had for some time begun their moonlight games at the canal bridge clearing. Their singing and clapping filled the air. Yaw joined the children in their games, humming along with them to "The Man in the Moonlight." *There was one African expression in that song. He did not know it then or he would have asked Yaw if he knew what it meant: myoko-myoko.* Word spread quickly that he was there, and several more villagers came out.

When the children sang:

Bessy down! Bessy down!
For the sake of the pumpkin,
Bessy down.
I ask Mr. Yaw to be bessy down;
For the sake of the pumpkin,
Bessy down.

He certainly "bessied down." They laughed at his initial clumsiness. Belle whispered something in his ear as she rejoined the circle, leaving him in it. It was his turn to name someone as the singing broke for him to do so. "I ask Miss Bayne to bessy down; / For the sake of the pumpkin, / Bessy down." Belle re-entered the ring, but instead of singing, the children shouted, "Not fair! Not fair!" They settled on someone who had not yet been named, and the game resumed.

Baisser. The flotsam and jetsam that made up the language they spoke! "You want me for bessy down to you? Is that what you want? Well, me don bessy down for nobody." Something left by the French. Je demande à mam'selle Belle de se baisser; / Pour l'amour de la citrouille, / Bessy down. No joking.

71

And that pumpkin! Guess Jung didn't look at Africa or Puritan America when he was getting together his archetypes, or the pumpkin would have made it right beside the snake. More than Cinderella's coach. Essential ingredient in Thanksgiving: eating the god. But, in Africa, where they go to the heart of things, it was the thing. "And the man couldn't bear it any longer. More he try for catch the woman, more she put distance between them. He meet a pumpkin, and he let it go in the pumpkin, and the pumpkin explode, and seeds scatter all over the world. And that is why today you find pumpkin everywhere." *And people too, he supposed.* "You must wash yo pumpkin inside." *And outside too, of course.*

Maybe the pumpkin had something to do with the hallucination he repeatedly had during his first bout of madness. There was always this giant pumpkin on top of which were the heads of Mr. Bunyan, Miss Blunt, and Miss Anderson. The whole floated like a hovercraft, only it did so on air over the street. Whenever it met someone, one of the heads extended like a tentacle and sucked the person in. Each time the hallucination returned, the pumpkin was bigger, like it was getting fat or was constipated. And every time the pumpkin came upon him, the head closest to him would stretch and begin to swallow him but would spit him out. Twice it was Miss Anderson's head, and after she'd spit him out, she'd yell, "Contaminated!" *Immediately the other two heads cleared their throats; he heard them spitting and felt the spit falling on his face. Once, the hallucination overpowered him when the patients were all in the cafeteria eating, and the commotion caused him to knock over two of the patients' food. Another time, it happened when he was on the grounds.* "For the sake of the pumpkin, / Bessy down."

When the singing and dancing lagged, Yaw asked whether they did not tell stories. Pointer Dublin pulled at his beard and said that once upon a time they used to. But now they did so only at wakes. The best storyteller wasn't there anyhow. It was old Zukki, who couldn't walk so well anymore. Pointer Dublin asked Yaw to tell them some stories.

"Crick!"

"Crack!" the older people responded, and the younger ones looked at them, surprised.

Yaw told the story about how death came into the world because of Anansi's greed and how Anansi outwitted the Python. The people applauded. But it was Yaw's drama they loved, especially in the second story, when he acted out how Anansi outwitted Brother Python: crawling from his hole, eating, Anansi's tricking him, tying him to the pole, feeling the edge of his axe, and slicing him to bits. It was good acting, and Jerome understood that the tales had some kind of function. It impressed him that the Ashantis linked death to greed. *At least that was one belief the Spirituals have held on to.* Zukki never made it; he was too feeble to make the journey, and his memory had begun to fade. Soon after that, the people returned home.

Next morning the villagers brought their choicest mangoes, soursops, and bananas for Yaw. His father slipped away to the farm alone. Jerome began to wish the time could go faster. He wasn't jealous of Yaw. Why should he be jealous of Yaw?

That evening, shortly after nightfall, String and three young men from the village came to get Yaw. Jerome did not know he had arranged to go hunting with them. That night he was vaguely aware of Yaw coming into the house, bringing with him forest and manicou smells.

Next morning he found his mother busy, seasoning several manicous—the sight and smell nauseated him. His mother was preparing Yaw's portion of the catch. String came into the yard then. "Miss Comsie, that boy faster than manicou. You should o see that boy climb tree limb and shake manicou down! He frighten we. Not a single manicou get way. Woohoo! We catch manicou for eat for days."

Henry came out of the hut. "Next time you all must carry Jerome with all you."

"Uncle Henry, you will ha for do that yoself. I ha for go look after my food now."

The day will come, he'd told him himself, when the likes of String will have to come crawling to beg him for favours. *Some crawling! At forty-five he was still going around in circles and semicircles, like the wet and dry seasons, apart and telescoped. String owned a truck. String was building a four-bedroom house on land he bought near Compton. He was spending his life in and out of the mental asylum.*

On Sunday Yaw and he returned to town. Almost the entire village was there to see Yaw off. Beside the canal bridge were four baskets of ripe bananas, oranges, grapefruits, mangoes, avocado pears, pineapples, a breadfruit, and ground provisions. Mrs. Buntyn, the mother of Bertrand, who was the guide for Yaw's Mosshi colleague, Kofi, had arranged to come and get them. He watched her nervously fingering her pearls and squinting at the crowd of semi-naked men, women, and children huddled together at the canal bridge. She looked from Yaw to the plastic container he was holding. She sniffed, and Jerome knew that courtesy alone prevented her from holding her nose and keeping the stew out of her station wagon. Mrs. Buntyn flushed when Yaw embraced Jerome's mother and father and called them Mom and Dad, and she turned her head away when he began to embrace the shirtless and barefooted steelbandsmen. Jerome became aware for the first time of the strong odour of sweat. Mrs. Buntyn, he was sure, couldn't disapprove of his hygiene. He'd carefully noted what the Eurafrican boys wore and did his own shopping not to be left out. And no one could ever say they smelled his perspiration.

They drove silently for about three-quarters of the way, then Mrs. Buntyn asked Jerome, "Is the White woman your mother?"

"Yes," he replied.

Why didn't she say Eurafrican? Anyone could see that, even if his mother was on the White side of being Eurafrican, she was nevertheless Eurafrican.

Mrs. Buntyn was a shade darker than his mother, though her hair showed no Black mixture. She tried to bury the darkness of her face under deep layers of pink powder. But everyone knew who she was. She was the only one of three children who showed up with a dark complexion. The mix had taken place three generations before. On Isabella Island, her ancestors became the only plantation owners with known Black blood.

Bertrand, who sat with Kofi and Jerome in the back seat, was silent throughout the trip.

When they were near town, Mrs. Buntyn said to Yaw, "They've told me that your father is a university professor in Ghana. I don't think he will approve of that *wild* life you have been leading here. Off all over the place in the backwoods where there's nothing civilized!"

"I see," Yaw replied. A while later he turned, caught Jerome's eye, and winked.

Mrs. Buntyn dropped them and the baskets of food off at Expatriates. Yaw had hardly put down the manicou stew before all the other boys pounced on it. "Where did you get this? You've been getting all the good things in the country!"

"It's not my fault if they farmed you out to White people."

"Farmed out to White people!" Kofi exclaimed. "Jerome's mother is a *White* woman."

"No," Yaw said, "that's only her colour. She's a Black woman. I know."

"Stop talking about my mother that way. My maternal grandmother was a Black woman—blacker than all of you— and my mother has never lived among White people."

"Even Mrs. Buntyn said your mother's White," Kofi rejoined, laughing.

"Well, Mrs. Buntyn sees with her own eyes—I can't help that."

"What the bother is about? Chauffeurs have been taking my comrades everywhere. You should take up a collection to buy Jerome and me two pairs of shoes."

"Chauffeured! It would have been better if we had used our feet," Kwame said, "like that we could talk with our cousins. The only Black people we talked with were the maids and gardeners."

"An it jus like the White people in Ghana," added Omar. "No sar, yes marm, and always peeping around the door and around the corner to see if the mistress is coming before they answer owah questions. You should see them opening their eyes wide and shaking their heads. Like eef they afraid something happen eef they talk to us."

76

Gertie Sauls came into the room, and they stopped talking. Jerome left shortly afterward.

Around ten the next morning, he returned to the girls' pavilion. All the Ghanaians were in. Three of them were eating fruits Yaw had brought from the country. Gertie Sauls came into the dining room then, smiling faintly and walking erectly and sinuously, graceful like a palm tree, her molasses-brown face ringed by two thick braids of salt-and-pepper hair. The Ghanaians looked at her appreciatively. Omar hugged her. "We will meess owah mother."

"Oh no, we won't. *We* are taking her back to Ghana," Kofi said.

"Why do you boys want to flatter an old woman like me?" she said, smiling, her perfect teeth showing.

He got to know her quite well after the Ghanaians left. He had dinner with her family two Sundays, and he went with them on a picnic one bank holiday. Her older boy had already finished school and was in the civil service. The younger one was in his last year of elementary school. When he was expelled from high school, she wrote him a nice note, telling him that we all learn from our mistakes. When she found out he was taking lessons from the Morrisons, she offered her help, if he thought he needed it.

Shortly afterward, Yaw and he left for a day at the beach. The beach could be reached only from the next valley, which meant they had to climb the promontory where he sometimes watched the sunrise, walk over another spur and down the other side. It was a distance of three miles. On the way he pointed out Miss Dellimore's dwelling. *He had never thought of it before, but now he wondered if he would have done so if Yaw hadn't visited his parents in the country.*

From the high point they could see the three beaches that were just outside Hanovertown. Yaw asked him about them. There were huge hotels and palatial houses fronting Farnborough and Ambrose. They were not open to the public. The entire area, including Glendale, the beach they were going to, used to be the Ambrose estate. He told Yaw how the beaches got their names. Ambrose after its owner, Farnborough because that was the maiden name of the mother of the founding Ambrose, Glendale because it was the maiden name of the founding Ambrose's wife. When the price of land went up and tourism became valuable, the Ambrose family sold out the estate, keeping most of the beachfront land for their hotels. Two of the students assigned to the Ghanaians lived in Ambrose. Two of them, including Bertrand, lived at Farnborough. Quite a few of the residents were owners or part-owners of the large country estates, where they also maintained houses. No Blacks and very few Eurafricans lived in Farnborough and Ambrose. Glendale was open to the public because the British government had bought the adjoining land for an airstrip. With planes landing only a few hundred feet away, no one wanted to live on this beachfront, and so the public was allowed to use it. There was no road to it, only a track beside the airstrip. At the beginning, zealous airport security guards would turn the bathers back, until a bather knocked a guard unconscious, prompting the British administrator to announce that, if the bathers "are orderly and clad decently, their access to the beach must not be impeded."

At a small food shop a few yards from the airstrip, they bought meat patties, coconut tarts, and carbonated beverages. A little farther on they bought a small bag of ice cubes.

It was a bank holiday but few people were on the beach at that hour. He and Yaw stretched out on the sand, allowing the sun to burn them, and then dived into the water to cool themselves. The beach sloped gently seaward, and the frothy lips of the waves played at the edge of the sand. The air swarmed with seagulls. About a hundred yards from where they were, where the sand ended and bare rock pushed out into the sea, there was a wood fire, and a man, naked except for his swim trunks, was roasting fish there. Yaw wandered in his direction and returned about thirty minutes later with a bonito cooked in a pepper-and-lime sauce in a banana leaf. They ate it.

"Jerome," Yaw said, washing the remains of the fish from his hands, "I didn't thank you for taking me to your village."

"They really appreciated you. They never notice me."

"You're upset because of the fuss they made over me?"

He said nothing.

"Oh, Jerome. That's because I'm a stranger. If you came to Ghana, it would be the same way. In my father's village everyone keeps a hut for visitors."

Jerome remained silent.

"Some of your people are Akan. That's why they know about Anansi and Ntikima. My comrades don't think that Isabellans are African. The people of your village are still close. But there are many Africans who are not African. My father says that Dr. Busia is the whitest man he ever met. A lot of Africans educated by missionaries don't know who they are. That Pointer Dublin is a *Nama*."

"A what?"

"*Nama*. Somebody who holds all the knowledge about the origins, practices, and so on about the group. The one you

79

go to whenever there is trouble interpreting the laws of the group."

He thought about the time Pointer Dublin was arrested along with his father and the others because the British felt they were inciting people to revolt.

"What I want to know is, if you don't have chiefs, who settles the disputes in your village?"

"We have a magistrate who comes to the nearby town once a week for that."

"Is he of your clan?"

"What's a clan?"

"Well, it's like I'm an Ashanti, and only Ashantis have the right to judge the behaviour of other Ashantis. What are you?"

He thought for a while. "Nothing." His mood changed to sadness.

There was a prolonged silence.

"Our disputes are settled by our chiefs. And most of the time it's the people listening that decide the verdict."

"Strange you say that. The Spirituals, the group Pointer Dublin heads, aren't supposed to take one another to courts." *"You ever know," Pointer Francis said to him, "anybody that put poison in the river they drink from? Well, is just so we have for be to one another. When the belly empty the hand find food, the teeth chew it, the throat swallow it, and the belly feel glad. But if the hand say, 'What concern belly is not my concern,' pretty soon hand will get weak and not able to work. We is one body. Every part of it useful and every part of it depend on the other parts. No part of it must suffer."*

Yaw plunged himself in the water. He swam quite far out and waved to Jerome to join him. Jerome shook his head.

He had never ventured beyond waist-deep water, though he always liked to sit at the bottom and let the water cover him. *His mother said that when he was nine months old—they had not yet built the bridge across the canal—she slipped one day on the planks they had put for crossing the canal and fell into the water with him. "You didn even cry." But he knew it had to be more than that.*

When Yaw came back ashore and once more lay on the sand, he said, as if talking to himself, "This is a beautiful island, but I feel there isn't much happening here. Not like Ghana, where we are independent and building a great nation. Now we give the orders to the British. It feels good. Nkrumah will make Ghana a great nation. We are going to free the rest of Africa, watch and see."

Youth! Youth! The folly of youth. "A boy's will is the wind's will, / And the thoughts of youth are long, long thoughts." Freedom! Who could ever be free? Freedom from yourself!

"We should have been getting our independence in the next three years if our federation didn't break up," he told Yaw.

"The way White people lie around here on your beaches, even owning them, you think they'll ever let you control these islands?"

Yaw didn't know how right he was. Trouble was he didn't include Africa. They were all independent now. But for whose benefit? A fellow called Harry Hazelton had published an essay, "Confessions of an Exile," on the subject. He read it and reread it several times because it made him wonder what would have happened to him if Peter hadn't screwed up that time he was all ready to go to England. Harry really had something to say:

The colossal St. Lawrence soundlessly hurries to its destination in the reservoirs of the Atlantic, never to alter it. Each year the birds return to mate in the trees bordering it, the gulls to feast on the food abundant in it. I too go to it, for comfort; or is it for an axis? I remember the ending of a poem—"Island Streams," I think the title was: "...and now I've taken to rowing in green water silently moving." The author might have added, "treacherously."

Here I am an alien. Among my own people I am equally an alien. I have no sacrifices to burn on this altar. Daily I am other people's real and vicarious offering. How long, I wonder, before they turn me to cinders? The Portuguese, the Spanish, the British, the French... all searched for Eldorado in black flesh; they still do. The mind before and since has been imprisoned in that old alchemic formula: Blackness is the source of gold-creating power.

I have come to realize that I am the night in this Manichean scheme of things. And all the light from the millions of suns in the universe shone upon or inside me would not convince White people otherwise. Being Black makes me evil, lecherous, irrational, unpredictable, raw, savage, unquantifiable, dangerous. It's impossible for White people to look upon me without one or the other of these constructs obtruding on their consciousness. Their needs, naturally, determine which of their playthings they make me. Some come expecting sexual pleasures free from the restraints of civilized behaviour, or to get wealthy harnessing the brute force they see in me (the ox hauling diamonds from the quarry); still for others I am proof that reason can conquer or at least contain irrationality—the bullfighter triumphing over the bull. But none of this saves them from being afraid of me. Guess the matador does not underestimate the bull. After all I am the devil, I am Proteus, I am the dragon— all these rolled into one. And so the operative words— contain, control, and in the process, gain. Fighting this is like catching ghosts. How to reform the collective psyche of a race? Sometimes, I'll admit, it's pregnant with humour. A young lady who was at one time married to a Black man told me after she had gained my confidence that her mother had told her to stay away from Blacks because at night their tails come out.

"Did you ever see his tail?" I asked her.

"No," she replied, "but I used to look. And one night he woke up and caught me. He wanted to know what was going on. I promised to tell if he didn't get mad at me."

"Did you tell him?"

"Yes."

"What happened?"

"He left me. Is it true?"

"What?"

"You know what I mean. Is it true that Black people have tails that come out at night?"

"Of course they do!"

"Will you show me yours?"

"No. Not really. Besides it isn't dark and I'm not asleep."

But the group hardest hit by this Manichean reality are those Indians who come to North America and, driven by the wealth ethic, become prosperous. They knock loud on Canadian doors—a little too loud for comfort. I've watched them present their credentials of possessions and I've watched and heard those doors slam in their faces—deaf to the plea, "But I too am Aryan."

They withdraw, dazed from the slap. For, long subject to Euro-American propaganda, they too believe that Blacks are "lazy and lecherous," "moronic, savage," and "dangerous." "We cannot serve you," all six cashiers told me in a bank in Bombay. "That's because they class you among Untouchables," the European hotel manager later informed me. "You are lucky," he added, "they did not stone you; it is common here to stone Black Americans."

They have no defences for the Manichean slap. (It would be interesting to see what alliance they'll forge with Blacks—after they recover from the slap.)

"If you cannot beat them, join them," a Dominican once said to me. "For every Malcolm X, let's face it, there are five million Booker Ts. A lot sooner than later the Malcolm Xs become Booker Ts and are tolerated for that very reason."

"You don't understand," I told him. "Our pride, our oil, our minerals, our traditions, our souls, are and have been the building blocks of White industry."

"Why should you give a fuck if you make a living from it? Go on and git yours, like the Black Americans say, cause every man jack is a pig and we all got to

scramble down there in the trough. Scramble or starve. Jump in, that's all you got to do. You guys who study all that crap fooling yourselves. Every nigger should study business. Life is about taking, brother. You better learn how to take, take and make the taken think they're getting. Soon's I finished my degree, I'm heading back to Dominica into politics. And don't think I'm joining no opposition party!"

Sheer simplicity!

I long to return. Do I return to prison and death? To a stage of torture in a theatre of greed? To be paraded in the people's mind as a microbe bringing disease? Consummate ape of our former and present masters. (Slaves adopt their masters' gods; aspirants to freedom burn them.) Return home to promote reality designed in Washington, London, Paris, Tokyo! Become whipmaster enforcing policies that fatten the Metropolis!

So, by the banks of the St. Lawrence, it's gone beyond weeping to numbness. Imprisoning numbness.

For weeks, article after article attacked Hazelton. Someone even suggested that the government invite him home under the guise of showing him the falsehood of what he'd written, then arrest him, hold him without bail, and put him on trial for libel. Some said his attack on the Indians had been uncalled for; it would damage the delicate relations existing between Indians and Blacks in the Caribbean; besides, the Indian prime minister had been very vocal in calling for sanctions against South Africa. Such an essay might cause him to change his mind. This gem of a response came from the half-Indian civil servant in the ministry—he was now assistant comptroller of works: "But what sort o joker Hazelton is? Me hear White woman a-Canada just a-rub themselves all over you, tears in they eyes! And he a-waste time, a-write stupidness! Some people just don know how for use them luck!"

He'd thought the essay a trifle long and a bit overdramatic, but it had helped him understand a few things. After all, a small island was just a small island. Had he migrated, he might have been one of those weeping by the Thames or the Hudson or the St. Lawrence.

The essay had been published in The Nationalist, *the newsletter of the Association of Isabella for Isabellans. The association's lease was cancelled soon afterward.*

Within a year its president, who was also the editor of The Nationalist, *was arrested. The newspaper, television, and radio carried the story. Some believed that the real reason for the harassment came from the fact that* The Nationalist *had published a cartoon, shortly after the US invasion of Grenada, showing the prime minister of Isabella Island phoning the White House after he'd found out on television that he'd invited the American president to invade Grenada. He asked the American president how many troops he was to send and what date he should put on the invitation letter.*

The number containing the cartoon also had the following announcement:

> *KEEP EYES PEELED FOR OUR NEXT NUMBER*
> *WHEN REAGEY WILL PLAY HOPSCOTCH AND*
> *OTHER PASSIONATE GAMES ON*
> *CARIBBEAN LEADERS' BACKS*

The advertised number was never published, nor was any other. The police destroyed the printing press and smashed the windows in the office of The Nationalist. IBS television showed pictures of twenty pounds of marijuana the police reported finding in Humphrey's home. Rumour had it that the police had destroyed the windows and the furnishings of his house. The media were forbidden access to the premises. And a government decree made it illegal to broadcast any interviews with Humphrey or any member of his family.

The justice minister was asked about this. He said that, although the major charge against the editor would be the peddling of drugs, there were also charges of treason, and where the latter was the case, the state had to take unusual measures to defend itself. The reporter trod lightly. Radio and television jobs were patronage appointments. "Do you mean treason or libel, Mr. Justice Minister?"

"Treason, libel? That's for our lawyers to decide."

"But, Mr. Justice Minister, does a charge of libel necessitate the suspension of a person's civil rights?"

"Are you trying to teach me the law? I'm the justice minister."

"But some people would say, Mr. Justice Minister, that there appears to be a double standard here, especially in light of the recent controversy regarding the prime minister's son."

"Now don't drag the prime minister's son into this. They are completely different situations, as different as chalk and cheese."

The prime minister's son had defied the ban on sporting and cultural exchanges with South Africa and had gone there to play cricket. The prime minister had been asked whether his son's behaviour did not fall under the definition of treason. He said no, it was his son's affirmation of his individual rights, which were guaranteed under the Isabellan constitution. A team of lawyers had appeared on television a week later to say that the prime minister's assessment of his son's conduct was correct.

"If you need any further clarification," continued the justice minister, "I will suggest you talk to the prime minister himself. He will certainly straighten you out."

The reporter was briefly stunned as the veiled threat sank in. "Thanks for this interview, Mr. Justice Minister."

"Any time."

But why, he wondered, had they put the marijuana in Humphrey's house? Why? Why?

That day sitting on the beach, he burned to ask Yaw about cannibalism. There wasn't a Black, White, or brown person on Isabella Island who didn't believe that Africans ate one another and that White missionaries were working hard to change Africans from this custom. Black West Indians were ashamed of Africans and looked forward to the day when they would hear that Africans had stopped eating one another, for only then, they felt, would White people begin respecting them, so each year they gave a lot of money for these missions. In his French text, there was a picture of a naked African pointing his spear at a White explorer wearing a bowler hat and sitting in an iron pot under which firewood was already arranged. Beside the picture was the question "Qu'est-ce qu'il dit?" The books were outdated texts, a gift from a Canadian school board. A former student had written beside the picture, "Mange-le, nigger! Mange le limey-son-of-a-bitch!"

Yaw was tossing pebbles out to sea. A crowd had built up on the beach. There were cooking fires here and there. Jerome's hands were sweating.

"What's wrong with your hands?"

"They sweat sometimes." That was true. But they also sweated when he was nervous.

Yaw glanced at him between the pelting of the pebbles.

"I want to ask you," Jerome faltered.

Yaw looked at him intensely.

Jerome could not continue. Yaw broke into a big grin, then gave a bark-like laugh. "I knew you had to ask. I don't know why you didn't ask me the first day we met. I'm not going to eat you, Jerome. For one thing, you're not White." He paused awhile. "Seriously, Jerome, putting ritual cannibalism aside, we don't eat people. White people try to teach us, even in Africa, that one reason they stole our continent was because we ate people. But our memories are not short. We didn't keep written records, but we kept live ones. Our historians say that's the worst lie the White man ever told on Africa."

Listening afterward to the calypso, he couldn't help thinking that the calypsonian really envied the Congo man all that white female flesh to dine on (fear must have made it even whiter) and was hopeful that one day he would put a White woman (maybe two) in the pot and eat another live—he'd already perfected the grunts; he lacked only the flesh. Guessed the moral of the calypso was: White women, avoid Africa if you don't wish to be eaten. All things considered, those two women discovered a new meaning to the expression "swallowed up in darkness." Had the calypsonian been literate, he'd have read George Lamming's essay about English factory girls who pestered Black males with demands to see their tails. They must have been amateur taxonomists.

Basil Davidson's books show that Yaw was right. Still, all nations at one time or other in their development were cannibals.

He must have read that in the Encyclopaedia Britannica. *He'd checked it after Yaw returned to Ghana, to see what it said on cannibalism. The Polynesian and Irish used to eat their dead. It said also that the Bantus were cannibals. But recently he read— he could not remember where—that what Europeans called cannibalism among Africans and native Americans was nothing more than the practice of eating the heart or the brain of their slain enemies, as a way of adding their vital forces to their own.*

Yaw had exploded: "Your good-for-nothing calypsonians have nothing to say about our independence struggles, about White injustice! They know a fucking lot about cannibalism. They carry on so much about thick lips and black skins, you would think they were fucking White people! They praise Kennedy and scorn the Mau-Mau. Well open your ears! We know that you people hate us, we know that you hate yourselves. You West Indians would be the first to trample us or spray us with poison gas, if you knew that afterward White people would accept you as White. Because we are Black and you are not White!"

Yaw didn't know, and neither did he then, that those calypsonians knew on which side their bread was buttered. All those islands were still colonies. Their songs could only be about ideas acceptable to the British. Praise the Mau-Mau and the calypsonian would have found all sorts of things happening to him. The Spirituals were put in prison for following their religions. He was old enough to remember the big fête at the canal bridge the day they abolished the law. He asked his father why they were dancing and singing, and his father replied, "We making merry cause now we can serve we own God without worrying that they might lock us up." He was seven at the time. What did the British do to you? *What did the Ashantis do to us? They hired Whites to train their army to catch slaves. Incredible! Every man jack selects what he wants to remember from history!*

6

THE FOLLOWING MORNING he went to Mr. Bunyan's office in response to a note Bunyan had left him. Bunyan sat quietly at his desk, his face tanned a cinnamon brown, his ice-blue eyes expressionless, his jaw firmly clamped. He picked his pipe up from his desk as soon as Jerome sat down, filled and lit it, and began puffing away.

He wanted the Ghanaians' addresses and telephone numbers because, he said, he wanted to enter the African art business when he returned to England.

Jerome did not visit the Ghanaians that day. They had gone on an outing down the Leeward coast, at Jeremiah's Cove.

The next day was his mother's birthday. (He did not know his father's.) He wanted to surprise her with a gift. He also had to pass by the Education Office to pick up his "envelope."

After he had given a Compton woman he met at the market the gift to take to his mother, he began to walk uphill to Miss Dellimore's. It was around noon. He met Miss Anderson at the bottom of the hill. She was wearing a wig with a pigtail that reached halfway down her back and was huffing and puffing because of two heavy baskets she was carrying. He offered her help. She wanted to know his name. He lied to her. She spoke to him in dialect. She was obviously pregnant and spoke about a husband who was studying in England. She turned off at the junction about thirty yards below where Miss Dellimore lived. Her house was just a little way in, a rambling affair. The galvanize was rusting and the yard was overrun with weeds, as if its occupants were away on vacation.

She died in childbirth about a month later. The obituary note mentioned nothing about her husband. It mentioned the same mother the cane cutter had spoken about. Eventually everybody came to know that the child's father was the education officer who had introduced her as having come all the way from the capital to teach them. Naturally, he could not say that he was the father of Miss Anderson's child. But Isabella Island was too small for such information to remain hidden.

About sixty people attended the film/discussion/exhibition that Wednesday. Mostly the faculty, their spouses and children, the mothers of the host boys, a couple of their fathers, and a few people from the community at large. Mr. Bunyan was absent, but Miss Hunt, looking a little less like Miss Blunt, accompanied by the son of a White merchant, whom it was rumoured she was dating, was very present in a saffron dress.

In one room was a display of iron, bronze, wood, and ivory carvings of ancestral figures, fertility dolls, and dance masks. On the walls were various lengths of kente cloth, all hand-loomed and dyed; they were like paintings.

The film was an hour long. It began with an introduction of the organic Ghana in the heyday of Ashanti power, went on to discuss the political Ghana that resulted from the Berlin Treaty, the fierce prolonged war that took place between the Akan and the British before conquest was finally achieved, the splitting of several nation groups, the Ashantis being divided between Ghana and Togo, and another group whose name he did not remember being split three ways: one part in the Ivory Coast, another in the Upper Volta, and a third in Ghana. Independence dominated a large part of the film.

When the film ended there was a dazed look on the faces of the Whites and Eurafricans and a look of relief on the faces of the Blacks: the Whites—he was sure—surprised that Blacks weren't running around naked and eating one another; the Blacks relieved that such wasn't the case.

The discussion period was quite short. Only two questions were asked. One of them criticized Nkrumah for being a communist. The other was from a man wanting to trace his roots and to know whether, from looking at him, the Ghanaians could tell where he was from. There was scattered laughter.

Thursday was party day. It was held at Ambrose Bay, at Mrs. Morkham's home. Everybody knew her from her photograph that appeared annually on the front page of the the *Isabellan*. It showed her handing over a cheque for a thousand dollars to the chairman of the board of governors of The Good Shepherd Mental Asylum.

When the chauffeur got through the ring of tamarind trees that blocked the view from the front of the property, they spied her, semi-enclosed by the bougainvillea and ivy that curtained off the front porch from the open air. She was fanning herself. Rumour had it that she was a "weedropper." But that was only because she had black hair. Somebody among her grandparents was dark-skinned—Spanish or Italian. She was in her early forties and slightly corpulent. She was wearing black lace, several strings of pearls, and diamond earrings. She belonged to the more outgoing of her class. It was known that she had been inviting non-White professionals to her parties long before the civil rights battles in the US prompted others to do so.

There were trays of food on tables arranged along the patio, which was about a hundred feet in from the sea. Classical music came from a speaker in the ceiling. He liked the view of the sea, which was partially blocked by sea grapes and almonds, and the blue outline of the offshore islands. He enjoyed, too, the cooling breeze coming off the water, for it was a hot day. They sat at the northern end of the patio and began eating sandwiches. Within half an hour, all the guests arrived.

Father Mulgrave overshadowed them; he was a short half-White man with a rich baritone that had begun to crack. He wore a black soutane, a white collar, and a pendular cross. He spoke of "a fellow quite dark but *very* bright and of exceptionally fine manners, one Joseph Antoine," who had been at Codrington College with him and who had gone off to Ghana as a missionary. Did any of the boys know him? No, they did not. Well, it was a pity. He himself had once had the missionary itch, but "my darling here" had cured him of it. He pointed to Mrs. Mulgrave, a White woman who spoke with a deep Scottish accent and whose skin looked like paper that had been crumpled, partly smoothed out, and left to yellow in the sun. Were the boys Christians? No, not entirely. One, Omar, was Moslem. One, Yaw, was "animist." Two were African Methodist Episcopalian, and two were Roman Catholic.

"No Anglicans. *Tch, tch, tch!*" He winked and shook his head as he said this.

The Ghanaians laughed at his antics and seemed to appreciate his attempts to be fatherly.

He wandered away after this to talk with the other guests.

Mrs. Buntyn, all decked out in red—dress, shoes, hat, and handbag—kept herself busy circulating trays of sandwiches. Nothing disturbed the engraved smile she wore as she eeled her way among the guests.

"Eat up!" Mrs. Morkham, never far behind Mrs. Buntyn, was saying. "We prepared it all in your honour. Eat up! We prepared…"

The gardener and the maid were nowhere in sight. But he wasn't fooled. They had done all the work. And if something was missing Mrs. Morkham would know exactly where to find the maid to supply it. As soon as the guests left, the maids would reappear to do the cleaning up. She covered up well, though, sending her son Terrot for ice for the fresh punch she was pouring into the punch bowl.

Kwame had brought some Ghanaian records with him, and the Ghanaians were debating among themselves whether they should ask to play them. Newesi, who was assigned to Terrot, advised against it.

At that point the Ghanaians and Jerome were together at the northern end of the porch and the Eurafricans and Whites were together in small clusters at the southern end. It was as if they had divided the porch into separate territories.

Gertie Sauls told him the first time he went to her place for dinner that, on the morning before the party, Mrs. Morkham had phoned to invite her. She told her she would not miss it for all the world, meaning, of course, the opposite. She wasn't interested in the charade. "What was the point of helping them put on a solidarity show, false impressions for the young men to take back to Ghana? No way was I going to be used that way! Can you imagine? They planned that party before those boys came. I had the itinerary a week before their arrival. Out of guilt they invited me. And I, I suppose, should feel honoured to sit on Mrs. Morkham's porch and look at the beach where people who look like me dare not set a foot."

Terrot must have overheard parts of the discussion over the records, for he came over to ask them if there was anything he could do. He was a tall, string-like, freckle-faced youth with hair the colour of honey, and looked as vulnerable as brittle firewood over a country woman's knee. His picture in his Boy Scout uniform was frequently in the *Isabellan*—the proprietor was his uncle, and his parents paid his fare around the world to represent the Boy Scouts of Isabella Island.

"We are fine," Newesi told him, exchanging a glance with Kofi.

"What have you got in the sack?" Terrot asked him.

"Records. Highlife music," Kwame replied. "Better than this——" Yaw's hand came over Asofua's mouth.

The Eurafrican-White enclave had noticed, and all eyes were on the Ghanaians. Terrot looked from one group to the other and finally focused on Jerome, as if to say, "Well, you're an Isabellan; take my side; tell me what's going on." But Jerome put on his deadpan look.

"You see," Omar broke the suspense, "we brat you some of the music of owah country so you can hare how eet sound. Eef eet sound gout and you like eet, we leave you eet." It was the first

97

time Jerome noted his difficulties with English pronunciation. He was embarrassed for him because of the hostile Whites and Eurafricans present.

Yaw turned to Terrot. "Is this the only kind of music you play in the West Indies?" He was obviously playing the devil's advocate.

"No, there are two kinds, depending on your class. The better class plays classical music. The other class plays mostly calypsos. Calypsos are funny and have a good beat. The church is against them, and in point of fact, they are quite vulgar. The better class does not permit calypso music in their homes."

This time the Ghanaians looked at one another and raised their eyebrows almost imperceptibly.

"Since you are our guests, I shall ask Mother whether or not she'll let you play your music."

He must have been sidetracked, because the subject never came up again.

The party dragged on until seven. About half the guests, those who had probably come out of obligation, politeness, or curiosity, left before six. A chauffeur arrived in a minibus from the Island Paradise Hotel, owned by Mrs. Morkham's husband, and took the Ghanaians back to town.

There were several exchanges between them in the remaining days.

"I know as a guest I must not say things like this," began Yaw, "but you must excuse me. You all did not have a single storyteller in that village. And the young people don't have a clue what's going on." They were standing outside the main entrance of the general market.

"All that storytelling business," replied Jerome, "isn't it for people who can't read and write and who don't have anything better to do with their time? I heard a lecturer saying something to that effect on BBC. He called it the oral tradition and said that once people get literate, they abandon it."

"Are your people literate?"

"A lot of them are."

Yaw was silent for a long time, but his forehead kept rippling and unrippling, and he kept pulling at his chin. Finally he said in an angry tone, "You are wrong. Every British boy knows about King Arthur and St. George. Every Jew knows about Abraham. The first things missionaries do is spread propaganda about their heroes and force others to give up their own. You know why? Because when we adopt their heroes, we begin to think like them, we become destabilized, we begin to want to be like them, and then they can do whatever they like to us."

St. George or George Saint or Saintly George; Arthur King (there must be somebody with such a name and round too and underlined). And Blacks sang that they were going to go to Abraham's bosom and Jews would certainly not want to be with all these Hams—probably one reason they did not eat ham—who came about because their founder had seen his father's dick after he'd removed it from his daughter. Chant on, Yaw, Yaw, Yaw!

"My father told me that the difference between Protestants and Catholics is because of the beliefs Christians found in those places. It's because of the way people there thought before they accepted Christianity. I can't remember the full explanation he gave me. He said that the people of southern Europe were accustomed to others making decisions for them, something about some Delphic oracle—"

99

A girl named Delphina lives at the edge of the village. She receives lots of men, but they return more pleased than wise.

"—and depending on the answer some priests gave them. So now they confess to their priests and he tells them their sins are forgiven."

Who gives a wet damn about this brittle shit. Go lather yourself with it. The expression was Peter's.

"The Catholics in Ghana don't tell their priests everything. In the earlier days my people used to notice the colonial police coming to their huts, but only to certain huts. It had them puzzled. Then somebody figured it out. You see, it was because the Catholics used to tell their priests—they were all White—what they had stolen from their employers."

That certainly wasn't Catholic, or was it? "What about the Protestants?"

"You see, they were more independent. They believed in making their own decisions. So they didn't want to be in the confession box. They found it was like a coffin, you see. They believe in making deals with their gods. I give you something; you give me back something."

Like making America and Africa coffins for their inhabitants. He was cheating. He did not think that then. He did not know that then.

"Your father is crazy. You know that? Crazy, crazy, crazy! When does he have time to teach, thinking up crazy ideas like that?"

"When your people stop being shadows and start becoming people, then you will understand why my father thinks like that. You have to keep a step ahead of White people."

More than a step ahead, and not just of White people. Yaw

certainly didn't need to tell him that now. And by now he must know a lot about shadows. Africans could teach Jung a thing or two about that.

"Take it from me, Jerome. When you start imitating the culture of a people that despises you, they spit on you for doing it. And *you* end up despising yourself. You become a shadow society. You become shadow people. We have lots of beliefs in Africa about capturing other people's shadows. You have to be proud of your culture. We Ashantis used to boast that nobody could push their culture on us for very long. That belief made us strong. For a long time we controlled the nations around us. When the Europeans came, we bought weapons from them and got the Dutch generals to train our troops because we knew the time would come when we would have to fight them."

Yaw, Yaw, ya-ya-yaaah. Yaw on, Yaw.

"You see, my father says if you want to have your own culture you have to fight for it. Better to be a king in a hut than a slave in a palace."

You have a lot of gall! The Ashantis bought their guns and paid their Dutch generals from the sale of slaves caught in raids on the very people they were collecting tribute from. I wonder if your father told you that. But he did not raise the subject. He did not want to begin again what had occurred on the beach on Monday. He let him drone on.

"You must have something to hold you together. Society is like a tree. That's why the kum tree is sacred to us. That's why we hold a lot of our ceremonies at the root of a tree. We are all trunk, branches, twigs, flowers, and fruit."

Fruit, for sure, and vegetables too.

"The thing that protects, the bark, is our past. In another way it is the water that keeps our roots alive, even in the dry season. Without it we would become shadows or dead wood for other people to make carvings with. That's why in our ceremonies we form circles and link hands and dance. Dance. There's nothing to create unity like dance. And it's everybody that creates the unity. That's how we act out what we feel. The soul of the group. We make it come alive. Everyone gives it life. And the soul of the past preserves us in the present and gives us a future. It is that past that your people lack.

"Look at Mrs. Buntyn. Neither Black nor British. And dead. Those people are moving corpses embalmed in their pearls, their diamonds, their silver, and their money. They need your people to keep them from rotting."

Just the same, there must have been something to what Yaw had been saying, for he remembered a conversation he overheard between his mother and Eunice during the months he was at home after he had been expelled from school.

"All like Mr. Manchester so done dead, and the Bible say we must leave the dead for bury the dead."

"Comsie, how you mean he dead?" Eunice had asked her.

"Eunice, when the dry weather come, what does happen to the tree them?"

"Them stop growing else them lose some o them leaves. But what that got for do with Mr. Manchester?"

"Eunice, you ever see a time when Mr. Manchester stop for shed off what he got? Try eating and eating and don't shit and see what happen."

"Comsie, me no get yo point at all."

"Eunice, it ain't no point to it. Money is like dirt. If you don

102

wash it away you gwine stink, and it sit in yo soul like shit in yo bowel."

"Comsie, gal, yo might be right. But me wouldn mind some of that shit right now."

"Well, you not going get it cause it in White people bowels."

He stared at Yaw, transfixed. And then it occurred to him that Yaw was delivering a speech his father had written for him to give if the situation called for it. Yaw did not want to go back to Ghana without giving his speech. He was tempted to say, "Good speech that," but kept quiet. He listened to Yaw for about ten minutes more and then suggested they move on.

The Friday before the Ghanaians left, he dropped by to see them. They had just finished supper, and four of them were going off with their charges to the cinema.

Yaw left the common room and returned with a box that he presented to Jerome. "You open it only after I leave."

"There's something I have to ask you," Jerome told him.

Newesi looked at Yaw as if to ask whether he and Jerome needed privacy.

"It's all right," Jerome told him. "It concerns you too."

"So, go on, ask it."

"It has nothing to do with me, please understand that."

"Break the suspense, brother," Newesi said.

Newesi looked at him intently. He was quite lean, with a very narrow face. He and Yaw were of the same complexion, but Yaw was stocky, more like someone from the Congo, from the pictures Jerome had seen of various African types. Yaw's nose was broader and somewhat flat and was definitely closer to the African stereotype than Newesi's. Newesi's eyes were cold, revealing none of his emotions, whereas Yaw's were forever twinkling—with mischief, for sure.

"What's in the box?" Jerome asked.

"You'll find out after we are gone. Actually there's a little African soul in it. Newesi, you better give him a little of yours. It's the only way we are going to keep him alive. Africanly alive."

All three of them laughed.

"Now, Jerome, what do you want to ask me?"

"It's about Mr. Bunyan, the school's principal."

"We know who he is. He met us at the airport."

"And came to see you several times."

Yaw looked at Newesi. Newesi looked at Yaw.

"When?" they asked together.

"Well, he said he did. He's interested in African art. And he thinks you and your comrades can help him."

"Tell him," Newesi said, "we have a national repository where all the national art treasures are collected. The remaining pieces we auction off, at international prices."

"I can't tell him that."

"You'll have to," Yaw said. "Newesi's father is the curator for the Ghana National Museum. You got it straight from the source, brother."

"Tell him to hire an army and stage a raid. That's how they did it in the early days. And they burned a lot of it too while singing hymns to their God."

"He wants your addresses and telephone numbers."

"Does he want our balls?"

"No, that's in America," Newesi said.

"You can have our addresses, but not if you are going to give them to Bunyan."

"Guess I'll have to tell him, 'No go.'"

"Guess so," Yaw echoed.

"How are your ears, Jerome?" Newesi asked after a brief silence.

"Okay. Why?"

"Because you've spent all this time with Yaw. This boy talks! His mother had to birth him before time. He just kept chattering away in her womb. She couldn't concentrate on anything else. And that's not a lie. His mother told me so herself."

"Don't listen to him. He never met my mother."

He stayed with them, politely chewing kola nut and talking about mainly nothing, listening to them teasing each other and trying to draw him in, until the other boys returned from the cinema.

Next morning there was a crowd to see them off. Gertie Sauls dropped him off in front of Miss Dellimore's house afterward. He was glad that it was over. But he also knew he would never again be the same. He did not have the words for it then, but they'd unburied a part of his African self. A depression came over him, and he felt listless.

Miss Dellimore called him for supper around six. It had been a cloudy day all along, and it had begun to rain. You could not see beyond a few feet. The fog had come down from the hills and buried the town. The rainy season had started.

Supper was very thin cabbage soup with two slices of bread and a cup of cocoa. He could not eat. He was even slightly nauseated.

Miss Dellimore eyed him.

"You is not feeling well?"

"I'm all right,"

"Then why you not eating?"

"I'm not hungry."

"Okay then, I gwine divide up yo supper between the other two boy them. Them gwine glad fo the extra. You sure you is all right?"

He clenched his teeth.

"You sick? That what it is."

He shook his head.

A week after the Ghanaians left, his mother came to town. She said she had come to see the doctor. They spoke a bit about Yaw, and then he asked her why she had come to see the doctor. If anything, she looked fat to him. It struck him then. At sixteen, without brothers and sisters, he had settled into believing that he would remain an only child.

His mother must have seen the V between his brows. It was always there when he had an unasked question. "Yes. Me think me was too old for this. But is God will. Round bout December or else January, you will have a brother or sister, God willing."

After Miss Anderson died, his mother's pregnancy caused him to think about death a lot during those months before his brother was born. He had never before entertained the thought of what it would be like to live with either or both of his parents dead.

He was pleased to hear his mother say, "You see how hard yo father working Miss Bensie land? Things is little better for we now. Henry and me decide is time we put a little money aside for buy a piece a land and build a house, cause like now we not working on Mr. Manchester land, he liable to ask we for go anytime. Is true his son that take over the plantation not as bad as his father—he does even say howdy when he pass you in the street—but like the old people say, you musn take any more chance than you have for."

"Oh, Ma, that is so good! I can't wait to start working to help out! I don't want my brother—or sister—to grow up in a mud hut like I did."

He walked with his mother downhill, passed the tennis courts where some of the sixth formers from Expatriates were playing, accompanied his mother to the hospital, and waited until the doctor had seen her. He stayed with her until her bus was ready to leave.

7

On September 3 his third year started. Because he'd been moved ahead a year, it was to be his fourth year in English language, English literature, history, geography, and biology, subjects he was going to have a shot at in GCE later that year. There was some doubt on his performance in the Easter exams. It was the first time, too, that the academic year started in September. Until then it began in January. They met in the auditorium for assembly: to be reminded of why they were in school. Following tradition they sang:

> Lives of great men all remind us
> We can make our lives sublime
> And, departing, leave behind us,
> Footprints on the sands of time.
>
> Footprints that perhaps another,
> Sailing on life's sultry main—
> A forlorn and shipwrecked brother—
> Seeing shall take heart again.

On stage, as was the habit, Mr. Bunyan and the deputy principal, Mr. Boggs—an Australian who taught physical education—stood at the front while the remaining twelve teachers stood in a single line behind them. Miss Blunt, her hips noticeably bigger and her hair quite golden—corn ready for plucking, one of his classmates had told Peter one day while gesturing at her back—was very present in a red dress.

That year, the first period was English composition, and the teacher was still Miss Blunt. On Tuesday they were to familiarize themselves with various narrative techniques and were therefore to read ten pages in their composition text.

As soon as she finished speaking, Allan said, "Peter is going go get us all in trouble. You all watch and see."

He hadn't been near enough to Peter during assembly, but he had seen the strain those close to him were under to keep from laughing.

"It's not my fault," Peter said. "I don't believe in fairy tales. If they're going to force me to go through this, at least grant me the right to have some fun."

"You don't believe in God!" Percy exclaimed in his squeaky, tremulous voice.

"Who believes that rot?"

"Don't say that!" Randolph exclaimed, his eyes bulging with fright.

Peter turned to look at Randolph, sitting directly behind him. "You actually believe that nonsense? I thought everyone goes along with it like my dad does."

"You mean the 'old bloke,'" Rajan said. That was Peter's usual name for his father, whom he frequently mimicked with irony. They'd deduced that his father had Parkinson's disease because Peter could never repeat a statement without reproducing the accompanying gestures.

"'We have to keep up appearances, you know,'" tremors, cigar-puffing and all.

"Your father doesn't believe in God!" Alfred exclaimed.

"Of course not! No intelligent person does."

They were all silent after that. *He later understood why. Peter was from England, where ideas and books came from and where their rulers, including the Queen, lived. They weren't permitted to challenge what came from England, just as they couldn't challenge those sent from England.*

Rajan placed a sheet of paper on Jerome's desk. On it was written Peter's parody alongside what seemed to be the correct words of "Awake! Awake to Love and Work." Jerome had the opportunity to read

"Awake! Awake! To love and work,
Awake, awake! come suck me off.

The Lark is in the sky…
My dick is hard and high…"

before Miss Blunt approached his desk. He held the sheet under the desk, ready to pass it to someone else should Miss Blunt ask him for it.

"What yalls fidgetin about?"

"Miss, 'The Intimations Ode' is a superb poem, isn't it?" Peter asked her.

"Yes, one o ma favourites," she replied, already heading back to her desk.

It was one of Peter's favourites too, one he always used to get himself out of trouble. "The child is father of the man, Miss. Now don't you forget it."

"Who has my songs?" Peter asked.

Jerome gave him the sheet.

"I'll bring copies for everybody tomorrow."

At that point they all began to read the work Miss Blunt had assigned.

That Tuesday afternoon, he went to see Bunyan to tell him the Ghanaians had left without giving him their addresses and to return fifty-one dollars he hadn't spent. As he was exiting from the school grounds onto the main road, he heard Peter calling to him from halfway across the grounds, "Wait for me!"

What did Peter want with him? He stopped walking. Be careful, he told himself. Peter's mouth's "an unsphinctered arse," one of the White boys had said, and Philip, who was from the country, had answered, "It ain't so you say it, White boy. Is, 'He mouth a-run like sick pickney batty.'" Peter approached him, smiling, and Jerome remarked how muscular Peter was. Apart from being mischievous, his only joy seemed to be playing soccer. His blue-green eyes were roving Jerome's face as though it were fine print.

"Why don't you like us?"

"Who's us?"

"The lads in class. All of us. Who else?"

"How did you arrive at that conclusion? Tell me. I'll add it to my list of theorems."

"How funny! I tried to talk to you at recess. Your head was in a book. You're always reading!"

"Well, if my head was in the book, what did I use to read the book?"

"Go to hell!"

He'd been trying to finish *Heart of Darkness* to find out why Yaw's father had objected to it.

"You read to avoid talking to us."

"Well, I don't see anything wrong with my reading."

"I do. It's to give us the cold shoulder. You don't fool any of us. Why don't you play soccer with us after school sometimes? The other Black boys play with us. We do all sorts of things together. You don't even listen when we talk to you."

Well, he didn't know that a person listened with his mouth, but that was another story.

"We're going to see a film on Saturday morning. Why don't you come with us?"

"I promised to do something for my mother. I can't go."

"Bosh! You don't want to go with us."

He resumed walking toward the main road. Peter followed.

"Your father's chauffeur must be waiting for you."

"I told him not to come."

They were now under the huge white cedars that bordered that section of the main road.

"It's not my fault that I'm *White*. And it isn't *my* fault that I'm British."

"Is it mine?"

"I'm serious."

"Who said you weren't?" He knew that Peter was fishing. Among his mother's favourite expressions was one about people throwing sprats to catch whales. He was going to let him waste his bait.

"I know how you feel. You know that?"

Posturing isn't one of your strong points, Peter. Even Miss Blunt knows that.

"I hear what the bastards say. I know what you read. I peek at the articles in the magazines and I look at your books."

"Do you know what will be on the GCE exams?"

"Stop laughing at me! I'm serious."

There was silence.

"If I was Black, I'd hate every White son of a bitch—"

"You don't have to be Black to do that."

"I want you to know I'm not my father, only his son. I know what's going on. Especially in Rhodesia. They talk about nothing else at home. We visit a lot of the plantations on Sundays. Do I know what they think about your people! And it makes me angry! I know why you goddamn well don't like us. I see who live in the shacks. I see who cook and serve the food and look after the children. I'm not blind, you know.

"One Sunday we were at this planter's place on the north coast, and you know what the conversation was about? Too many schools on Isabella Island and too much power in the hands of the field workers!"

"What did they say?"

Peter hesitated. "I'm not supposed to repeat what I hear."

"So why did you start telling me?"

"You don't know! It's because I like you. You aren't fake. Most people are fakes. Almost everyone in class is. I fight with my father. All the time. You know why? Because he has a conscience. He seldom shows it, but it's there. Forget about Mother."

Did Peter think Black people were fooled? Maybe the dunce White boys thought Blacks didn't know what was going on. There were all sorts of opinions expressed in the Isabellan. *About six months earlier there had been an article that read:*

113

It is now a known fact that it is only a matter of years before the traditional occupations into which our secondary school graduates go become saturated. What will happen when we find ourselves with large numbers of educated, unemployed youth? We must not forget the calamities of the 1930s. Moreover, the individuals involved then were barely literate. I do not think we will want to see the scenario occurring presently in America duplicated here.

  Joseph Moton, Esq.
  Planter

Mr. Grover had written in support of Mr. Moton:

It's a terrible thing to have to say I told you so. Now I have lived long enough to see that I was right. When the idea of free primary education was pushed down the throats of taxpayers thirty years ago, I and the majority of planters—almost unanimously—opposed it. But the British government imposed it.

  Any fool at the time should have known that once the labourers became schooled they would not want to work in the fields. I argued too that if primary education became free it would lose its prestige: only the education that people have to pay for is respected. But for our vigilance in opposing the construction of new secondary schools, not to mention paying the salaries of an increased number of teachers, every estate would be idle today. Heaven knows enough of them have had to close down and sell out the lands.

There is a simple solution to this problem. Reduce the school enrolment by a third. The large number of secondary school graduates is a bad example, anyway. It gives every young boy and girl the idea that he or she too can avoid working in the fields, which we know is the principal occupation of ninety percent of the negro workers of this colony. I will therefore recommend that we maintain present admission priorities—the children of the planters and merchants accorded first priority, since it was their endowments that founded the school; then the children of the mulattos, for they have proven to be able administrators; and the remaining places, if there are any, to the children of Indians and negroes.

I know many will say that my recommendations look like a turning back of the clock. I predict that if they are ignored, not only will the economy collapse, but blood will gush in the gutters, the blood of the very negroes whom so many irresponsible people have of late taken to filling with unrealistic hopes.

So he knew what Peter had been hearing on the plantations.

After Isabella Island got its independence, a historian who had graduated from the London School of Economics began to publish information that the public hadn't known about. He published the transcript of some of the consultation over free primary education. A certain Mr. Brown, he wrote in an introduction to one of these transcripts, had been sent by the Foreign Office to inquire into the schooling system. Messrs. Munro and Morkham were planters and also members of the legislative assembly, and they'd been delegated by the planters to communicate the planter viewpoint to Mr. Brown. They told him that schooling spoiled good agriculture workers, that putting children to work early taught them the value of thrift and hard work, and that too many literate people on the island would become a source of trouble for the colonial government. The historian published the exact transcript of what they told Brown.

Peter went on to say to him, "Each time you look at me, you accuse me of being like other White people. I want you to know that I'm not. I'm just Peter. I could have been Black. Or I could have been Chinese. But I'm White and can't change it."

"You've misunderstood me, Peter. I've never accused you of anything." He was afraid of having friends but couldn't say so. *"Friends bring you but they don carry you,"* he'd often heard his grandmother and his mother say. And they were right. Many times he'd wondered how different his life would be if he had been able to follow all the wisdom they'd tried to teach him through proverbs. Maybe, just maybe, he would have been as successful as his brother. But his brother got his perks because he was of the independence generation.

Peter stretched out his hand. Jerome took it.

"Let's just be two human beings and forget the rest—our race, our parents, *everything!*"

They continued to look at each other in silence.

Jerome turned to begin climbing the hill.

"This conversation must stay between us," Peter said.

"No problem."

He thought about Peter a great deal while walking up the hill. He felt tender toward him. He even remembered that he'd figured in one of his erotic dreams. Still, he had to be careful:

"Is them what hold the handle and we that hold the blade."

The following morning Peter winked at him and smiled. Assembly passed in the usual fashion. For some reason Miss Blunt had to leave the class right after she assigned the work, and so they did not do it.

"There's a joke I have to give," Alonzo said. "I rolled with laughter last weekend. We have this new maid. You should see her stepping! First day Mama asked her what time it is. The clock staring her boldly in her face.

"'I don't knows, mistress. I ain't wearing my specs.'"

Everyone except Jerome tittered. Randolph tiptoed to the door and looked around the corner to see whether Miss Blunt was coming.

"So later the same afternoon, Mama asked her if she knows how to make Yorkshire pudding.

"'No, mistress, I never heards about it.'"

"That's not how Black people talk," Philip told him.

"Quiet! So Mama gives her a five-by-eight card with the recipe on it and goes down to the beach. When she gets back, ready to serve supper, no pudding.

"'Harriet, didn't you make the pudding?'

"'No, mistress, my eyes runs too much waters when I reads without my glosses.'"

They all laughed, he in spite of his discomfort.

Almost instinctively they looked at the door.

"When Daddy got home, Mama told him.

"'Alice, let's try something. You remember those mood cards I brought back from Florida?'

"'What are you talking about? I told you to burn them.'

"'Let's put five of them on the table—'"

117

There was a lot of throat-clearing and they exchanged lewd looks, smiling.

"Your daddy doesn't have much imagination," Percy said.

"I have a better idea," Allan said. "Tell him to stick a thermometer in your mama to see when she's in heat."

Percy tiptoed to the door and peeped around the corner.

"'BEWARE, HEADACHE, TIRED, MAYBE, NOT TONIGHT. Put them all together and tell her to bring MAYBE. She can't make any excuses. You can read those cards a mile off.'

"After supper, Mama put the five cards on the kitchen table while Harriet was washing the dishes. From the parlour, she called, 'Harriet, see those cards on the table, bring me the one that says MAYBE.' Harriet brought all the cards.

"'Harriet, tell me the truth. Can you read?'

"'Shore I reads alls the times.'

"'So why you brought me all the cards?'

"'Cause I feels likes its.' You should see how she swelled her bosom.

"Mama thought for a while. Daddy and I were laughing. Harriet was standing there staring at the floor.

"'Look, Harriet,' Mama said, 'you better get your "glosses," as you call them, and if you still can't read, remember you won't have a job and I won't pay you for two weeks. But, if you can't read, you better tell me now. You do your work well. I won't dismiss you.'

"'You is rights, mistress. I nots can reads.'"

"That's the joke, Lonzo?" Peter asked.

"Some joke!" Percy said. "I've been hearing that before I could talk. You didn't tell it right."

"Why you don't tell jokes on your own kind?" Philip asked him.

118

"We have to find a joke school for Lonzo," Peter intervened. "Right now he can't even recognize jokes."

Miss Blunt entered the room and they began to look serious.

She questioned them on the comprehension questions they should have answered. She asked the questions, waited, then read the answers from the Teachers Manual—priest and congregation in her own litany.

Next day, Percy collected their homework. When he was finished, Miss Blunt, blushing and looking a little suffocated in her yellow miniskirt, said, "Today, yall, I got somethin excitin fer you. Yall know many great poets came outta simply writin poetry in the classroom—" They looked at one another, puzzled. "I thought we'll commence by writin sonnets." She pronounced it *saawnnets*.

She passed out two mimeographed sheets of sonnets and told them to examine them and then use them as models for their own work.

"She can't even write graffiti," Randolph exclaimed, "but she wants us to write poetry."

"Let's hand in some of Peter's songs," Rajan said.

"Give her your balls," Peter told him.

"It's yours she wants," Rajan replied.

Miss Blunt was leafing through the homework assignments. Then they noticed she was holding up one of Peter's songs. She blushed as she read both pages. Everyone sat tense. They waited for her explosion, but she proceeded to mark their work as though nothing unusual had happened. That period they worked enthusiastically. When the period ended, she said very quietly, "Peter, I wanna see you in this classroom raat after school."

After school, they all waited for Peter to return from Miss Blunt. He spent about thirty minutes with her. When he came out he was laughing.

"Tell us what happened," Allan urged.

"Calm yourselves," he said, extending his arms and outstretching his fingers as if about to soar. "'Why don't you shave this off?' she said, touching the fuzz on my chin. Then she showed me the sheets with my songs. 'Yous guys are careless bastards, you know, yall is. How many o these you got going round?' I didn't answer.

"'What you're going to do, Miss?'

"'I gotta mind to show em to the old boy.'"

They all laughed.

"'But, if you sing em for me, I won't now. All raat now, let's hear you sing em.' You should see how her chest was rising and her titties were jumping."

"Did you get a hard-on?" Philip asked.

"Fool," he replied, "you don't get one when you're scared."

"Why didn't you lean her over the desk?" Lonzo asked.

"Because your father wasn't there to show me how. My hands started to sweat. 'I can't sing, Miss.'

"'You wrote em and you're gonna sing em.' So I sang them."

They all knew Peter couldn't sing. Whenever he did, it was as if they were all listening to a tape with several gaps in it. His throat moved, but often no sounds came.

"You know what she told me? 'Peter Pinchley, you're such a heartbreaker!'

"'Miss, I never broke anybody's heart.'

"'How you gonna know, loverboy? Handsome young men always break the younguns' hearts.'"

"Loverboy!" they guffawed and began to stomp and clap.

"'Hold on to ya sheet. If ya compositions were's good as this here smut you'd a been gittin better marks. If you got more o em floatin round you'd better round em up and burn em. If the headboy finds em your goose'll be done proper. Gotta admit, them songs is really funny. And I been quite lenient with you so's not to git the other boys in trouble, cause they ain't got neither the looks nor the position to git erway with it.'"

"See?" Rajan said. "That's just what my father said to me."

"Rajan!" they shouted. There was an unspoken agreement among them not to mention their school mischief to their parents.

"You all carry home news on Mr. Morrison."

There was silence.

To this day he did not understand why he came to Peter's defence. "Rajan, you shouldn't be talking about him at home."

Peter walked halfway up the hill with him. He thanked him for taking his side against Rajan. "It's great that it's you who defended me."

"Why?"

"Because, you see, you never take sides. And everybody knows you're bright. So, when you say something, it's respected."

He had answered Peter out of reflex, for it was long afterward that he started to pay very close attention to what his villagers said in private. Guess you have to break your bones before you know why you shouldn't race on a slippery slope.

When Peter turned to go down the hill, Jerome thought about Rajan's remark that they gossiped about Mr. Morrison. He wondered if Rajan knew why the petition against Miss

Blunt had been shelved. *In the weeks at home following his expulsion, he had thought, among other things, that the White parents could not bring themselves to do anything about Miss Blunt. For one thing, she was White, and they had to show solidarity. They certainly believed, few in numbers as they were, that a chain was as strong as its weakest link. And the Eurafricans were so dependent on them for everything, they couldn't initiate any action against her. Mr. MacIntosh was the exception, and when he wasn't in jail on charges of sedition, the* Isabellan *called him "the brown monkey doing Bolshevik tricks."*

Mr. Morrison was their English literature teacher. In complexion he was the only Black teacher on staff and one of three Isabellans. Of the other two, one was Eurafrican and the other White. Three were from other Caribbean colonies. The rest were from the White Commonwealth.

Mr. Morrison was a tall man in his mid-thirties, just beginning to thicken in the waist. The top of his scalp was bald, and the hair at the back and the sides of his head was noticeably grey. His face was roundish, his nose broad and bridgeless, his lips big to the point of appearing swollen, and his forehead usually greasy, though he was always wiping it to remove the grease. He wore gleaming white shirts, narrow ties, dark trousers, and polished black or brown shoes. If he liked you, he smiled. If he didn't, you couldn't know what he was thinking.

Discipline was never a problem in his class. If they talked, he merely lifted his eyebrows and they fell silent.

There was always a lot of discussion in his class. He encouraged them to give their opinions on the works they were studying. He always praised a good analysis and encouraged them to see the arbitrariness of a poor one. Often he'd agree with certain interpretations, but he'd tell them not to write them on GCE if the occasion arose; occasionally he pointed out why.

They studied Defoe, Dickens, Shakespeare, Wordsworth, Pope, Milton, and George Eliot. But he also added Kipling's "The White Man's Burden," on which they wrote analyses. When he handed back their work, he'd corrected only their grammar, punctuation, and style; he made no comments about their opinions.

Trouble began when he taught George Lamming's *In the Castle of My Skin*. There were thirteen White boys in the class, and Jerome realized later that he should have expected trouble, for they had all been silent throughout the discussion. Peter had asked a few questions but, probably sensing the hostility of the other Whites, soon became silent. Philip, who was the only pure Black boy in their class, and the six darker-skinned ones, including Jerome, agreed with Lamming's portrayal of the plantation owner. Philip's uncle was a union organizer. Philip usually ranked fourth or fifth in performance, outdone only by Jerome, Peter, Rajan, and occasionally Eardley. His hatred for White teachers and students, even though he rarely spoke, was evident to Jerome. *Jerome met him in town several years later and had seen in the* Isabellan *that he'd got seven GCE O-level subjects. Philip was getting ready then to go to America. He told him that it was his aunt, who was a registered nurse in the US, who'd paid for his schooling. He was going to study engineering at Hunter College. They'd refused him a job in the civil service on account of his uncle's activities. Philip had been working for about seven months at the school where Mr. Morrison's wife taught when Jerome met him in town. Strange, he'd got a job in the civil service, still had one, for that matter.*

Mr. Morrison knew what went on in Miss Blunt's class. He laughed whenever they spoke about her. "Miss Hunt," he'd say, "is a teacher. She wouldn't be if she hadn't received the requisite training."

Some fifteen years later, when Isabella Island was no longer a colony and the Canadian government had helped to build ten secondary schools and several Peace Corps teachers taught in them, very few of the students, in some schools none, passed GCE. When Cambridge threatened to strike those schools from its exam rolls, a commission investigated the schools and found that the Peace Corps teachers spent their time entertaining the students and being entertained by them. Their attitude was that of people on vacation. The commission found that many of them lacked basic mathematics and reading skills. It recommended that they be tested before being allowed to teach senior high school classes and that they be kept to under twenty percent of the teaching personnel. He wished Mr. Morrison was still around, to find out what he'd truly felt about Miss Blunt.

Peter was very fond of Mr. Morrison. One day while he was seated at his desk, Peter had begun massaging his bald spot. "I know something that will make your hair grow back."

"Where's it? In a tomb under Stonehenge?"

They'd all laughed.

His wife was a White Canadian who said she wasn't at home in Canada or with White people. She told you this within the first five minutes of getting to know you. Mrs. Morrison taught French at Bethel High School, run by the local Baptist Church. It was a small two-storey building, not far from the cemetery. There were no partitions between the classes. Some of their classes were held in the cemetery. During the rainy season the students took turns sitting down—those with reading assignments standing, those who had to write sitting. There were about a hundred and fifty of them in the building, which leaked and sometimes drenched the students because the church lacked the money to repair the roof. Water and light, too, came in from holes in the termite-eaten wood. Occasionally those parents who were masons or carpenters gave their labour free to repair the building, but the school rarely had the money to buy the materials. A committee of parents took turns doing the cleaning and caring for the tiny plot on which the building stood.

During the fifties, when police were occupying Compton, some neighbours near Bethel saw a White man drive up, enter the premises, and soon leave. Within fifteen minutes, the building was on fire. They contained the fire, pouring buckets of water on the flames, until the fire engines came.

Bethel never turned away any students who passed the entrance exam. Other than the principal and Mrs. Morrison, who refused to teach at Expatriates, none of Bethel's teachers possessed university training; a couple of them had A levels in the subjects they taught, but most had only O levels. Their pay was just about half that of Expatriates' teachers, their classes bigger, and their hours longer. A girl called Magdalena, who lived in the house above Miss Dellimore, went there. Jerome had helped her once with a composition. She told him that Mrs. Morrison had got her friends in Canada to send them crates of books to create a school library. But, for three years, the books stayed in the crates because the government had refused to give the school the money to build the extra room to house the library. Eventually termites got into the crates, and they had to burn the books.

Jerome still wondered why Mr. Morrison had married Mrs. Morrison. He would have liked him even more if he'd married a Black woman. *Years later he understood, from examining his own self, that most Black people who lived under colonialism were milder versions of Miss Anderson, and he'd seen the wisdom in Mr. Morrison's choice.* She was a tiny, fragile-looking woman who seemed always to be in a hurry. She talked as if she was in a hurry too, and she rarely smiled.

Jerome had seen Mr. Morrison's father. Both he and Mr. Morrison's mother had taught at the school where Comsie and Henry spent three years before their parents removed them, finding the two cents they had to pay every Monday morning too onerous. Mr. Morrison, Sr., had gone on to become a head teacher. Mr. Morrison, Jr., had won a scholarship to study English at the University of Toronto. It was there that he met Mrs. Morrison.

Shortly after his classmates abandoned the idea of a petition against Miss Blunt, Jerome waited outside for Mr. Morrison one afternoon after school. They walked together to the nearby elementary school, where Mr. Morrison went to pick up his daughter every day. He begged Mr. Morrison to read compositions that he would submit to him every week, because he was uncertain about Miss Hunt's comments. Morrison hesitated and agreed on condition that Jerome not breathe a word about this to anyone. Teachers had their own classrooms, and he met Mr. Morrison in his on those occasions when he had to hand in or discuss a composition.

Mr. Morrison's class was the third of the eight daily periods they had. It came right after recess. One day, when Mr. Morrison entered class, they knew, in spite of his controlled expression, that something was wrong. His face wore a crucified look. Everyone sat stiffly, eyes fixed on him.

He stood silently at his desk for about five minutes. Then he said, "I have a letter here which I would like to read to you. Perhaps I shouldn't involve you, but I'm going to. In a couple of years, you'll be governing this island." He read:

Dear Mr. Bunyan:

On behalf of the governing board of the Expatriates Academy, I wish to register my protest over the sort of material Mr. Morrison uses in his class.

The issue in hand is that Mr. Morrison is using a book call *Uncle Tom's Children*. This book is written by a Communist and it can do no good, only harm, causing the children reading it to hate the White race. Let me tell you that all of this Wright's books have been removed from American libraries and people in America burned them.

This colony is a very peaceful one. Whites and negroes here get along together well. If we allow teachers to teach writers like Wright don't you see it will cause race riots, atheism, and destroy democracy?

We would like you to insist that Mr. Morrison sticks to writers like Shakespeare, Huckleberry Finn, and Silas Marner. [Mr. Morrison paused to let the laughter die down.] They are the writers our children should know about.

I will even go on farther, which is to say that the Wright book is full of broken English. We work too hard to get these children to speak good English. I think it will hinder the children from learning good English. [Laughter.]

I demand that Mr. Morrison be duly informed about our feelings and of our readiness to execute a plan of action if he ignores us.

Signed: Mrs. Janet Motley
Secretary of the Board of Governors
of the Expatriates Academy

"The ruddy bitch!" Peter spoke. "What right does she have to tell you what to teach! And illiterate too!"

Everyone else was silent. No one would openly criticize Mrs. Motley. The Motleys owned four medium-sized estates around the colony, a bank, and several of the commercial buildings in Hanovertown.

"You should send it to the *Isabellan*," Peter said.

"They won't print it," Jerome said, surprising himself. He'd better watch his comments. They all turned to look at him.

He expected Philip to say something, but he remained silent. He looked around the class, wondering which of the boys' parents had started it. No one could be certain. It could even be a Eurafrican who started it. There were a lot of people on Isabella Island who were frightened of communism and who denounced those who made Marxist-sounding remarks.

About five years later, he discovered that Mrs. Morrison was Marxist; it was her Marxist principles that made her refuse to teach at Expatriates and eventually leave Isabella Island. The colonial government had promised to fund Bethel but had insisted that the school dismiss those teachers who were openly communist. The school began to harass her and two other teachers. The Isabellan began to harass both her and her husband, quoting out of context and distorting certain things their ex-students had reported. Mr. Morrison told him it was tiresome to have to deal with "phantom accusations," and so he and his wife and their daughter went to live in Canada. Monsieur Dusseault was still at Expatriates, now renamed Hanovertown Secondary School. He had come on a two-year contract but never returned to Canada. His wife was a Black Isabellan. Very few of his students failed French.

It was around that time, too, that he found out Morrison had read them Mrs. Motley's letter with Bunyan's permission. Bunyan, he said, had promised to support him against her and showed him his reply, which said that he had confidence in Morrison's judgment, that Richard Wright was an acclaimed writer and some of his works were published in England, so there could be nothing wrong with them.

They were to discuss the last story of *Uncle Tom's Children* that day. "Should we continue with 'Bright and Morning Star'?" Mr. Morrison asked.

"I'm in favour." Peter's hand went up.

"Me too!" Philip said, also raising his hand.

Jerome raised his hand. Slowly, hesitantly, the hands of the Eurafricans went up; even more hesitantly did those of the Whites.

"We continue," Mr. Morrison said.

In Miss Blunt's class the next morning, Peter asked her

if parents had the right to tell a teacher what to teach. She thought about it for a while and answered yes. Peter told her about the letter. She said she would have to see the letter and read the book before she could give an opinion.

When Wright's book on Ghana was reprinted, the Isabellan *quoted extensively from it. It praised Wright for "telling the truth about Ghana." "There we have it, straight from the mouth of a negro; Africans have a long way to go before they are civilized." There'd have been no fuss if Mr. Morrison had taught that book.*

When Miss Blunt's class ended and they were heading off to other classes, Rajan asked Peter why he wanted Miss Blunt to support Mr. Morrison.

"Because I don't want him to get lynched!"

"They don't lynch people here," Rajan told him.

"Well, I think they're about to start, and I don't want him to be the first victim."

"Peter—but Miss Blunt!" Rajan said. "Don't you know innocent people sometimes hang because of dotty witnesses?" He entered his classroom. Jerome and Peter continued to theirs, down the corridor.

After that the term appeared to progress uneventfully. Miss Blunt's classes got worse. Most of them simply forgot to do her homework, and it didn't seem to bother her.

One day just before school closed for the Christmas holidays, Peter told him that he was going to follow him home. Jerome said he had things to do in town. He started walking toward the commercial district, eventually going into the market. Peter stayed with him. "Are you going to remain with me all day?" he asked Peter.

"All day and all night too," Peter told him.

He didn't know what to say or do. He stood still in the market, refusing to speak to Peter, hoping that he would leave. Peter eventually left, but when Jerome was nearing the top of the hill where Miss Dellimore lived, Peter emerged from the side road where Miss Anderson used to live.

"I won this round," he said to Jerome. "You mustn't be ashamed of where you live."

Jerome continued walking, and Peter came along. No one was at home. He invited Peter in and offered him a seat. There were things scattered about the room. A dishpan full of dirty dishes sat on the table. The kerosene stove Miss Dellimore used smoked, and the ceiling was badly smudged. He observed these things intently for the first time.

Peter stayed for about ten minutes. He too said nothing. When he rose to leave, he said, "Now it's my turn to take you home. We are friends, see? And friends must know where one another live."

Miss Dellimore wouldn't have minded. She might have even asked Peter if he knew anyone who would give her daughter a job, for that was a contentious issue between them at the time.

He never did visit Peter's home. He would have gone there on Peter's birthday, the following May, but he was already expelled.

The Christmas holidays came and ended. His baby brother was born on January 2. Jerome promised to go home more often now. He was quite glad to have a brother. His brother was pale and his hair blondish—heavy on the milk and light on the coffee. But that didn't bother him.

When the January term started, he spent less time on incidental reading and began to concentrate more fully on the subjects he was writing at O level that year. All but the brightest students had five years' preparation. There was about a sixty percent failure rate for first-time takers of the exam. The White students did worst. The Blacks, followed by the Eurafricans, were the best achievers because only the brightest Blacks and Eurafricans got into Expatriates.

Miss Blunt's class continued as usual. They were focusing on compositions. She had trouble with the number of words like *each*, *its*, *their*, *anyone*, *everyone*, *none*; she confused them no end. Mr. Morrison continued to grade his compositions and to teach him correct usage.

Miss Blunt continued to wear her miniskirts to class. She had three of them—one lime green, one yellow, the other marine blue. They still continued to move farther up her thighs whenever she was writing on the board. Peter had stopped focusing on his erections but would cup his hands and put them behind the cheeks of Miss Blunt's buttocks as if he were going to massage them. One time he actually stood up but managed to sit down just before Miss Blunt turned. She sensed the tension in the class, squinted, returned to writing on the board but turned around in thirty seconds. Peter stopped for the rest of the period. Over the next couple of weeks Rajan and Jerome joined in.

It happened one Tuesday morning. She was writing away on the board, and Jerome was making signs at her bottom and looking around at the class to see how they were reacting, when Miss Blunt turned. It was her scream that alerted him. She ran into the corridor, and all the teachers came out of their classrooms. They couldn't get a word out of her. She pounded the wall and emitted a high-pitched screech.

Bunyan arrived and questioned them. Eardley said, "Miss Blunt turned and saw Jerome making obscene gestures at her bottom and she became hysterical." He said it as if he had been cutting up a dead cat in the biology lab.

"Come with me," Bunyan told him, "and bring your books."

Jerome eyed him and made a dash for the door. He didn't stop running until he got to the market.

8

THAT EVENING HE WAS sitting on the bleaching stones when his father entered the yard astride a donkey Jerome didn't know he'd acquired. He dropped his machete before dismounting, and Jerome watched him silently surveying his seated profile against the growing dusk.

Earlier that afternoon, he had told his mother that he'd had a serious quarrel with a teacher. She wanted to hear the full story, but as he looked at the deep lines under her eyes and the pain already etched in her face, he postponed telling her.

After securing the donkey, his father returned and stood towering over him. "What you doing home in the middle o the week? It not no holiday."

He didn't answer.

"Look, boy, you see I jus come from the land tired and everything, don get my spirit vex up. I ask you a question and I expec a answer.""

Jerome still did not answer.

"Father in heaven, give me patience."

Pongy and Millicent came out in their yard. String was in his. Comsie hurried out from the kitchen.

"Henry, leave im alone, please." She said it pleadingly. "He get in trouble in school today with one o his teachers and he not ready for talk bout it."

"Woman, you done gone out yo head? What you mean he not ready for talk bout it?" His shouting brought more people out into their yards.

He watched his father turn to look at the gathering people. His father bowed his head and walked into the hut. Yawesi started to cry then, and his father picked him up.

Jerome ate no supper. His father ate sitting on the bleaching stones and then summoned Jerome into the hut. "Now tell me everything that happen, from A right down to Z. And you better tell me everything, cause although this two by four build pon Mr. Manchester land, is still me that build it, and longst as I still have breath in my body when I ask you a question in here I want a answer, cause, as you well know, two bo rattah can't live in the same hole. Now tell me what happen today."

"Don't be too rough with him, Henry. Go easy with that boy. I never seen him like this before. We don want a nervous breakdown pon we hands."

"Shut up, Comsie!"

His mother already knew that he had left his books at school and that he hadn't even gone to Miss Dellimore's before coming to the country.

He hesitated.

His father pounded his fist on the makeshift table and it came crashing down. Henry got up and walked out of the hut. He came back very late that night.

Next morning his mother took the bus to town. She

felt she should apologize to Miss Dellimore for the anxiety his absence must have caused her, and she wanted to see the principal.

He awaited her return at the canal bridge. She had his books, and there were scaly patches below her eyes where the tears had dried. He was deeply saddened that he had pained her. He loved her dearly. But he'd already decided to put on a brave face. He knew he didn't matter in the scheme of things. Not even Bunyan was important. Bunyan too took orders. After his classmates' parents had heard the story, they would threaten to withdraw their contributions to the school or fire Bunyan if Jerome was permitted to return. He understood that very well. Yaw had opened his eyes and set him thinking long after he left. Not about the things Yaw would have liked, but thinking nevertheless.

When Comsie got into the yard, the weight of the day's woe seemed to be upon her, and she sank onto the bleaching stones.

"Go bring Wesi let me nurse him," she said, putting the sack of books down on the stones.

He brought out Yawesi, and his mother took out one breast and later the other, and his brother noisily sucked away at her milk. When he was finished, she handed him to Jerome, went into the hut, changed into her home clothes, and set about preparing supper.

When his brother had fallen asleep, he joined her in the kitchen.

She shook her head, brought her bare hands up to her eyes, and wiped the tears that had begun to flow again.

"Mr. Bunyan not taking you back. I never think I would o

live to see the day when I would go down on my knees in front of a White man. I do that today cause I know it important for you to get yo schooling. Is yo only hope. I didn know yet what you do. When he tell me the teacher catch you playing with she bottom, he self had to help me get up off the floor. Jerome, I never did know you was so stupid. I never know that."

There was a long silence while she peeled away at the tannias and occasionally adjusted the firewood under the iron pot.

"Well, Mr. Manchester estate out there. And when no work on it you can help yo father on Miss Bensie farm." She said not another word to him until his father's arrival. It was as if she'd settled the matter once and for all. He could not understand it.

His father came home sooner that day. He came into the kitchen. "Comsie, what the head teacher tell you?"

"Henry, Jerome finish. Jerome try for feel up a White woman teacher from Merica behind."

Henry walked into the yard. He came back about five minutes later. "Tell me the rest, Comsie."

"Nothing for tell, just that them expel him. That mean he caan go back to school. Henry, that is one coalpit that burn to ashes. Tree waste, labour waste, everything waste. God make mouth and He provide bread; is not so the world go?"

His father went to sit on the stones outside. His mother served him his dinner there. Jerome ate his in the kitchen.

After she finished washing the dishes and nursing his brother, she said to his father, "Henry, you and me and Jerome have for sit and talk this whole thing over. When you have a half-rotten onion you does use the piece that ain't spoil."

They sat on the makeshift bench inside the hut.

"Who name Peter?" she asked him.

"A White boy in my class."

"I didn know you go to town for friend up with White people. I did think you have better sense than that."

"Peter is no ordinary White boy. It's he who pushed his friendship on me."

"Go on! Dig out me eye!" his father responded.

"Well he say for tell you," Comsie said, "that he really sorry for what happen. He see me when me leave the head teacher office and he come up to me and he say. 'Are you Mrs. Quashee?' I nod my head and he say, 'Tell Jerome I'm coming out to the country to see him as soon as I find out where he lives. Tell him he must come to town on Saturday and see Mr. Morrison. Mr. Morrison gave me the message and I went up the hill to look for him and the lady I met there told me she didn't see him after he left for school. I told her he got into trouble at school and she said he probably went to the country.'

"Next thing, what you been writing in yo book them?"

That question surprised him.

Well, the head teacher read some things from one of yo book them and it really frighten me. I don know what for say. I never did think anybody what win scholarship so stupid.

"What he write in the book, Comsie?"

"You know the blessed are the peacemaker part in the Bible? Well, Jerome take them and add his own words to them for make them sound blasphemous. And the book even have in rude words too bout the same White woman that he try to feel up. Henry, we can't save this. It done gone sour."

"Go bring the book."

"He don got it. Mr. Bunyan say he keeping it."

Jerome was frightened. He'd written everything in that book. He carried it around with him because he didn't want it to fall into anyone's hands. He had written a lot about Miss Blunt in that book, his feelings about White people, his growing affection for Peter, his opinions about Mr. Bunyan, the dreams about having sex with Errol and later Peter and the big question he was asking himself. He knew he could never stare Mr. Bunyan in the face again. Would Bunyan tell all the teachers what was in the journal? Did Miss Blunt read it? Was that all he had told his mother or was she hiding part of it from his father?

He never found out how much his mother was told. Once when she asked him whether he was seeing anyone, he had become suspicious. When Hetty had started telling people that there was something between them, his mother had looked relieved. He knew she wouldn't have told his father about that part and he was sure that if she knew, she would have hoped for a miracle.

Boy-boy, his mother's first cousin, was gay. He'd been present many times when jokes were made about him and even more than jokes. He was a constant point of reference for what the society would not accept:

"You not no man, you is like Boy-boy."

"I see you talking with Boy-boy. What happen? You turning weird??"

"What you know bout oman? Is Boy-boy you interested in?"

The first August he was home on holidays, his mother had sent him to the shop over in Mercy Village to buy salted cod, and Boy-boy was in the shop. Alice Bolton, who boasted sometimes about all the men she had slept with, and sometimes threatened to tell their wives—her tongue never stopped going just like her fat body that rippled in the see-through fabrics she sometimes wore—was there too. She went up to Boy-boy, placed her hand on his crotch, and shouted to the men drinking and playing dominoes in the far corner, "I never taste this yet."

"What you wasting yo time for? That ain't gwine raise it head for you," said Alfred Boatswain.

"It gwine raise it head if you promise fo let in by the back door," said a young woman Jerome did not know.

Everyone in the shop laughed.

"It have fo smell shit first," said another rum drinker called Hardup. "Ain't me is right, Boy-boy?"

"You not saying nothing on yo own behalf?" Alice asked him.

Boy-boy remained silent. He moved only when Alice took away her hand, and Jerome could see that he was trembling.

During the first year when he went to work in the civil service and was living on his own in the capital, there was a very handsome fellow who worked on a road repair crew who had smelled him out and sent him messages. He refused to speak to the messenger; he didn't like him; he didn't look careful enough. The one who sent the messages was quite different though. Jerome never knew how he found out where he lived, but one Wednesday, when Jerome only worked a half day, Jerome had met him standing at the gate to his rooming house.

"You don take my message them, so I come in person."

His biggest fear was that someone might see him talking to this fellow; that would have been enough for them to conclude that he was that way too. He didn't answer. He walked past him and began climbing the steps to his room. The fellow began to climb the stairs too. "If you follow me," Jerome told him, "I will call the police."

The fellow stared him straight in the face and said, "Who you think you foolin? I can see in yo eyes that you love me and you know I love you. What you so fraid for? You will live for regret this."

Jerome said nothing more to him but did not climb the stairs right away. He stared at him and remembered Boy-boy and the pain Boy-boy's mother and cousins and sisters were living through. Never. Never will his mother ever have to face that on account of him. And he had stifled his desires over the years. Each time he saw this fellow on the street, a slight chill went through his body. It happened for others too.

For twenty-seven years he kept the promise.

If Mr. Bunyan had told Mr. Morrison about it, Jerome did not know because Mr. Morrison had never mentioned it. If he'd told Peter, Peter had never mentioned it to him either. How many people knew his secret? How many people had secretly passed on his secret? Was he a deaf person wondering why the world was so silent?

While they were talking, Ramcat, one of Mr. Manchester's unacknowledged, illegitimate children, called on Henry. Mr. Manchester, he said, was aware of what Jerome had done and expected Henry to discipline him.

"I gwine flog him," Henry said. "Tell yo father that."

When Ramcat left, Henry said, "Comsie, the White people them want blood. Them done send and tell me the jumbie-bird wha Jerome do. Jerome, where yo sense is? Under yo foot bottom? Is walk you does walk on it? You can win scholarship, you can come firs in class, and you still don know you caan make White people know what you think? You think cause I laugh, cause I use for work on they estate, cause I live pon they land, I like them? No sah! But I don ha for tell them that, and I don ha for show them that. Deep down in here, there is where they is." He pointed to his chest. "Plenty thing yo grandmother uses for say I gree with. But yo grandmother was a damn fool. Excuse me for saying that, Comsie, but me have for say the truth. If you hit a empty barrel cause you want people for hear the sound, that good, but when you hit it cause you want them for know it empty, then you is a damn fool. I uses to hear she say all sort o things, and when I take stock that she didn have a stitch o power, I uses for just laugh and laugh.

"Well, Mr. Manchester want me for give you a good cut arse so you better, if anybody ask you anything, tell them what I wale yo behind good and proper.

"I always uses for tell you it got plenty things for learn what you ain't going find in White man book."

He had thought then about Philip and just how different Philip was from him, always knowing how far to go and then slipping back into silence. Philip. It was as if he was seeing him now. Skin the colour of asphalt and smooth as polished ebony. Eyes that were wells of dark light. He must have been around five-eight. He had the streamlined body of a runner and the thighs of a soccer player. He was a runner too. The year he was expelled, Philip won Expatriates' first Caribbean-wide medal: he took the silver in the 220-yard race. He had never dreamt about him. But he had been embarrassed by his reactions in his presence, and once he'd had to turn his back.

Something he could never understand about Philip. You'd see him on the left of the crowd, and when you looked for him again, he would be in the middle, and if you looked again he would be on the right. Or sometimes he would be there but as if he had faded into invisibility. Somehow Philip had never elicited the curiosity of the other boys, certainly not Peter's. It was because he challenged them at times. He played with them sometimes too. He had inoculated them against curiosity. There was nothing in him to be curious about. That was it. He stayed in Lower Town (Corbeauland) with an aunt, under what circumstances he did not know. Most of the residents in Corbeauland lived in single rooms, even with three or four or five children. Philip made it so that everyone thought they knew him. Wasn't that something?

He had a good sense of humour. One lunchtime Philip showed him a reaction he wrote to a piece in the Isabellan *about government expenditure in the colony outstripping revenue, and the colonists' refusal to accept any increase in taxes.*

Dear Mr. Editor:

I read the article about the revenue problem in the Isabellan *last Saturday. I think I have a solution for your revenue problem.*

In an article about three months back there was a complaint that the residents of Hanovertown waste water because they flush their toilets too often. I think you could solve the revenue problem and the water problem with one stroke.

Here is my solution: install a meter to each WC to record the weight and volume of the stool deposited in the toilet bowl, the weight of the person depositing it, as well as the frequency of use. You needn't tax people whose stool is less than average size. The bigger stools will come from the wealthy people because only they can afford to eat plenty, considering the cost of food in Hanovertown. The poor don't have indoor toilets, so the tax won't affect them.

How would this solve the revenue problem? Well to begin with, a lot of wealthy people are gluttonous, so your taxes won't discourage them. Some, it is true, will cut down on their eating; but they will get slimmer and won't be candidates for health care due to overweight in the near future. Those who eat less will also use the toilet less, and so less water will be used. But there will be another benefit too. Some will be too cheap to pay the extra taxes for flushing and will only flush their toilet once a day, once every two days, or maybe even once a week, regardless of what's in it. You're wondering what the benefit will be? Don't you see it will cut down on water use and give them a chance to smell their shit and realize that just like normal people's, their shit stinks too.

Signed: Bartlett Boyers
(a future economist and toilet meter vendor)

PS. Some might even decide to hold it in. What a blessing that would be! But we won't get into that.

He had laughed a lot. "Let's show Peter," he told Philip.
"You out yo head?" Philip pulled the letter from him and tore it up into tiny bits. "If you ever breathe one word bout this

144

to them coffee-cream and bonny clabber friends you got, I will ram this ya fist down yo throat."

Philip must have kept a journal too. Jerome longed to know what he had become. Hope he wasn't one of those who went to the States and got hooked on drugs. He could never envisage Philip getting hooked on drugs—or on anything. There was no net big enough to trap Philip. He slipped through the one the colonists had spun when he got into Expatriates. And by the time they realized he'd got away and tried to catch him by refusing him a job in the civil service, he'd already found an escape route to the US. Indestructible Philip. Bravo for him.

His thoughts returned to that night with his father. "Listen to this story here and draw yo own conclusion. It never too late for start learning sense," his father said. "A long, long time ago they been a little boy who been bright, bright, bright. That boy uses for learn everything what anybody teach him. That boy look up in the sky one day and then he turn to his mother and he say, 'Mama, why hawk can fly and me caan fly?' His mother say to him, 'Child, why hawk caan talk?' 'Cause hawk not human,' he answer she. She answer back to him, 'And you think you is hawk?'

"Later the same day the boy go off in the woods, and he see a crocodile sleeping with the jaw them open wide. The boy go up to the crocodile and he peep down the crocodile throat cause he want for know what inside o it. When he couldn see nothing, he push his hand down the crocodile throat. Paps! The crocodile bite off his hand.

"The boy watch his wrist bleeding and he say to the crocodile, 'Why you bite off me hand?' The crocodile swallow the hand and then he say back to him, 'Did you look down me throat?' The boy say, 'Yes.' 'I did bite out yo eye?' The boy say, 'No.' 'Did you push yo hand down me throat?' The boy say, 'Yes.' 'Well,' say the crocodile, 'me throat is mines, no? Anything in it is mines, no? You got yo territory and I got mines, no?' The boy start for cry. 'Give me back me hand,' he beg the crocodile. 'I done swaller it,' the crocodile tell him.

"If you don understand the meaning of this story, you ain't ha no business winning scholarship for go a secondary school."

His father went off to bed. A few minutes later his mother did too.

He undressed and lay in his own bed thinking about what was in his journal:

Blessed are the poor in spirit:
They hate not life;
They only miss it.

Safe are the poor in purse
When the wealthy don't curse.

Blessed are the meek
If they're eaten like sheep.

...

Why I come here nobody knows;
Miss Blunt writes not nor understands prose;
And what she knows in verse
Is not worth the hiring of a hearse.

...

Pretty Miss Blunt, of sexuality the fount.
Knowledge she'll never mount.
She should have known Leigh Hunt
He never had enough of juicy —.
…

When you are Black and poor
You're White people's door.
If you're a man, they make you a boar;
If a woman, they make you a whore.
…

Bunyan is a keg of yaws.
Why he has hands I do not know.
His character suits claws.

In his mind he went over and over similar passages. What did Bunyan think when he read them? Bunyan must have remembered what he'd said in his office—"Careless! Impossible!"—when Jerome told him the Ghanaians had left without giving him their addresses. White people thought they came to the colonies for the natives' good. A waste of time, Bunyan must have said: they're mostly savages, they can't show gratitude.

He heard his baby brother crying. He opened his eyes to the dark. There was someone beside him.

It was his mother. "Wake up, Jerome!" he heard her say. "What wrong? Henry, light the lamp."

He was wet with perspiration, he was already feeling chilled. His father approached with the feeble kerosene lamp. Jerome sat up.

"You was shouting down the house, bawling for help," Comsie said.

"Yes, I dreamt I was—in a thick forest—and a White man was chasing—me—with a lasso. I kept running—and bumping my head on trees. I fell down and couldn't get up. That's when I started to scream."

His mother brought him a clean pair of pyjamas.

"Go back to sleep," his father said.

"Things will work out," his mother said.

His father blew out the lamp and he and Comsie went off behind the canvas partition where their bed was.

He woke early and went outside to sit and to think about nothing. After breakfast he headed toward the sea and sat under a clump of pingwing and thought about nothing, occasionally allowing himself to be distracted by the cries of the plovers or the change in the water level as the tide rose or fell.

At home that evening he listened to the steelband, which had expanded. He dreaded what its players would say to him when they found out he'd been thrown out of school. The boys from the neighbouring villages had banded together—young men between thirteen and twenty-one—with those from his own. Compton being the most central of the villages, it was here they met, at the canal bridge clearing. They'd enlarged the thatched-roof hut. They spent much of their spare time cutting the large oil drums they'd stolen, bought, or begged for, and hammering out the notes: testing them, adjusting them to sculpt the pitch. Often this went on past midnight; it did not disturb the villagers. At nights these sounds interlaced his thoughts. When they could play "Abide with Me" at three different pitches on the new pans, they considered their work done.

They looked happy. They weren't like the island Whites whom the Ghanaians said perfumed their bathrooms because they couldn't acknowledge that anything they did stank. But cruelty flowed from them as readily as water in the mountain valleys—as long as they weren't speaking directly to Eurafricans and Whites. They greatly admired and were deferential to pale-skinned people, even the poor ones. And they were very critical, sometimes abusive, of the half dozen or so successful Blacks in the neighbouring communities.

Next day he decided that he could not face Mr. Morrison, so on Saturday morning, when his mother woke him at five, he told her he wasn't going.

"How you mean you not going? He probably get Mr. Bunyan for change his mind."

"No, Ma, nobody can get Mr. Bunyan to change his mind."

"I want you for go see Mr. Morrison."

"Ma, I'm not going today. Maybe next week."

He got up then, though, and went walking along the sea coast. He didn't want to have to explain to his father why he hadn't left for town. He was afraid of running into his classmates. He couldn't bear the thought. It was as if he'd come last in his class. It was failure. To have fallen so low after all the secret thoughts he'd had about them, after all the secret laughter at their expense!

He returned home after he knew his father had left for the farm. His mother was singing.

"The cross is not greater than his grace.
The sun will not hide his blessed face.

I am satisfied to know
That with Jesus here below
I can conquer every foe."

She had left his breakfast on the table, covered with a towel. He ate in silence, listening to her sing. His brother lay quietly on a blanket on the floor, sucking his thumb.

Around ten o'clock he took his school books out of his school bag and began to leaf through them. He thought about the O levels he should have been writing that year. With three O-level passes he could get a job in teaching, in the civil service and other places. Suppose he studied on his own? Would he make it? He decided to read a chapter in his history text and make notes in the margins just as he had done when reading ahead at home in preparation for the next day's lecture. His mother came into the hut and nursed his brother and placed him back on the blanket. Later, when he started to cry, she took him outside with her.

He had no idea what time it was when his mother came into the hut and said, "The White boy come for see you." He got up and saw Peter outside in the yard, grinning. Jerome kept shaking his head and smiling.

"At least you've kept your pecker up, as my old man says. Why didn't you come to see us this morning?"

"Us?"

"Yes, didn't your mother give you my message?"

"Yes. But I couldn't face anybody this morning."

"Oh, it's not so bad. My father says that in England they'd have sent you home for a few days or given you a caning.

But things are different here. You know the boys in our class respect you for your brain."

"How's Philip?"

"Quiet. He told me, 'If Jerome gets thrown out of school I'm going to make sure you get thrown out too.' He went to see Bunyan too. When he came back he was quiet and he hasn't said a word since.

"I went to see Bunyan too." Peter had begun walking toward the road where his father's chauffeur was waiting. "I can't stay long with you or I'll get the driver in trouble. They don't know he's out here. I gave him a fiver to bring me."

"Why did you go to see Bunyan?"

"To tell him what my father said. He told me, 'You'd be better off staying out of adult matters. I should have thrown you out of here a long time ago. You will cause your father more pain than you are worth. Now get out of my office!'"

"Was that before or after Philip went to see him?"

"After."

"How did you find out where I live?"

"I asked Mr. Morrison. Bunyan showed him a letter he was sending to your mother, and he remembered that it was Compton village. This morning when we waited for you and you didn't come, Mr. Morrison was worried, so I said to him that if I knew where you lived I would come and try to convince you. He told me the name of your village and said that it was near to Campden. I know Campden and my father's driver knew where the village was. We couldn't come tomorrow, and I have school all next week, so I persuaded him to bring me today.

"Mr. Morrison's coming here tomorrow to discuss

something with you and your parents, so don't go away. You didn't come to see him, so he's coming to see you."

They were standing at the canal bridge, and the chauffeur was blowing the horn. "Wait a minute," Peter called to the chauffeur. There was nobody at the canal bridge when they got there, but now about seven people were present, listening and looking without appearing to do so. The presence of a White person always brought them out because, if it wasn't a missionary, it meant trouble. They'd come to make sure it wasn't trouble. They would be curious as to why a White boy who had a chauffeur would come to see Jerome.

Peter stretched out his hand as he saw the chauffeur approach. "I'll see you next Saturday."

As the car drove away, Jerome realized that they hadn't spoken about Miss Blunt.

He had an idea around what time Mr. Morrison would arrive. People who drove in from town usually did so after they had eaten, so he knew Mr. Morrison would arrive between two and three. His mother went to Campden to buy eggs and flour and butter and a bottle of wine and baked a cake so that she would have something to offer him to eat.

He positioned himself at the canal bridge at two. He saw the car approaching around ten past three. It stopped and Mr. and Mrs. Morrison and their seven-year-old daughter got out, and Jerome led them to the hut. His mother had borrowed a chair from Eunice to add to the two they had, and she offered them seats. Mr. Morrison chose to stand and insisted that Comsie sit.

"Mr. and Mrs. Quashee, I'm sure you must be very vexed with Jerome. Be patient with him. What happened to him could happen to almost any boy his age. We're all silly at that age. I'm sure I did sillier things. I didn't get caught, that's all."

"My parents have been more understanding than they should be, Mr. Morrison." His mother and father smiled, pleased, he was sure, to have had their judgment approved. He felt proud of his mother; she had kept his father under control.

"Good. So we can get on to the rest. Your future. You can pass the O-level subjects at the end of the year, if you continue your studies."

There was a long silence, and he stared at Jerome intensely, as if saying to him, Don't be foolish! Think about your future. Don't throw it away.

"You're going to have to continue as if you were in school. You will get out your timetable and spend the school hours on the subjects, and at nights and on weekends you will go over everything. Forget about mathematics for now. Work on the GCE subjects. My wife will help you with Spanish. Drop the French for now. You must come into town to see me on Saturdays, so that I can monitor your work and answer any questions you have in English. I can't guarantee you help with the other subjects, but I'll go over them with you to see that you're following your schedule and ask you spot questions to see if you remember what you're reading."

Afterward they all ate cake and drank wine, and his father told Mr. Morrison that he and Comsie had been students of his father, and he remembered that when Mr. Morrison was a little boy his father used to bring him to the Methodist Church when he preached there some Sundays. He wasn't a Methodist but he used to have a girlfriend who lived facing the Methodist Church in Campden.

153

Mr. Morrison took the opening to tell them that his paternal grandfather had been illiterate and his mother's parents not much better. They had been labourers on the estates where they lived. His parents had got ahead because they were bright and because the Methodist minister at the time, a Reverend Jones from Wales, had taken a deep interest in them, taught them to speak standard English, and coached them so that they could become pupil teachers and pass the Junior Cambridge exams.

Mrs. Morrison said her parents were Irish peasants who had immigrated to Canada. When she was about sixteen her mother took her to visit Ireland. She was astonished by the large number of her relatives she found living in hovels.

His father and mother thanked the Morrisons for the interest they were showing in him. When they were about to leave, his mother motioned to Henry and him to take two boxes of ground provisions and fruits out to the Morrisons' car. No one had seen her pack them.

After the Morrisons left, his mother didn't fail to tell Eunice and, through her, the village that the two people who came in the car were two of Jerome's teachers who had come all the way from town to visit him.

The following day he resumed his studies. At his favourite spot by the sea, he did most of his reading. When it was raining or when for whatever reason he chose to remain home, his mother took Yawesi outside with her. They gave him no family chores, and his mother rarely worked on the farm now that she had Yawesi to look after.

Peter gave him copies of all the notes he took in class. They generally spent an hour together after his lessons at the

Morrisons'. The buses left for the country at one. Sometimes Peter sat in at the sessions he had with the Morrisons.

Every Saturday his mother always had something to send for the Morrisons, ground provisions, even when they weren't in season, and ground provisions and fruits when fruits were in season.

9

A LOT OF INCIDENTS INTERESTED him during those months at home. One day his cousin Laurel called from the canal bank asking for his mother. He told her she was in the kitchen.

"I hear them throw you outta school."

He winced.

Laurel descended the canal bank. Eunice came to the door of her hut. She was now too weak to work in the fields—every four or so steps she took would cause her to pant and pause for breath—so she depended solely on String's earnings and the neighbours' charity. His mother came out of the kitchen. Only the deaf would miss Cousin Laurel's metallic voice.

"Comsie, how you do, gal? Eunice, how bout you? Me hear Clipper break outta jail and he hiding in the cane field? We ha fo watch out?"

Cousin Laurel worked weeding for his father, now that his mother had to stay home with Yawesi. Even when she didn't work for him, he supplied her with vegetable staples just the same. His father and she had been raised by a grandmother. They both lost their mothers quite young. His father's mother had died giving birth to her second child when Henry was only four. Laurel was nine when hers died in Aruba, poisoned, they said, by the wife of the White man who had lured her there. So his paternal great-grandmother had raised them both, and they looked on each other as brother and sister.

Cousin Laurel lived in the village just across the stream. They merely had to go down two houses, skip the stones, and in five minutes they'd be at the house. She still lived in his great-grandmother's house, which she had inherited. It was a two-room wooden house; most of the boards were rotten, and weeds were growing in the shingles on the roof. Once she tried to persuade them to move in with her. "You all can come and live with me. I don have chick nor child, and when I go, I leaving the little place fo Jerome." He had smiled, thinking it would be all rotten long before Cousin Laurel died.

After Laurel left, his mother had said, "I not living there, Henry. We will stay on Mr. Manchester land till we can afford a place o we own. When two oman live in a house like that, them fight like dog and cat; and me have no interest in fighting with Laurel. She all right as long as we not living under the same roof."

When Cousin Laurel left this day, Eunice said, "Comsie, what she ha fo worry bout? Ain't them say the doctor stitch it up?"

"How you expect me for know?"

"Well, is you that did tend to she after."

"Well, I don know what the doctor do from what he don do."

"She right. We should keep we eye out for Clipper cause with him outta jail, none o we is safe," Eunice remarked with a lot of excitement in her voice.

He watched the faint smile on his mother's face. They were sitting on the bleaching stones. He was sure she was thinking like him that an orgasm would have finished off Eunice.

That was the third time Clipper had broken out of jail. He had never seen him in person, but he had read the news in the *Isabellan*. It carried a front-page picture of him and news of the breakout each time it happened. "Rapist at Large," the headline always read. He was said to have raped a widow, the mother-in-law of Mrs. Buntyn's sister—a Lady Cumberbatch, wife of Sir Ralph Cumberbatch. The servants said that Mrs. Cumberbatch the younger had engaged Clipper as a yardboy. He was sixteen at the time. He spent so much time in her bedroom that they privately called him the chamberboy. Sometime afterward, according to the servants, she gave birth to a Black child (like her sister, she had a touch of Black blood in her, but her husband was a White Englishman), who was given up for adoption in England.

Clipper was said to have attempted the rape one afternoon in the walled-in orchard behind the mansion. No one witnessed the act. He pleaded innocence and even became violent in the court. "Who would want to fuck a dried-up bitch like that!" he was said to have screamed after the judge pronounced the final sentence. That did not prevent his co-workers from saying that "cause Miz Cumberbatch cry out fo it so, Chamberboy get a notion that every White woman can't do without him."

Even with his breakouts from prison, Clipper wasn't known to have raped anyone. But the *Isabellan* gave a lot of advice about how people should travel, what they should do if they should be attacked, and his breakouts were the most important topics of conversation among all classes every time they occurred. Some felt that they should remove Clipper's genitals and then set him free.

His community rarely talked about Ramcat. *He* was a rapist. He had raped several young girls in Compton and the surrounding villages. They were always the daughters of the field hands. He wore a pith helmet in imitation of his unacknowledged father. Ramcat had an unusual complexion, like Jerome's stool that time he'd had jaundice. Ramcat's face was dagger-shaped and inflamed and pustular from pimples and beehived where other pimples had healed; his lips were large and red and couldn't close because of his oversized teeth. A dead dog if there was one. He probably had congenital syphilis. His legs were deeply bowed and his back curved, giving him at thirty the physique of someone seventy. Jerome had once seen him blow his nose in his hand and wipe it on his trousers, and each time he saw him thereafter, he shuddered at the thought that Ramcat might touch him, and his stomach would get ready to expel whatever was in it.

A Compton man had stood up to him. After he raped Harry's daughter, Harry had hidden in the cane field one evening, lassoed him off his horse, and dragged him into the cane field. Henry and Errol's stepfather had hidden behind a clump of grass and seen part of the action. Hours later someone saw his wandering horse and found him in a heap beside the road.

He couldn't understand why Ramcat raped people that way. For centuries White men had simply ordered Black women to sleep with them. His mother was a product of that, and his grandmother had been a broken woman because of it.

All around him were people of all ages who were the results of such demand sex. *Drop yo drawers—if you could afford them— or starve.* A comparable situation existed in Hanovertown, where the dives swarmed with children of White sailors to whom the mothers had hired out their bodies; there was one in his class whom the town Eurafricans called Sailor Pickney behind his back, simply because he lived in Corbeauland.

Usually the White fathers never acknowledged such children, though occasionally they bequeathed them an acre of land or a hundred dollars. A sort of deathbed plea for forgiveness.

Ramcat liked girls who were between thirteen and fifteen, before labouring had coarsened them and other men had had them. "Is only new clothes me like for wear. Me don eat nothing what other hand done touch up," he was reputed to have said.

Most of the parents quietly went to him. He paid them to keep quiet or threatened to dismiss them from the estate and evict them if they raised a stink. They usually gave in, knowing that the judge, regardless of his race, would consider it imprudent to convict Mr. Manchester's son, acknowledged or not. On occasion, usually after a couple of drinks at the rum shop, he named those who had been virgins and those that hadn't been, those who had enjoyed it and those who hadn't.

Jerome remembered the incident that gave Cousin Laurel her nickname. He was around eleven. The fellow she was living with had suspected her of sleeping with someone else. Someone had knocked on their door early one morning and said that Pedro had cut out of Laurel's "business."

His mother and father went over to the house. An ambulance sped her to the hospital. He overheard his mother telling Eunice that she found the razor and two chunks of flesh when she went back to wash away the blood. Eunice replied, "Comsie, you ever hear more foolishness? That is like well water. You don miss it. What wrong with Pedro?"

His father had donated blood to save Cousin Laurel's life. When she came out of the hospital people began speculating about how that part of her looked, whether it could still function, and settled upon calling her Razor Pussy, mostly behind her back.

Pedro was in jail still. He got a fifteen-year sentence.

He understood why for the sake of power the British did what they did; it was true that some of it was as bestial as Ramcat's actions. But Ramcat, Pedro, and String's father enjoyed humiliating people.

It was around this time, too, that he became involved with the Church of Saints Militant. The interest coincided with his reflections on the suffering in the world. No doubt the offshoot of his own suffering. He'd already read Freud's *Civilization and Its Discontents*, and it had helped him understand that man created God. God was a response to human need. It forced him to reflect on how religious the poor were—the astonishing number of hours they spent in church, the way their conversation was garnished with biblical quotations. "Seek ye first the Kingdom of Heaven and its righteousness and all things shall be added unto you." Or wanting a shepherd and green pastures to lie down in—wanting to hand over to others the responsibility for their lives. How many times did he hear even his own mother say that Black people were cursed! Once he had asked her why and she told him it was because a long, long time ago, Ham had looked upon his naked father and was cursed for it. "That's a story someone made up," he told her. "Look who have the power, the money, everything!" she had replied. Another favourite story of the villagers was that "when God make the world He give the race them three choice—pen, book, and hoe. White man take book, the Indian take pen, and the Black man take hoe." Freud helped him realize that his people were trying to work out what they felt was some sort of inherited curse. After all, they were the descendants of slaves; since their lot had been to be worked hard and beaten when it wasn't hard enough, they had to conclude that they were not righteous. The Bible said so. On the surface it looked like a huge joke, but there was no comedy in its consequences, unless you were like Ramcat.

And so it was that he became interested in the evangelical group that came to the village on Wednesday evenings. They operated from a rented house on Mr. Manchester's plantation. The mission was run by a White American, Pastor Oberon.

For several Wednesdays, as he lay on his bed or sat at work on his courses at the makeshift table, Pastor Oberon's ("O'Bum" was the villagers' name for him) words dressed up in a southern American accent came to him. At first he was shocked by the grammar. Eventually he made an association with Miss Blunt, and he began to wonder just how well people in America were educated. Occasionally echoes from the jokes of the irreverent about preachers would interrupt either what Oberon was saying or his school work. "Some preach the gospel for love o riches, some for love o the sisters, and some for love o the brothers." What was this Southern White man, who most certainly did not consider Black people his equal, doing it for? Why did Albert, whom he suspected the Methodist minister was grooming to become a minister, who was popular with girls and was passing all his exams, join them?

The following Wednesday he decided to attend. The little band suspended a Coleman lamp and the horn of the loud-speaker from a self-supporting extendable steel stand. The official gathering numbered five (O'Bum had his work cut out to get it up to twelve, Jerome mused): the schoolteacher and three women whose faces but not names Jerome knew. A grandmother, her grandson, and he were the only villagers present.

Pastor O'Bum was a short, pink, pot-bellied man who looked like a clothed rum barrel. He had the microphone around his neck, and it in turn was connected to the speaker via several feet of wire.

They began the meeting with the hymn "Hear the Blessed Saviour Calling the Oppressed." The light from the lamp made the darkness around them all the more real. It was as if this oasis of light in which they found themselves represented truth, civilization, hope for humanity. It was as if the sounds of the hymn were intended to push back the frontiers of that darkness.

Pastor O'Bum addressed the darkness when the singing stopped. "Folks out there, we're gonna pray. Now bow yer hairds, open yer hearts, don't let the Dervle tickle you. He's a wicked one, and yer gotta tie him down.

"Allmaity Gawd, we come to yer gracious throne, fore Chris, er mediator n er judge, who Paul tells us is the proprietor fer er sins. Great Gawd, we beg yer ter keep us from sinnin, cause the Bible done told us that them that's been sanctified by yer can't sin. We ask yer ter grab a-holt o these here hearts, the hearts o these here villagers. Lawd, we know yer greatness.

Yer build this here world in six days, just like it was clay in a potter's hands. Lawd, we know there ain't nothin, ain't no miracle, yer can't do. Lawd, wring these here hard hearts. Enter em with yer lubricatin power. Oil em, Lawd. Take the rust o sin outta em, Lawd, n polish em fer yer service. Lawd teach em ter come while yer's their saviour n not their judge. Send out the Hol Sperrit like a durv ter spread yer holy wings above em. Even if their hearts like lumps o ice, send the warm sperrit o repentance, n let em melt. Hear our prayer, Lawd. Ermen."

The next hymn was "There Is a Fountain Filled with Blood." They sang lustily. "Drawn from Immanuel's veins / And sinners plunged beneath that flood." When they got to the crescendoing line "Lose all their guilty stains," Pastor O's voice failed, so he passed the microphone to the light-skinned sister; she sang well.

The music seemed to suffuse them with a knowing enthusiasm and a certitude that set them apart, like the Coleman lamp that created an islet of light in that ocean of darkness. The tonic syllables issued solidly, cementing the inscrutable, convincing them that they had conquered earthly sorrow. This could only happen at night, he thought, when it was dark, when they did not have to worry about feeding their children.

Long after they had finished the song, even while Pastor O'Bum was reading from the Bible, his mind dwelt on the words:

E'er since by faith I saw the stream
Thy flowing wounds supply,
Redeeming love has been my theme
And shall be till I die.

The image of perpetually flowing blood from Christ's wounds revolted him. And the determination motivated by that blood was a gorier ugliness. Little wonder so many massacres had been committed to further Christendom. "And sinners plunged beneath that flood, lose all their guilty stains"—it made you want to vomit, watching that blood clotting all over their bodies, watching the traces their footprints left; and what happened to it? Did it rot eventually and leave the same smell as the abattoir? Or did it just keep flowing red and fresh and unclotting, mystically, everlastingly? What were his stains? They'd say it was his sin, but Whites and Blacks deeply believed it was the colour of their skin. "Wash me in the blood of the Lamb and I shall be whiter than snow!" Blacks did not know how ridiculous they sounded when they sang that.

His attention returned to O'Bum's reading:

"Say thou thus unto them, Thus saith the Lord God: As I live, surely they that are in the wastes shall fall by the sword, and him that is in the open field will I give to the beasts to be devoured, and they that be in the forest and in the caves shall die of the pestilence.

"For I will lay the land desolate, and the pomp of her strength shall cease, and the mountains of Israel shall be desolate, that none shall pass through.

"Then shall they know that I am the Lord, when I have laid the land most desolate because of all their abominations which they have committed."

It had taken him years to understand the cruelty in those words, which he understood now as the cruelty of those who had institutionalized them.

When Pastor O ended his reading, he said to the fat woman whose round oily face glistened in the lamplight, "Sister Biddows will now sing a solo fer us." He slipped the microphone over her head. She cleared her throat, straightened—she wore a long-sleeve burgundy dress that reached almost to her ankles—and stepped forward, in front of the lamp, so that her front became a silhouette, abstracted, perhaps the way sculptors perceive the models they use in their work. Now a pillar of darkness, she cleared her throat raucously and vibrated the darkness with the first few cataract notes of "Does Jesus Care?" He listened attentively. Her voice was as powerful and haunting as Mahalia Jackson's. "When my heart is pained / Too deeply for mirth or song." When she got to the lines "And the daylight fades as I nearly faint / And the way grows weary and long," her voice assumed a pain that suggested the climbing of steep slopes. *When he became an atheist, as opposed to the doubter he was then, he remembered Sister Biddows singing this song and wondered where she had been going so rapidly. It must have been to heaven, because Isabellan life was a mere whirlpool in a cruel colonial ocean.*

She did plummet once, too, to the less laborious valley of "Oh, yes, he cares! I know he cares! / His heart is touched with my grief." She sang her way through the hills and valleys of belief until the song ended and she rejoined the illuminated and liminal.

When Pastor O (it was the name he called him by after they got to know each other well) repossessed his microphone, he told the night, "That was a cheerming solo by our dear sister. Sister's faith in Gawd is as she sings it. Solid as the rock o Zion. You too can have a same faith if yer jes heed the voice of the

Hol Sperrit talkin ter yer right now. We gonna now sing the hymn 'Are Yer Washed in the Blood o the Lamb?' Jes don sing it, heed it. Are yer washed in the blood of the Lamb?"

He passed the microphone to the light-skinned sister and they sang, "Will your soul be ready for the mansions bright? / Are you washed in the blood of the lamb?" A third sister carried a tambourine, which, up until then, she hadn't used. Now it carilloned away. She slapped it alternately against her thigh and the back of her hand. He waited for her to skip a beat, but she didn't.

When the singing ended, Pastor O called on the light-complexioned sister to "testify." She stepped in front of the light. "Brothers and sisters, where you all is out there tonight, I want all you for know what a sweet feeling it be for lay down pon Jesus bosom. If I been know how sweet it be, I woulda make the decision long time ago. When I been a little girl, I hear the story bout the Wise Virgin them for the first time, but I didn understand the meaning. Now I know the meaning. Brothers and sisters, I beg all you for make Jesus all you bridegroom, make him put him soothing hand pon all you, make him breathe the Holy Ghost pon all you—"

"Amen!" shouted Pastor O.

"A-me-amen-men," the others aped.

"I beg all you, give Jesus all you heart. All you gwine find him a frien, a husban, and a father."

Whew, he thought: friend, husband, and father all in one. And bridegroom for all the brothers and sisters!

The next hymn was "Peace, Perfect Peace," which Pastor O started unannounced and the others picked up. "The blood of Jesus whispers peace within…"

The rhythm of the hymn had the calm, unhurried aura of sheep grazing on the rocky dry slopes overlooking the seldom ruffled sea a few miles north of the capital. "Peace, perfect peace / By longing duties pressed / To do the will of Jesus, / This is best." It was as if he were on the beach, with the gentle waves like a puppy's tongue licking his feet, the blue sky above him, the blue sea before him. Pastor O clearing his throat, the loudspeaker amplifying the crackles, awoke him from his reverie.

"Only in Jesus yer fin peace, my friens. Only in Jesus, like the lovely woman o Samaria, yer gonna fin that wadder that gon quench yer thirst forever. Oh, yes, friens, yer better give yer hearts to the Lawd. Tonight, friens, I wanna warn yer bout the wrath that's a-comin. I wanna tell yer that today Jesus is yer redeemer. Today he's a-sittin at the right han o Gawd, n he's a-makin intercession. N all yer's gotta do is drop down right now on yer knees n say, 'Lawd, I ain't worthy! Lawd, speak the word. Lawd, save me.' Friens, that bloord he spill out on that there cross on Calvary can bleach yer heart so white, there ain't gonna be no sin lef in it. It's like chlorine to bleach the blackest stain. It can work miracles." He covered the mic with one hand, faced the little band that shook their heads from time to time as if afflicted with St. Vitus's dance, and made a sign to them.

"Amen! Amen!" they said, bowing their heads so as not to look him in the eye.

"Yer fin it hard to stop cheatin yer husban?" he spoke again into the mic. "Let Gawd into yer life—"

"Amen!" the soloist shouted.

"Amen!" the others echoed.

"Yer fin it hard to keep yer hands from robbin? Let Gawd into yet heart. Yer fin it hard to keep from livin in sin? Let Gawd into yer life—"

"Hallelujah!" exploded the soloist. The others looked confused.

The sermon continued and the small band shifted from foot to foot and fanned away the moths that made them resting stations on their way to the lamplight. Pastor O grew more and more excited by the rhythm of his own voice. The cord of the microphone now looked like a tether and he a goat at the end of it. Now he dashed forward a little too far and the pole and lamp began to tilt. The light-skinned sister jumped forward and saved it from falling. She stayed beside it just in case Pastor O got another power surge.

Pastor O was yelling, "Repent! I say repent! There's gonna be many a-wailin n a-gnashin their teeth. I say repent! Repent! Repent."

Instantly he began to sing, the others joining in, "Jesus Is Tenderly Calling Today," and he handed the microphone over to the soloist. She stretched the sounds out mournfully. When she attacked the refrain, one would have thought she had changed places with Sisyphus.

But no doors opened, no one came. The grandmother shook awake her grandson, lit her flambeau, and left.

When the singing had ended and the final prayer was said, Pastor O came over and shook his hand. Jerome stared into his eyes, at the round pink cheeks and hanging jowls illumined by the lamplight. He felt a twinge of pity for this White man who had come all the way from America "to win souls for Christ." Perhaps he was fleeing his own racism.

"Yer mus come ter er Bible wership on Sundays," he told Jerome.

"I'll think about it," he replied.

Next day Jerome received a letter from Mr. Bunyan giving him permission to write the O-level subjects for which he was already registered. "Perhaps you should drop French and Spanish." The letter also said that at some point in the future the board of directors of Expatriates might lift the expulsion order, if they thought he had been "adequately chastened." He'd be dead, Jerome thought, before that board, comprised of plantation owners who'd permitted Blacks into Expatriates only because the British had forced them to, lifted the expulsion order. *A couple of years afterward, when his reinstatement was no longer relevant, Mr. Morrison showed him a copy of the school's constitution. It had never been revised—only ignored. It permitted the enrolment of Whites unconditionally and "outstanding mulattoes of the lightest hues whose sound character had been attested to by an outstanding merchant or planter. All said mulattoes must be interviewed by the principal and a member of the board of directors before final acceptance is given. At no time should the mulatto population surpass the third part of the student body." "Negroes" were not mentioned in the constitution. "Expatriate" did not include them. They must have been part of the Europeans' baggage.*

When he attended classes with the Morrisons the following Saturday, he showed them the letter.

Mrs. Morrison was delighted. "This is good news. Continue with French and Spanish and biology; you'll need them to get into university. I expect you to go to university. Every bright

Isabellan should. Only you will take the development of your country seriously. The foreigners who come here as advisers are tourists in disguise. Even the teachers."

Morrison listened to her, his eyes fixed on the floor. His daughter was standing beside him, holding on to his knee.

"Mary, you know why they elected Buckingham chairman of the board of directors?"

She shook her head.

"For the simple reason that he feels Isabella should be like Rhodesia. They know that with him there the school will oppose all attempts by the colonial administration to expand and increase the number of Black students. Bunyan knew before he wrote that letter that you won't be permitted to re-enter Expatriates. It's true that the pocket of Blacks has quietly grown larger and the mulattoes are getting browner, and these days, with what's going on in the States, they are quiet about it. But they're not *happy* about it."

"What a people!" Mrs. Morrison was shaking her head.

He learned that day, too, that both Bunyan and Miss Blunt would leave at the end of the year. They had both come out on contracts. Bunyan had extended his to four years. Miss Blunt wasn't extending hers.

Off and on for several weeks, he went to watch the barrel-shaped man run up and down and scream to the villagers while tethered to the lamp-and-microphone pole. There was something about it all that suggested penance. Quite often Jerome was the only villager present.

One night after the shenanigans had come to an end, Pastor O said to him, "I been makin inquiries bout yer. I hear yer got a mighty fine brain. Yer should be in the service o the Lawd."

He paused. Jerome could see that he was studying him for a reaction.

"I been thinking," he resumed, "that if yer give yer heart ter the Lawd, our church might have blessins aplenty in store fer yer. We might even sen yer ter study in America. Think bout it."

That night he hardly slept. That explained why Albert had joined the Militants. They must have made him an offer the Methodists wouldn't have dared to imagine. *When you in a trap, every little hole might come a bigger one fo let you out.* He would not ask Albert about it. That way they could both pretend they had joined the church of their own volition. *Albert did get to America, where he became an engineer, but Pastor O had nothing to do with it. Albert and the light-skinned sister left about six weeks after Jerome joined. The light-skinned sister—her name was Mavis Blanche—was already three months pregnant by him. He denied having anything to do with her. But he left the Militants and eventually went back to the Methodist Church.* Yes, he would give his heart to the scheme to get him to America, but for now he would call it "The Lawd."

He waited for three weeks before doing so, and that Wednesday night, while they sang "Come Home! Come Home! Ye Who Are Weary, Come Home!" he went home to his dreams. He was indeed weary, exhausted completely by his anxieties for the future. Pastor O knelt and prayed with him and declared him saved. The sisters and Brother Albert looked on gravely with bowed heads. When Jerome opened his eyes about a dozen villagers had come to look on. They'd obviously heard the excitement in Pastor O's prayers and had come to see who was in the net.

A rainy Sunday five weeks later he was baptized in a stream that had been dammed for the purpose. Thick fog descended from the mountain during the ceremony, and neither he nor Pastor O could see each other clearly as Pastor O ducked him under water in the name of the Father, Son, and Holy Ghost, and he went down limply in the hopes of getting to school in America. The sisters and Albert stood on the bank, invisible.

Shortly after he joined the Militants, the young men in the village began to tease him. "So now we know, you like yo cousin Boy-boy."

"Miss O'Bum," someone called him.

His mother told him that the villagers believed that Pastor O was a bullerman. His father said, "Is me earnest hope that you grow outta all this nonsense you gettin yoself in. Don give up yo studies in all o this nonsense. You start off trying for feel up White oman bottom. I hope White man don end up in yos." It cooled the affection he'd started developing for his father.

Hetty came frequently to their hut. She lived near the river in one of the huts they passed by to cross over to where his Cousin Laurel lived. She was the same age as Jerome. Her mother and Comsie worked in the same weeding gang before his father had stopped her from working. He called Hetty's mother Nennie Lucy, and Hetty called his mother Nennie Comsie. Hetty had made it to standard seven but was one of those who had failed the exam by a few marks. She had an aunt who worked as a maid in Trinidad and who sent her clothes from time to time. She was better dressed than the village girls. She was never barefoot. The young men whistled at her and called her fresh.

Nennie Lucy still worked in the fields. During the day,

Hetty spent much of her time with Nennie Comsie, helping her bathe the baby or babysitting him, while Comsie trudged off to the farm to take Henry's food. He'd told his mother that he would look after Yawesi whenever she had to go off, but except for the odd time, she left him with Eunice, whom they compensated with ground provisions, or Hetty took him away to her mother's hut.

In a quiet sort of way, he liked Hetty. She spoke English well, when she had to. She was very black with smooth skin; some Kalinago ancestry, which was visible in her mother, showed up in the length, blackness, and texture of Hetty's hair. She was slim and graceful as a palm. She walked upright and smiled when the men teased her.

One day she was seated on one of the boards that formed the rough steps that led into their hut, Yawesi on her lap. He heard Mullet calling to her from the canal bank, "You see all them smooth stone what does come outta sea, them been rough one time. But the water smooth them down. What you playing? You can only hol out for so long. You gwine spile jus like all the rest. Why you not let me do it? Me gwine treat you nicer than the rest them."

Comsie came out of the kitchen and told Mullet, "You go long and leave people gal pickney alone."

"Is want you want she for Jerome. But Jerome no want oman."

"If Henry been home you wouldn'ta say that to me, Mullet. But I won't tell im. You not worth a jail, Mullet, you not worth it." She went back into the kitchen and Mullet moved on.

There was something in Hetty that stirred him. He had heard her say that her aunt had promised to send her the money to pay for a course from International Correspondence Schools. She had heard that with it she could get some GCE subjects, and after that she might be able to study nursing in England.

Hetty and his mother discussed everything. One day he overheard them talking about wife beating. "The Holy Ghos can work miracles. You not see when Betsy get saved she go back to her husband," Hetty was saying.

"Husban, my foot! Is the blows them she couldn take. She join Adventis fo get way from kick and box from that man she take up with after she leave she husban. All the same, you know, if Alfred used to put his hand pon her from the beginning she wouldn'ta lef him in the firs place. She never been one for satisfy with one man."

"I can't gree with you, Nennie Comsie. These men here have only one woman? What good for man good for woman too. Anyhow, no man going hit me and live after that."

"Don talk so. You is young yet. If you talk like that you will never get a man."

"I don't want none o these around here. I certain bout that."

"Me hope you don live for eat them words. You young still. You will larn." His mother lowered her voice to a whisper. "Eunice tell me the other day that if she did know better she wouldn'ta leave Boysie."

That was why, he thought, she used to sing:

I must have the Saviour with me
For I dare not walk alone.
I must feel His presence near me

And his arms around me thrown…
I will go without a murmur
And his footsteps follow still.

That was before her lungs had begun hissing. He was tempted to alter the words, as Peter would have done.

"If she did stay with him," Hetty said, "she would o say, 'If she did know better she would o leave him.'"

"You got a point there. You is a regular lawyer, Hetty. I hope yo auntie help you finish yo schooling."

"But Nennie Comsie, I never hear anybody say Godfather Henry does beat you?"

"Well, with Henry it different, child."

"So why you think it going be different for me?"

"Me didn say that. Child, life ugly, ugly, and is pure chance that make some people life good and some people life hell. We dare not choose our lot."

"I will choose mine."

"We going see."

One day, when Comsie went off to take his father's lunch, Hetty did not take Yawesi down to her mother's hut. She came into the hut where he was reading. It was drizzling outside.

From the moment she entered, he felt a certain tension. His eyes roved over the words, but it was Hetty's presence he was aware of.

"Jerome," she said after about two hours of silence, "why you don't talk to anyone? I come here every day and you don't so much as look at me."

He looked at her where she was sitting on the floor with Yawesi asleep on her lap. He smiled but he did not speak.

He resumed his pretence at reading. Finally, he said to her, "You're all right, Hetty. I'd be proud to call you my sister."

"Sister! *Sister!* I don't *want* to be your *sister!*"

He really liked her. But she didn't magnetize him the way Peter, even Philip, and Errol did. But, if she did, she would have been the girl he'd have taken a chance on.

They talked a lot more on different days and eventually got around to kissing. But, when the big day came and they took off their clothes, he ejaculated as soon as his body touched hers and he became afraid of what they were doing.

That night he thought it had been a providence. What if he hadn't ejaculated and had had sex with Hetty and she'd become pregnant? Pastor O would have been forced to excommunicate him, and that would have been the end of his dream to go to America.

Next day he told her their act was sinful. She offered to join the Militants. "That won't make it any less sinful. We must stay away from each other. You are a temptation."

She'd begun to cry, and he was unable to bear it, so he left the hut and went for a long walk, returning only when he knew his mother had returned.

He was shocked to hear his mother say, "Jerome, Hetty is a nice girl. You musn frighten she away. One day she will make you a good wife."

He looked at his mother with silent anger.

She did begin her course, and sometimes she told him about it. Sometimes she brought the work with her, and while he was working at his she worked at hers. She got good results, but had to drop the course after a while. Her aunt could not spare the extra money. She became a store clerk in Campden, the first visibly

Black girl to do so. The three stores were owned by Eurafricans, who employed only Eurafricans. The owner hired her in a pinch, was impressed, and kept her on.

Irony of ironies, she married Pinchman, who'd fantasized about raping girls and having an oversized penis. Chance was indeed a strange thing. Pinchman was injured in Florida, where he'd been recruited to cut canes, and he collected four thousand US dollars in insurance. They thought he'd injured his spine. But he recovered after he returned home. He used the money to buy ten acres of mountain land. Within three years, he acquired twenty-five acres of coastal land. Now Pinchman and she owned over four hundred acres and had several labourers working for them. Their first son was studying engineering at Oxford—a Rhodes scholar! The other one had just entered Cave Hill. Hetty kept the accounts and was probably the force behind their success. He suspected his mother had borrowed money from her when she built the cement house they were now living in. A good thing she didn't marry him.

10

PASTOR O SEEMED VERY FOND of Jerome and invited him to visit the estate the house whenever he wasn't studying. It was a huge house constructed of wood, except the bathrooms and kitchen, which were cement additions. Its large living room was where the church services were held.

It was the dry season when he started to visit Pastor O, and the poui trees that were scattered about the two acres of lawn intersected here and there by flower beds were ablaze. The grass was brown and the flower beds, now full of weeds only, contained only the odd fleck of green. The whole gave the property a sunset look that contrasted with the green of the miles and miles of half-grown canes in the distance, all the way up to the foothills of the mountains. He always enjoyed the scenery from there.

The estate house was now twice its size, they told him. Pastor O finally found a way to serve people instead of the Lawd. Rumour had it that he had a lover, a Barbadian, living with him. The last time he passed by the property had been during the dry season, and there were sprinklers going from what he was told was water drawn from a well Pastor O had got drilled. The grass was a lush green, and he could see lots of blooming hibiscus just a little within the gate. The old walls that hid ninety-nine percent of the property from view were still there, except that now the holes from which the cement used to crumble had been filled in and, instead of green from the moss that grew on them after the Manchesters had stopped living there, they were now white.

Pastor O loved to talk. He reminded Jerome of those children who couldn't sit still, whom parents described as having nettle in their skin. As soon as there was a lull in the conversation he began swivelling in his chair, or smoothing down his trouser legs, or wiping a film of dirt from the windowsill, or picking up crumbs with the tips of his fingers. If he was near a balcony table and a glass was on it, he'd pick it up and begin rotating it to watch the way it reflected the light. He asked Pastor O a lot of questions and Pastor O said a lot, even though he never quite answered the questions. It was as if Pastor O was afraid of silence.

One afternoon they were sitting on the porch. He was staring out at the sea, which was unusually calm that May day. He was feeling restless and irritable and was about to leave when a blackbird alighted on a nearby cherry tree. Pastor O muttered, as if in a dream, "His eye is on the sparrow and I know He watches over me." He gave Jerome a side glance quickly followed by a direct look. Sometimes he squinted but he didn't now. His face was unusually pink.

"Jerome, have yer been thinkin bout that speshull gift yer got ter offer the Lawd?"

"Yes, but I haven't received an answer yet."

"Well, I been thinkin, now—bout all them questions yer been askin me? Huh? And I think yer gonna make a mighty fine preacher."

Jerome felt the intensity of his eyes on him.

"If yer was ter pray, yer gonna fin that that's what Gawd done chose yer fer."

His hands began to perspire and he trembled slightly. He placed his palms on his thighs. But Pastor O had already noticed.

"I can see the Holy Sperrit possessin yer already. Le's kneel n pray.

"Almighty Gawd, we thank yer fer possessin er dear brother Jerome with yer holy power. Take him into yer service, Lawd. Barb his tongue with the fire o yer power. Let his tongue be a whip ter flog sinners ter yer throne o mercy…"

By this time the sweating hands and feet had given way to a generalized cold sweat. Pastor O noticed this as soon as he opened his eyes. He glowed with delight.

"A mee-ricle! A mee-ricle!" he shouted, leaping up and down.

About ten minutes later, chilled to the bone and shivering, Jerome left. He remained ill with influenza for about five days. *Over the years, whenever he got the flu, he thought of the Holy Ghost.*

Two weeks later he went off to the capital to write his exams. The Morrisons had invited him to stay with them. His last paper, European History: 1500 to 1800, which Peter wrote also, was on June 13.

Early that evening he and Peter were seated on the wharf in the capital enjoying the last moments of daylight reflecting off the water, just as Yaw and he had done almost a year earlier. When it grew dark, Peter began to talk about racism. It was probably sparked by one of the questions on their exam:

181

"Discuss the extent to which the Thirty Years War resolved the conflicts that had engendered it." Peter wanted to convince him that he wasn't racist, that was for sure. He recounted many of the things he heard at the homes of the planters who entertained them. He even repeated a story he forgot he had told him the year before. "'Only hire a naigger if you can't get a mulatto. Now they tell me that the mulattos are hard to come by, but hold out as long as you can. You keep everything under lock and key, I hope? They carry away anything that isn't nailed down.'

"Even my mother—my mother, can you believe it!—was shaking her head on the way home. She fell in line quickly, though: the very next day. My father wondered who would think it worthwhile to cut their throats. They were cutting them themselves anyway. He said it was only a matter of time before Isabella Island got its independence, and if Ghana is any sign of what's to come, they would be in for quite an awakening."

"How old was this person that told your father this?"

"Old. In his eighties."

"That's why. They're out of touch with what's going on. That's exactly how old Mr. Manchester, who owns the plantation where we live, would talk, but his son knows everybody by their names and he says hello to them and calls them mister and missus." He had continued silently: That doesn't mean anything; Mr. Manchester is his father.

"Do you hate White people, Jerome?"

"Can't you change that tune?"

"You should. Look at how Bunyan treated you."

"He's not a whole race. Is he you?"

"The others aren't jolly well better. It isn't only here, in America, and in Rhodesia that they hate Black people, you know. You should see what happens in England!"

He wanted to say, "I don't give a shit."

"When we were leaving to come here, there were several newscasts, on the radio and in the papers, about the buzzards. They were refusing to rent rooms to coloured people. There were demonstrations too. To petition the government to stop coloured people from coming to England. My mother was part of that."

But he'd already moved beyond Peter, to look at how his own people treated everyone who was different. Boy-boy, for instance. What the BBC journalist or whoever it was said about people hunting their own kind had to be true. Black people on Isabella Island were not kind to the Kalinago. Many Black male teachers slept with their Kalinago students and left them pregnant, and the colonial administration did nothing about it. Black men treated Black women just as cruelly as Whites treated Blacks. Injustice for him was injustice. The rest was all pretence and that, he feared, he'd never be able to do anything about.

"Let's leave," he told Peter.

They walked up to Nelson Street and agreed to meet the following day, for Peter said he had something important to tell him. Peter turned right, toward the residences of the chief justice and the colonial administrator in the hills above the Botanic Gardens. Jerome turned left and walked up the short hill where the Morrisons lived in one of the fifteen small, identical, drab three-bedroom houses that the colonial government had built for sale to their local senior employees.

Next morning Peter and he met around eleven. The chauffeur dropped them off about half a mile from Crater Beach on the south coast, about four miles from the capital. There was a basket on the seat. Peter took it with him. They began walking toward the beach. Jerome had heard of the beach. It was a black sand beach and it looked as if it had been scooped out of the steep rock that surrounded it. Steps led down to the beach floor. Except for four fishermen who were at the far end mending their seines, the beach was deserted.

It was one of those June days that are the loveliest on Isabella Island. The sun sat in the middle of the sky, the water was smooth and glassy, and the sky was an untarnished blue tent with splashes of white. Maybe it was because his exams were over, because he was at a transition; he didn't know. But he remembered that he'd felt happy that day as they sat down on the beach under a sea almond.

The basket contained several cucumber sandwiches, which Peter said were his favourite, a large Thermos of ice-cold lemonade, and six very ripe bananas.

"Henrietta prepared these for me. When my parents aren't around I call her Aunt Hennie and tease her. She has a fat mole over her left eye. She wants it cut. I told her not to. She won't be Aunt Hennie without it. The other day I asked her to adopt me. I guess I was serious. You don't know how lucky you are to have real people for parents."

Jerome smiled. Case of the grass being greener on the other side. Peter had completely forgotten who lived in the huts and did all the hard and dirty work. *"A boy's will is the wind's will, / And the thoughts of youth are long, long thoughts."*

They did not go into the water. He had not brought swim

trunks, for he hadn't expected to go to the beach. Peter, he suspected, didn't want to swim. They were silent sometimes for as long as fifteen minutes.

When the sun began to dip and the sea to turn to grey, Peter said, "I'm returning to England in two weeks."

"Is your father being reassigned?"

"Not yet. His tenure doesn't run out for another year."

"Why are they sending you back to England alone?"

"Burnt Pan!" (Philip's nickname for Bunyan) "How do you like that for a nickname? The bastard! Told my father about Miss Blunt and me. He's afraid I'll bring 'disrespect on my office.'" Peter's fingers, lips—even his head was shaking— moved in imitation of his father's Parkinson's. "They're sending me to a boarding school in Kent. They announced it to me at dinner on Sunday. They didn't ask for my opinion. 'At this stage, my dear Peter, your opinion is worthless,' my mother said. She looked and sounded just like Agnes Moorehead. They tell me I'll be just like them when I grow up. Fat chance! That bitch!" He turned purple with rage.

"When I was eight I overheard my father telling Uncle Willy—the one who's the MP—a story about Mother. You see, when my father began working for the colonial office, he and Mother had to attend these parties where they met people from almost every country. Well, one night they went to one, and this is what I heard my father telling Uncle Willy:

"'When she got in the car she said to me, "Joseph, we have to do something about these uppity coloured people."'"

According to Peter, his parents' discussion continued something like this:

"What do you suggest, my dear?"

185

"I don't know! Anything!"

"Must we take urgent action? Or can it wait?"

"I'm *very serious*, Joseph!"

"Not for a moment did I doubt that you were. What's it now, my dear?"

"Well, the bloody nerve! That coloured whatever, the one with the vest that he didn't know he should button, asked me to waltz with him."

"But at a party where there is waltzing a man may waltz with a woman."

"Oh, but he meant something else. I heard it in his speech."

"His speech, my dear? Nigerians speak a heavily accented English."

"It was more than his accent, Joseph. It was that quiet smile that said I was a dish, or something like that."

"Are you a dish, my dear?"

"Stop turning everything into a joke!"

"Have no fear, my dear, of being eaten or getting broken. Why, you may also tell him you don't digest easily, or for that matter that you are unchewable. And as for breaking…"

Peter returned to his father and uncle: "'Willy, what will I do with her?' my father exclaimed. 'Sometimes I feel like lifting her up by the hair.'

"'Nothing, Joey, nothing. That's frequent when people marry their childhood sweethearts. It can't be helped. Settle down and enjoy what's there to be enjoyed.'"

Jerome listened attentively. "Your mother is a very special woman."

"A bitch, you mean!"

"Is your uncle Willy the Trotskyite?" Peter had told Miss

Blunt this and asked her opinion, and she'd replied that she didn't mix teaching and politics.

"Yes."

"So what will you do when you need to get away from boarding school?"

"I have an aunt in London. My father's sister. A spinster. She's the matron at Norwood Hospital. At least that's where my parents think I'll stay."

"What will you do?"

"Stay with Estelle and Judith, my Black cousins, or at Uncle Willy's, though Mother hates him for his views."

"Your what?"

"You heard what I said. I thought I'd save that gem for last."

He told him a drawn-out contradictory story about an aunt who married a Nigerian, who was now dead. His uncle Willy had secretly taken him to meet them because his mother had disowned her. He and his cousins wrote to one another, but his mother didn't know because there were no return addresses on the envelopes.

Jerome was silent, waiting for him to say more. A cooling breeze blew off the water. The fishermen were still there.

He didn't know how much of all of that was true. That his aunt and two Eurafrican cousins existed was probably so, because the next time he saw Peter, ten days later and three days before his departure, he showed him a photograph of a White woman who resembled Peter in some ways; an overweight, broad-faced Black man; and two half-white girls—as well as separate portraits of the cousins, Estelle and Judith. But the story Peter had told him about a racial attack he had witnessed on his

187

cousins was something he had either seen on television or in a film or had made up, because when he asked him about it later, Peter had forgotten the story. He'd felt let down and had to fake enthusiasm for the rest of the time they were together. The story had been so convincing! How much of what Peter told him was fiction? Peter had noticed his withdrawal and told him that it was normal for him to feel that way at the departure of a friend. He was half right. That should have immunized him against Peter's tendency to exaggerate.

Before they left Crater Beach, he asked Peter whether he had ever tried to discuss any of his views with the White boys at school.

"Not in a direct way, no. But I tried to find out theirs. Bullock's, for example. You know how stupid he is. I asked him why they didn't have any Black workers in their store. He said that Blacks are stupid and dishonest. I asked him if he thought you were stupid. He filled his mouth with sweets, I guess to give himself time to think, and when he found an answer, he swallowed, then said, 'What makes you think Jerome is Black? Look at him. He's brown.' So I said to him, 'But you don't have anybody Jerome's colour working in your store.' 'It's not *my* store,' he shot back. 'Jerome can work for me any day, when I take over from my father. Now it's my father who makes the decisions.' He'll need you, too, Jerome, to keep from going bankrupt."

"Fat chance that glutton will ever get me to work for him! Why don't you guys tell him to stop eating all that sugar?"

"You know he's nearly three hundred pounds! Rajan said the other day that B's brain's too busy distributing fat to have time to for anything else. Maybe, if he loses weight, he'll move up to second-to-last or pass in one or two subjects. We almost split with laughter."

Fireflies were already visible when they got back to the capital.

11

WHEN HE RETURNED TO the country following his exams, Pastor O pushed him to take an active role in explicating the Bible during the prayer meeting and Bible study sessions. They took place every Friday evening. Sister Biddows, Albert, and he were most probably the only ones in the congregation with more than two or three years of schooling, and he was sure the couple of years the others had received had already been lost through disuse. At the Friday prayer sessions, they uttered basically the same prayer in somewhat altered words—a string of sentences asking God to keep them from the temptations of Satan and to minister to their needs. It made sense—only Albert and Pastor O had reliable salaries. When they came to Bible study, Pastor O would select the text, usually one that underscored the doctrinal beliefs of the Militants. Only Albert and he could offer opinions, for, apart from praying and singing, women weren't supposed to speak. Once Sister Biddows asked Pastor O to clarify something. He stayed silent for a long while before replying, and at the next Bible study session, he chose to explicate Paul's argument in favour of silencing women in church. Sister Biddows interrupted him.

She might have been drawing him out. She asked him why some churches, like the Church of God, the Nazarenes, and the Pentecostals, had women preachers. Pastor O told her he would answer her question after Bible study. When the session was over, Pastor O took her out onto the balcony and told her that the Militants came into being because the churches she had mentioned had backslid and departed from the laws of the original church. He had nothing against women speaking in church, but the rules of the Bible were the rules of the Bible, and he wasn't going to break them. It was the word of God, so it couldn't be wrong. Sister Biddows was silent throughout his explanation, and she left without telling him goodnight. *She left the Militants. Later she joined the Spirituals. Guessed she found no abyss there between male and female.*

He preached the Sunday after his return from town, where he had gone to see Peter for the last time. That Sunday he read the passage about Jesus and the Syro-Phoenician woman and talked about the woman's faith and Jesus's sympathy for her and the universality of Christianity and the comforting qualities of Christianity. While preparing what he was going to say, it occurred to him, from what Jesus told the woman, that Jesus too was bigoted—the woman was a dog who did not deserve to be fed with the children's bread; only when she accepted her status, requesting the crumbs reserved for the dogs, was Jesus impressed. How different was she from the Isabellan women who were forced to sleep with the plantation owners and overseers or sell sex to sailors? Lear had said that our needs were no more than the beasts', only reason made us think they were, but reason made those women do what was necessary and on par with beasts: to eat. That should have been his sermon.

He followed the sermon with "Jesu, Lover of My Soul." *Long after he had left the Militants, he'd often find himself singing that hymn. If only the words were true! It had to be one of the most beautiful Christian hymns, and the rough poetry in it!*

Jesu, lover of my soul,
Let me to Thy bosom fly—
While the nearer waters roll,
While the tempest still is high.

Hide me, oh my Saviour, hide!
Till the storm of life is past!
Safe into the haven guide—
Oh receive my soul at last!

There was a lot of deep feeling tinged with fright, he afterward reflected, as they sang the stanza:

Other refuge have I none.
Hang my helpless soul on thee.
Leave, oh leave me not alone!
Still support and comfort me!

During the last two lines of the hymn, tears rolled down Sister Belle's cheeks.

Cover my defenceless head
With the shadow of Thy wing.

He was depressed for the remainder of that afternoon. How long, he asked himself, could he continue faking this? In a play, everyone knew it was make-believe, and the actor was rewarded for how well he could make the faking lifelike. But here he was playing with people's faith, beliefs that kept them out of the madhouse, from eating manchineel or hanging themselves from rafters. And for what? For a vague promise that he might go study in America? The image of a tearful Sister Belle left him distraught. *He was exploiting his own people.* He'd have to begin working his way out of this, America or no America.

Pastor O said it had been a good sermon. Afterward he squinted and said that the part about "taking no thought for the morrow" wasn't meant the way Jerome had interpreted it. His church encouraged the hungry to come to Christianity in order to be fed. But it wasn't the hungry in body, it was those that hungered after righteousness. It was only after they lived righteously that "all good things were added unto them." The example of Job was the best one and, even before Job, how the children of Israel gained the Promised Land. *Years later, as he thought about this gaining of the Promised Land, it had struck him that that part of the Old Testament sounded as if the Jews were bragging about their own colonial policy. Anyway, their sojourn there was sporadic, and rarely was it in freedom. Even now, with all their military might, which could kill a hundred thousand Lebanese in a matter of weeks, the Promised Land was no more than a luxurious prison. Promised Lands were illusions, adult versions of juvenile fairy tales.*

Pastor O invited Jerome to dine with him that Sunday on boiled beans, bread and butter, and tinned beef. It was an excuse, he later realized, to continue the discussion, for while Pastor O reheated the food and while they ate, he spoke about his personal experience as regards the "seek ye first the Kingdom of Heaven and its righteousness and all things shall be added unto you" doctrine.

Pastor O told him that God will always bless to rapid increase the labour of those who serve Him faithfully. His farm had lost money for ten years, but once he became a "sanctified Christian," the prices for farm produce rose: beef went to record prices, and there were bumper grain harvests on alternate years, keeping the prices high and the supply constant. Within five years he had paid off the mortgage on his farm and added another hundred acres. No, sir, he could not accept Jerome's interpretation. "Yer had ter plan—that was part o the meanin o the story o the Wise Virgins. All yer gotta ter do is look at America, the most God-fearinest country in the world, n see how prosperous tis. Look how American influence spreadin round the world! Soon all nations gonna want ter be unner American guidance. Yer only got ter look around the worl n see that where people's livin in sin, worshippin idols n such like, like in Africa, they's poor. When them Israelites obeyed God, He rained down manna on em n sent em quails."

Did they eat them raw? he had wanted to ask, visualizing the desert and an absence of fuel.

"He protected em too from their enemies with His own presence, a pillar o cloud by day n a pillar o fire by night. My God is real. His followers don't never suffer from wants such as hunger n disease."

Pastor O had to return to America instantly. That was why he was eager to hear Jerome preach. He needed someone "to look after ma flock…How's if me n you was to make a deal? You do all ma preachin fer me when I'm gone n take care o this here prapty? I gon pay yer fifty dallaz a week. I gon be gone tru da bignin o October."

He was silent for a while. "Yer don have ter give a answer right now. Jus think on it some, n the Lawd gon guide yer aplenty," Pastor O said, his eyes two mini turquoises in pink marble.

"Let me think it over," Jerome told him.

Pastor O was unusually quiet for a little while. They were seated on the porch, and his face was turned away from Jerome, in the direction of the sea. When he turned to Jerome, he said, "Yer remin me o maself when I been yer age. N sometimes I tremble fer yer cause I done been in some awful mess that I ain't want nobody ter be a-fallin in.

"I'm gon tell yer a lil bit bout maself. See, I done clear all this up with Gawd so it ain't no burden fer me."

Jerome developed a grudging respect for him. The story was long and rambling and full of digressions, many of which he no longer remembered.

Pastor O had grown up somewhere in Tennessee. He left school in grade nine, at age sixteen, and ran away to Memphis. "I didn have no head fer figgerin n memrizin n them thangs. N I just kinda feel I done had ma fill o smellin cow dung. Ma pa, he brought him home a thousand dollars he'd done borrowed from the bank to buy him a tractor. I stole me three hundred o it and took maself off ter the city.

"When I got there I been sittin all by ma lonesome. The

sun was already a-settin. N comes this here man up ter me, smilin n friendly like, all dressed up in a suit n tie. N says he ter me, 'Look lak yer be needin yer a place ter stay?' N I say yes. N he takes me home. N I lived with him some." He paused here for a good two minutes before he said. "N I was his lover.

"I stay with him fer bout three months til one day I look at maself in the mirror n I just spit at maself. N I heard my mother who been a Nazarene all her laf singin, singin lak she was there in flesh n blood, 'What a Friend We Have in Jesus.' N I fall on ma knees n prayed n cried. I prayed n cried some that day. N I asked the Lawd ter show me the way. N I packed n headed back home that selfsame day." There was silence again, like he was refuelling to continue.

At eighteen he forgot the pledge and returned to Memphis, where he fell into "awful vice. I just had ter sell maself ter survive. After I been there bout two years, mah skin jus come out in a rash all over. I had a dirty disease n the doctor he says, says he, I done had it fer too long. But I did some mighty prayin n Gawd He cured me. It had ter be a miracle. That doctor did done give me over. I went back home n I ask forgiveness. N they fergived me."

Three years later his father died and he found out that, upon the death of his mother, the farm would go to his younger brother. "Them temptations ter return ter Memphis was mighty perful. N even then there in the country I slipped me up some a few times. Wasn always what I shoulda been but I didn stay on the slippery slope. The Lawd he didn throw me over, see, cause I prayed ter Him ter work on ma mother. N when I approached ma mother ter raise me the money from her part o the farm, she jus went right ahead n done it. And ah bought me a farm.

"Gawd, He sure works in some mysterious ways. He make me sos not to desire womens, cause Ah woulda upped n married, cause Ah was mighty lonesome fer a lil love. But the good side was Ah could save mah money n pay off ma farm.

"Now Ah got ter get me back ter America, cause when Ah heeded the Holy Sperrit ter spread the gospel, Ah lease out ma farm, n the tenant, a mighty fine lad he peared ter me at the time, ain't been payin his rent like he shoulda done. So Ahma gon fix that.

"Ah been studyin too a whole heap bout thangs we can do here. Ah done speak ter young Manchester n he gon sell me this place if Ah can convince em in America ter buy. Ah got me some plans that gon be ter the greater glory o Gawd n that gon help yer people."

Jerome left the house around three, but he did not go home. He headed to the spot where he sometimes read. He sat there a long time, thinking and watching, just watching the waves hurling their grey-haired crests onto the beach, self-destructing; the steep cliffs on one side standing like sentries to the sea; the deep ruts scarring the slope, like wrinkles on an aged face; the plovers soaring from or diving into the water; even a little boy coming around the bend making footprints, which the waves quickly washed out.

There were times when this sea was so angry it reached beyond where he was sitting. The sun dipped behind the mountains and dusk began to descend: presences equal absences.

The sun was high when he awoke the next morning. He decided to go walking before going to see Pastor O. The wind swept the blades of sugar cane stalks, transforming the fields into green, undulating blankets. The black sand road, the mica in it glowing, stretched out like a monstrous serpent between the fields.

Where the cane field ended there was another squatters' village. The main street of the village was deserted until he got to the rum shop. Roughly a dozen men were loitering there, playing cards and dominoes, some of them at a makeshift table in the street just away from the shop, some of them on the concrete slab that formed a sort of porch at the entrance. They looked languid, like sacks of potatoes waiting to be carted or exhausted bodies waiting for someone to provide "them rest unto their souls." They certainly took no thought for the morrow, for they had only today. He reflected that he had seen them in every village he had gone to, on and off the plantations. And unless they were recent deportees from wealthier Trinidad, they had none of the lily's beauty or Solomon's gilt. Only deep, sunken eyes, papery skin, and lazy movements. The holes in their clothes suggested an element of war, but the damage had not been the result of struggle. They had laid down arms a long time ago. Some had never taken them up.

It was noon and the sun continued to beat down upon the earth, casting shadows that lay like fallen clothes at the feet of things. He passed Brammah, the area's Obeah priest, on the way out of the village. He took another road between cane fields. It led him down to a river—not the one that flowed through his village. He crossed it, resumed the road on the other side, and walked in an almost straight line toward the old Manchester house.

When he got to Pastor O's place, he was dusty, and his shirt was transparent with sweat. Pastor O suggested he take a shower. He refused. The day before, as he watched the sea's liquid reality, simultaneously settling inside and battering its container, he'd concluded that the container was to accept Pastor O's offer. The battering, he told himself, would come later.

12

"You see the lovely moon?" Sister Doris asked as she ascended the four steps leading up to the porch of the plantation house. The moon glowed in a cloudless sky. The lawn was a lake of ghostly sparkles; it had rained half an hour earlier. It was Friday, ten days since he had been on his own, and the first Bible study session he was to direct.

Sister Doris went into the living room-cum-church and left him leaning against the porch railing. She was a recent convert and a friend of his mother's. On mornings when work was available, punctually at six her wiry form appeared along the canal road, a hoe on her shoulder, a hand tugging at the rope of the goat that wasn't keeping pace with her. No one ever heard her swearing or saying anything bad about anyone. She had a ten-year-old daughter from a common-law union. She'd left the man shortly after the child had been born. There'd been no man in her life after that. Her mother was cantankerous and bedridden. Comsie looked in on her during the day now that she was home with Yawesi. No one ever heard Sister Doris complain about her mother, and no one knew how she managed to feed all three of them with the pittances she earned during seasonal estate work. But Sister Doris felt she needed salvation and had recently "come forward," as she put it, "to dip herself in the blood of Immanuel." It did not seem to have changed her much: her skin was just as dry and scaly, though she made an effort to improve its appearance with Vaseline each time she came to prayer meeting or Sunday worship, and her eyes had lost none of their blank sadness.

Gradually the others assembled, and soon the living room was full of their cheap perfume. Their dresses of browns, greys, and dark greens reached almost to their ankles, for Pastor O had warned them against clothing that would show off their bodies and cause men to lust after them; God would hold them accountable on the Day of Reckoning. For the same reason, they were forbidden to wear swimsuits. They could bathe in the sea, but they had to be fully clothed, and the fabric must not become transparent when it was wet. Wisely, they stayed away from the sea. Pastor O hadn't said anything about wearing perfume.

July was almost finished, and his plans had not fully crystallized. He'd heard from Peter. That Saturday he'd gone to see the Morrisons, and Mr. Morrison told him that he'd seen Bunyan about having him reinstated. And, after the puffing and habitual spiel about the ingratitude of the natives, Bunyan had agreed to write a letter to Expatriates' board of governors recommending that he be reinstated.

At home that Sunday afternoon he spent a great deal of time with Yawesi, who was now creeping and getting into a lot of delightful mischief. Jerome used coloured marbles to trick Yawesi into moving around, and Wesi simply could not outdo himself. He said to Wesi, holding up a yellow marble that Wesi was trying to take from him, "When you grow up, you must work for more than these." His mother and father laughed. "Ma and Dad, if I had a chance to go to England, would you be able to raise the money for my fare?"

His parents looked at each other. Both nodded at the same time.

"How you will get fo go? People caan go to Englan so easy these days," his father said.

"What make you ask this question?" his mother asked.

"No special reason."

"What bout school next year? I ain't hear you say nothing bout that."

He decided not to tell them about Bunyan's decision. Better not to get their hopes up and then have them dashed, in case the board rejected the request. "Well, you know if I don't get back to school and I pass four subjects, I can get a job in the civil service and begin to help out." Actually, it was three, but with three you could be squeezed out if there were enough cousins and godchildren of influential people applying.

"No," his father said. "I want you fo go back to school. Since I meet that fine gentleman, Mr. Morrison, I been thinkin you might even turn out like him—win a scholarship and study abroad."

His father did get his scholarship-winning son. But it was Wesi, not him. Still, if he hadn't been living in town and feeding and clothing Wesi on his civil service salary, things would have been hard for them because only Wesi's tuition was covered by his scholarship. That was like sprinkling a bucket of water in a dry field. Wesi didn't even get a book allowance in high school. But, when he got his first scholarship to university, everything was paid. Wesi was coming home from the University of Western Ontario in a month. "I have to cross the t's and dot the i's on my dissertation and change the odd thing here and there to satisfy the idiosyncrasies of my professor. That will take a week. Expect me home in about six weeks." It was nice to have a brother with a PhD in physics. To have an understanding brother, period.

But that Sunday his father wasn't sure that he could make it on his own in England. "You so shouldn leave home for go to no White man country. You never learn how fo take care o yoself properly. Book alone caan do it. Sometimes you ha fo use yo foot and yo fist. And *you* never learn fo do that."

"Yo father right, Jerome. They say that when Black people firs start for go Englan is the Jamaican them what put a end to plenty o the abuse they meet with. I hear the Bajan and the Isabellan them use for take all what the White people dish out. But not the Jamaican. When they start for kick and box for they rights, White people take notice."

"If you was like that African, I wouldn'ta worried fo yo, but you don know how fo take care o yoself. You is too sofie-sofie.

"If you really want fo go Englan and you know somebody there that will get you in the country, me and Comsie will find the money somehow. But we won't surprise if they bring you back in a coffin."

He did not tell them that Peter had offered to help him come to England. *What a joke that was!* Isabella Island was too small for him. He felt like a penned animal, put out to pasture at the owner's will. He'd already figured out that Isabellans worked for the benefit of the British manufacturers, bankers, and merchants. That was really what the Mercantile Policy had come to mean. It was better to be where the spoils were distributed, even if he wouldn't get more than crumbs, than in Isabella, where there weren't even crumbs.

After Pastor O left for America, Jerome would on occasion sleep at the plantation house. That Monday evening he put out the light and sat in the darkness, then moved onto the porch and eventually began pacing up and down the lawn. How long was he going to keep up this farce? Why was he being a tool for a semi-literate man who was using missionary work to run away from confronting himself? When the moon had cleared the west and gone down behind the mountains, he still had no answer. It was almost daybreak when he decided to go home to his parents' hut.

When he woke up that morning, his mother was in the kitchen and Wesi was on the floor waiting to play. In Wesi's smiling cheeks he saw the life of promise that adults longed for, and he understood why Christianity insisted that its followers become children. The Kingdom of Heaven was the domain of fools and children. Shelley summed up the situation for those who were not afraid to face reality. "We look before and after and pine for what is not." *Just last year, too, he read Nietzsche's statement that only idiots and children could be happy. How he'd wanted to quarrel with Arnold's ending of "Dover Beach"! Now he could truly say that his life had been a series of wounds with occasional respites for a little recovery. Sisyphus, dragons, Proteus! Never mind the St. Georges and the Ulysses: they were the real figments of imagination. But they probably had to be there, like life after death or taboos against suicide, to encourage people to go on living.*

An hour later he walked to his spot by the sea. It was a dry, windy day, and the sea was rough. The waves broke beyond his mangrove seat, so he had to sit on an unsheltered stone on higher ground. The high-pitched, frightened sounds of the plovers were audible above the booming waves and the grating drags of the pebbles. It made him think of an unoiled engine, even of worlds colliding. He felt, too, as if he were falling apart. He left almost as soon as he arrived.

On his way home he stopped in at the plantation house, where a letter from Pastor O awaited him. He wrote that he had a good offer for his farm and was selling it. He said he had convinced the missionary body to let him hire an assistant so he could be free to establish missions on the other islands. "You are my assistant now." He also enclosed a money order for three hundred US dollars "so's you can buy yourself some fine closes."

It was as if he'd left the turbulence of the sea to find another in the plantation house. Should he accept the money? It would be a good opportunity to leave the sham behind. But he was seriously thinking of going to England. He might need the money.

About a month after the letter from Pastor O, all his plans were finalized. By 6:45 p.m. the faithful began to arrive for Bible study. The house was dark. The door was locked.

"Brudder Jerome mus a forget we got prayer meeting and Bible study tonight," he heard Sister Doris say.

"Me not think so. Knock the door," Sister Matilda said. "He mus a fall asleep inside there."

Someone banged the door.

Five minutes later, he turned on the porch lights and emerged holding a blazing Bible.

The women stood still, their mouths wide open.

"Drop it befo it burn yo hand," Sister Felicia's young grandson told him.

He dropped the burning Bible onto the porch and movement returned among the sisters. Now they looked at Jerome and at one another, shaking their heads.

Sister Felicia said, "This is crazy people work! Boy you not fraid God gwine strike you dead?"

"It's the only way," he told them. "We have to burn our Bibles. Why do we have to wait for White men to come from America to tell us what to believe and how to live? Let White people in America teach White people in America to stop hating people, to stop burning people alive. Sisters, we are Africans—"

"Don call me no African!" interrupted Sister Amelia.

"Is you what is the African. Is you what burning God word," said Sister Belle.

"He mus think we is cannibals and that we live in tree," added Sister Felicia.

"Has any of you been to Africa?"

""Don ask we no questions. 'Has any of you been to Africa?'" Sister Betsy mimicked him. "You gwine go to hell, that is what I know."

"Amen," Sister Felicia said.

He closed the door, turned off the porch light, and left them muttering. By morning the village would know what he'd done, and within three days so would everyone in the neighbouring villages. He looked at his sweating hands and only then realized how frightened he was.

There was a knock on the door and his mother's voice.

When he opened it, she, his father, and Sister Doris were standing on the porch.

"What wrong with you Jerome?" his mother asked him.

"Nothing."

"How nothing? These past weeks. Henry, didn I tell yo I fin Jerome acking strange? Lord deliver us from tribulation." Her voice sounded tearful.

His father was staring at him from head to toe. "Jerome, you gone crazy?"

He shook his head. "Let's go home. Tomorrow morning you will see that I'm quite sane. This is enough excitement for tonight."

He had not planned what he did that night. The idea had come to him a few minutes before the women arrived. He hadn't even planned what he was going to tell them. *When he was around thirty, after having been reminded countless times of what he had done, always with the intention of wounding him, he'd come to realize how deeply the superstitions of Christianity had sunk their roots into his people. When at forty he'd had his first experience with insanity and had recovered, he wondered whether his act hadn't been an early sign of mental weakness. But, if that had been the case, he would have broken down when the telegram arrived from Peter's aunt.*

Peter had written to tell him that his uncle would find a job in the post office for him. He'd inquired and found out that, in order for him to remain in England, he would need an employment voucher. Peter told him to come to England as a visitor, and after he got there, his uncle would make the necessary arrangements to secure him permanent residence. He said he'd arranged for him to stay at his uncle's, but if that didn't work out, he could stay with his aunt Aggie. Jerome added the three hundred dollars he'd received from Pastor O to carry out his preaching duties to the money he had left over from his scholarship funds as well as what Pastor O had paid him in advance. Altogether it covered his fare. When he told his parents that he had booked his passage for England, they were quite surprised and wanted to know where he'd got the money. He told them that he'd borrowed it. His father got four hundred for him as travelling money, and the Morrisons gave him another two hundred as a going-away present.

The Morrisons arranged a little get-together for him the day before his departure. His father and mother and Wesi came in from the country. There was a bottle of wine, roasted chicken, and various cooked vegetables. His mother had difficulty eating. At one point she wept. She did not like his going to England all by himself at seventeen (eight days before his eighteenth birthday). She had asked around the village about people who had gone to England and had given him a wad of addresses of people to get in touch with in case he had difficulties or was lonely.

He was excited and frightened by the experience awaiting him. Several what-ifs crept into his thoughts from time to time. He had stood on the Morrison's porch a large part of that morning, looking out over the capital. It was raining off and on, the sea was choppy, and its blue hue had changed to a leaden one. Mist was sweeping down from the mountains and enveloping Hanovertown. Tomorrow would be a fateful day in his life.

By six they had finished eating and Mrs. Morrison suggested that he might want to be alone with his parents. They walked down to the harbour, each of them taking turns carrying Wesi. He always remembered that half hour as the closest he'd ever felt to his parents. Not to Wesi but to his parents.

When they returned, Mr. Morrison was waiting for them on the porch. He handed Jerome a telegram that had arrived while they were out walking. He took it and read it, laughed, and then cried.

It was addressed to Mr. Morrison and it was signed by Hilda Pinchley. It simply said: "CANCEL TRIP STOP IMMI-GRATION TOLD TO DENY ENTRANCE STOP."

He wanted to return to the country that night. Mr. Morrison drove them out. He begged for silence each time they tried to talk to him. He did not sleep at all that night, and just before dawn he left the house and went to sit at his spot by the sea, now calm. He returned home around sunset and found his parents quite worried, already thinking about getting a search party. He told them he was all right. He merely needed to spend a lot of time by himself. *He noticed that pattern all through the years. Whenever he was in difficulty, he couldn't talk to anyone, and it frustrated him when people tried to force him to listen to them. Whenever he chose to discuss a personal problem with others, it was either because he'd become reconciled to it or because he'd already found the solution. His mother considered his approach selfish; no one should live that way. But, after he had screamed at her to leave him alone and then apologized to her tearfully that he had not meant to be rude, he merely needed to work things out silently, she respected his wish. His father saw it as arrogance, a feeling that others weren't intelligent enough to advise him. His co-workers merely dismissed him as weird and saw his nervous breakdown as proof that they were right.*

That evening, after he had eaten, his parents handed him two letters from the Expatriates Academy. The first one was from the board informing him that they'd ruled negatively on a request that he be reinstated. It ended with the statement, "We wish you every success in your future endeavours." A postscript written by hand read, "We have just been informed that you were successful in your O-level exams. We wish to assure you that the school's personnel will be delighted to furnish you with character testimonials which will not mention the unfortunate incident."

The next letter contained his exam results. He had passed with distinctions in all but one of his subjects. He quietly informed his parents.

"You not even happy you pass!" his mother said.

"I happy for you," his father said. "When one door close another open. You will make it still, if you learn for humble yoself. And God will bless Mr. Morrison. Is not all Black people that turn their back on their colour when they succeed."

He didn't know what his father meant by humility. He didn't brag and he didn't feel he was better than anybody. He felt there were some people whose company he hated. He took nothing for granted and probably thought too much about consequences, so he didn't drink with the boys. Talking about how many women they screwed and trying to make him feel abnormal because he didn't do the same were reasons enough to avoid the company of boys his age. They couldn't tolerate you if you were different. All the men in his village considered his father abnormal, though they also admitted that his mother was a good woman and didn't need to get beaten. Still they protested: "But, Henry, you ha fo gi them a slap now and again, even if they don't nothing bad—so them remember who wearing the pants." His father ignored such advice.

When he was about ten, he had passed by the gate of some people who lived in the village beyond the first cane field. A fat woman was in the yard telling a man that Malva went into her garden that day and stole a hand of plantains from a bunch maturing behind her house. "Me catch she right in the ack." The man called Malva out in the yard, and all the neighbours, men and women, who certainly knew the story, gathered to watch the outcome. The man asked the woman if what he'd heard was true and she said yes. He removed the thick leather belt he was wearing and the woman stood still while he flogged her. After he'd given her about six strokes, the complainant said that it was enough and some of the others nodded. A female bystander said to the complainant, "You can always count pon Prescott for gi yo satisfaction when you complain bout Malva."

There was no room for difference. Difference was arrogance. At seventeen he already understood that, and the years merely confirmed what he realized then.

The following Monday he got a letter from Mr. Morrison congratulating him on his GCE passes and assuring him that even if the tactic for his reinstatement hadn't worked and his plans to go to England had fallen through, it wasn't the end of his life.

He said too that Peter's mother had come to see him and had accused him of putting up her son to take on responsibilities he wasn't ready for. "She even called me a communist and told me to watch my step. Isabella Island is still a British colony. We still call the shots here. God be thanked for that."

By the end of August, when the hoped-for explanation

from Peter did not arrive, he became plunged in thought. *Beggars on horseback and on foot! Some twenty years later, he had thought that if he ever discovered Peter's address, he would write him the following letter:*

Dear Peter,

Once upon a time there were two beggars, but they begged from different altitudes. You see, one owned a horse—better nourished than he, if you ask me. The other moved around on foot. But there was a time when the two met and realized that they had something in common on which they could build a relationship. Beggarhood must have been it. The one on horseback agreed that from horseback things did look somewhat more optimistic. He promised that one day he would let the other ride his horse and see for himself. The one on foot, never having been on horseback, could not comment. The one on horseback went on to say that on horseback you could easily whip those who refused you or laughed at you and make a quick getaway. Then, too, if you were of a mind, you could spit on your pedestrian brethren.

But they separated, and the more the mounted beggar thought of his promise, the more afraid he became that if he loaned his horse to the pedestrian beggar, the latter would keep it. So he broke his promise.

Now, Peter, this question is for you. Have you any idea of the risks mounted beggars run? From what I hear, it seems there are only advantages: that frequently they crack their whips over the backs of their brethren on foot, pillage their pence, laugh at their pleas for mercy, and exasperate at the readiness with which they bleed. I have another question for you: Do you think that one day pedestrian beggars might take up arms against their mounted brethren? Perhaps not, I suspect your answer will be, for some are born to beg from horseback and others on foot; some to ride horses and others to be horses.

My dear Peter, I'm very eager to have your opinions on the above matter.

Fraternally,
A footless and horseless beggar
that calls himself Jerome

In another frame of mind he had written a reply to Mr. Yeats about this poem. If there was more than a joke to the afterlife— Was this a joke within a joke?—he would present it to Mr. Yeats— that is, if Mr. Yeats would speak to him—but more of that anon.

If from the lash you've never been bent,
It is easy to say,
"We're beggars, on whipping intent."

If beggars are we,
a whipping beggar I'd rather be.
You see, W. B., to survey from horseback man's frailty,
to watch him mend, nurse, or drag
his broken, bleeding ends
is luxury
—and entertainment.
Horsebacked whippers

in beggaring bury their guilt.
And since the lash is all there is,
the whipper must become the whipped.

Let the beggars change places.
Let the erstwhile whip wielder become the whipped.

He'd been devastated to hear a professor say on BBC's Literary
Giants that Yeats had been a fascist, an ardent admirer of Mussolini,
and a passionate believer in eugenics. When he overcame the shock,
he'd wondered what Yeats would have written, since he said his
poems were his thoughts in poetic form, if Hitler had triumphed
and he had lived to see it. Maybe something like this:

But such pure forms as concentration camps
Of blackened flesh and blacker smoke
Leaving snow-white cinder piles
Monuments to a black world made white
To tell of evil past
And the greatest, goriest human glories yet to come.

The professor felt that, had Yeats lived to see the effects of
fascism, he would have invented paradoxes to encapsulate it. Well
maybe. But after he had got over his initial shock, he'd seen Yeats's
horror as part of his Celtic Twilight. The Irish, like Isabellans
and Africans, were wonderful storytellers. Many of the ones who
settled on Isabella had been swallowed up by the Blacks, and now
the stories of the two traditions have merged. That's what an
anthropologist had said, anyway. Guess when you have no bombs
to make others do your bidding, you try verbal conjuring.

Fat chance!

What sort of a beggar were you, W. B.? Mounted before the need for the monkey gland operation, no doubt. Quite another matter after. Or was that Michael Robartes rather than you? They said you came from a family of nuts. You must have had difficulty holding your many warring selves together. You succeeded though, a helluva lot better than me, and you did it magically: pentametrically.

He decided to go to town the following day and cash in his ticket and pick up a job application for the civil service.

The application was to be accompanied by two testimonials in sealed envelopes. One had to come from a former teacher and another from someone who knew him well—the suggestions were clergyman, planter, or justice of the peace. He spoke to his mother about it and she said nothing, but two days later she gave him the envelope. She had asked Mr. Manchester, Jr., to write it.

13

ON OCTOBER 1 HE BEGAN working as the dispatching officer of inland mail. He disliked the job. The mailbags were dust laden and filthy; it was his responsibility to open them and sort the mail they contained into local and international. Within weeks he developed tonsilitis and, eventually, a chronically inflamed throat.

It was a job full of responsibilities and hazards. His supervisor, Marian Myers, was a supercilious woman who had completely remade herself in the image of British acceptability, with straightened hair tinted blond, a face whitened by bleaching creams, a body encased in grey wool suits, speech with carefully enunciated syllables, no humour, and a walk in tune to some unsteady alien drum. They did not mask their contempt for each other.

He joined the staff at a time when mail from the United Stated came through Trinidad and when all the letter bags and many of the letters would arrive opened, the money they contained, since Isabellan emigrants to the United States rarely sent home "empty" letters, stolen. One lunch hour— he frequently had to work on his lunch hours and beyond five o'clock—he saw one of the sorters slip a letter into his pocket. Since the sorters were nominally under his charge, he confronted him, but the fellow denied he'd done anything wrong. He threatened to call the supercilious woman, and the fellow emptied his pockets.

Three months later, at his own request, he was transferred to the Ministry of Communications and Works. Now, looking back, he found it funny: his complaint had been that he was too tired or it was too late for him to profit from going to the public library. He'd also begun two A-level correspondence courses, literature and economics, and needed the time to get his work done. But he lived in a chronically depressed state then. The concentration the courses required was beyond him. But he continued reading at the library and even bought books from overseas.

From having lived at Miss. Dellimore's, he knew he wanted to be alone. He rented a room about a half mile from where he worked, nearer after his transfer to the Ministry of Communications and Works. It was a large but depressing room. The painters hadn't thought of covering the floor, and paint had splashed and dried all over it. Near the stairs that led outside to the backyard was a tap where the tenants showered and did their laundry. They all shared a single toilet on the floor. With a little bit of the money from his cashed-in plane ticket, he bought a small wooden screen, a two-tiered wooden stand, a Primus stove, a frying pan, a small pot, a second-hand single bed, a second-hand kitchen table for two, and two kitchen chairs. His mother bought barfleur in the country and mattress fabric and made a mattress for the bed. She brought him two pillows and bed linen. She laundered his clothes.

Apart from the last five years, nothing much altered in his routine. The friendships he made in the capital were superficial. He soon discovered that those seeking to befriend him did so for pragmatic reasons: they needed a drinking buddy, a moneylender, an emergency babysitter, or a distraction from their personal problems. He began to think that people were very ordinary, fond of routine, and truth about themselves or truth period disturbed them. He wanted friends with whom he could share ideas, but the people he encountered or who were drawn to him looked skeptically on ideas and considered those who pursued them strange. "Why you thinking all them things? I think was only for pass a exam that people think them things. What exam you studying for? You not studying for a exam! You strange! Boy, leave the book them alone and le think think fo imself. Life make fo live." Everything—every act—was calculated to yield a meal, a drink, an orgasm, a loan, or at the most innocuous, a forgetting of the self; occasionally it was a projecting presence for their problems that they needed. *He had been the first person to borrow Achebe's* Morning Yet on Creation Day, *right after the library acquired it; he'd laughed and laughed at Achebe's story about the Ghanaian girl who wrote to castigate him for not having exam questions at the end of his book.* His interest was in stripping away masks to get to the essence of things. People soon became uncomfortable with him and cooled their initial enthusiasm, for they treasured their masks. *Of late, too, he began to see human relationships as tennis games. The other panicked when he couldn't strike the ball, and the game ended: people would not invest their time learning how to send back the ball. The player was important only insofar as he knew what to do with the ball. The tennis model applied as well to his own social clumsiness, his non-conformity. A question of the wrong skills or an absence of skills.*

He spent a lot of time at the library. He took long walks up to the Botanic Gardens. During periods of peak political activity, he attended all the political meetings, which, in the capital, were always held at the Market Quadrangle—though he never supported any of the political parties and never once voted. Very skeptically he participated in the independence celebrations, if looking at others amuse themselves or make fools of themselves could be called participation. He was glad that British influence over his people would lessen. But *Black Skins, White Mask* and *The Wretched of the Earth* had already given him a good idea of what to expect from the future leaders. *They were among the books, along with* The Autobiography of Malcolm X—*all books that advocated "Black power"—the prime minister banned two weeks after independence: clearly he'd got independence to perpetuate White power.* Butler had already shown his colours as far as his own self-enrichment was concerned, and the British had not exposed him overtly—their press merely dubbed him P. L. M. Midas. (It was lost on his supporters; they knew nothing about Midas.) Butler could always be pointed to as a specimen of what the post-colonial leaders would be or were. He was often amused by the impossible promises the politicians made to their supporters, by corrupt officials calling others corrupt. And the practice each of the political parties had of firing thousands of road menders and petty workers each time they came to power to create employment for their own supporters was medieval, wicked. It nauseated him. Once, after an election and the mass firings had taken place, hundreds of dismissed, angry people crowded onto the grounds of the Ministry of Communications and Works and began yelling abuse at the minister. One of the workers from the general office was an ardent supporter of the newly elected party. He poked his head out the window, spat at them, and told them to eat shit.

Within a year of his return to town, he'd read all five books on psychology in the library. They were the dullest books in the world, but he was seeking a cure for his angst. Sometime toward the end of that first year, he came upon Machiavelli's *The Prince*, and it left him wide-eyed about political behaviour.

There was some modification to this routine during the six years Wesi lived with him, and even before that, he would let Wesi visit him for a week or two at a time, when Wesi was on vacation from primary school. Wesi's being with him, along with buying books for him whenever Jerome could afford them, was his way of making sure that his brother read. *During his convalescence following his second breakdown, when Wesi wasn't around to encourage him to regain his sanity, he had wondered whether his assumed responsibility for Wesi wasn't what had preserved his sanity, whether he had not made a tool of Wesi in order to remain sane.*

Between his first and fifth year, his monthly salary had increased from $116 to $146. He sent his mother twenty-five or thirty dollars each month. *It was only a year ago that he found out that, for the first two and a half years, she used it to pay back the three hundred dollars Pastor O had sent him. He had been angry with her for doing so. She had simply looked at him wide-eyed and said, "Where is yo pride? Is the only thing poor people got. You caan throw it way fo a few hundred dollars." He'd quietly laughed at her. She knew nothing—and was better* off not knowing anything—about capitalism. He went home only at Easter and at Christmas.

One such Easter—his brother was still in elementary school; it was a Saturday evening—Millicent called out to his mother that old Manchester had died about an hour before.

"Thanks for telling me," his mother replied, paused for a while, and added: "When you strip birds o they feathers, you can't tell one from the other."

He had laughed aloud from inside the hut, and so did his father, who was outside washing his feet on the bleaching stones. It took him back to the shower room about ten years earlier, where they had been showering after PE. Mr. Boggs occasionally showered with them, but he wasn't there that day. They joked about Donald. He was White to the point of being pink, his face and back covered with inflamed pimples that made him smell like tripe. He was tall and gaunt, with legs and thighs that angled outward when he walked. He carried his huge backside like a burden. It caused him to sway below the waist.

He suffered from something or the other that had caused him to lose all his hair by the time he was fourteen. His hairless, pustular body intrigued them. His dick hung like a limp plantain almost halfway down his thigh. They'd spoken about it among themselves, joking about how it would look erect and pitying the woman who would have to endure it.

"That is one bird that can't fly," Andrew had said, pointing to Donald's dick.

"You mean it like a ostrich?" Rajan giggled.

"Donald," Lonzo said, "where's your plumes? How're you gonna fly?"

Donald grinned throughout, his large buck teeth darkened by cavities, giving him the look of a jackass with bared teeth.

"*Tell him to send his sister to find out,*" Peter told Donald.

"*You mean—all o that—and is only a piss spout?*" Philip added, and everyone laughed.

"*Tell them,*" Peter said, "*that with a bird like yours, you don't need plumes.*"

"*You should know,*" Randolph said.

"*Yeah, I guess I'm into birds.*"

On occasion, they talked about Mr. Boggs, who was also well endowed but very hirsute—thick, dark brown, almost black body hair. "Now I bet you Boggsy can fly." Boggsy was a bachelor. Maybe that was why he showered with them. But there was nothing suspicious about him.

Donald's parents were poor. They lived beside the Coastal Highway about eight miles out of town in a rambling board house full of rotten wood and crying out for paint. An aunt of his had won a beauty contest and ended up marrying a foreign hotel owner. It was she who paid for Donald's education. There were lots of half-naked White children running around in their yard; they looked as malnourished as Donald, who must have been the oldest. His father was a grocery clerk in Hanovertown.

But it wasn't Donald who was the scapegoat of the class. It was Bullock, whose fat was thick, whose mind was thicker, and from whose sensibility the cruellest of jokes bounced off, deflected by an eternal grin. Sometimes they took away his candy.

Donald was never more than two or three places from the bottom of the class. The hotel proprietor divorced Donald's aunt before Donald could complete high school. He wouldn't have passed GCE anyway; that was probably the only advantage of having the papers corrected in England: the candidate's race was unknown. He became a grocery clerk at the store where his father worked. He was married, with a son, so he could fly—erotically, at least. They never acknowledged each other when they met.

Outside of this he had gone back home one May, nine years before, when Wesi, about to go off to Cave Hill to begin his BSc, told him that his father was sick. Two weeks later Henry's testes were removed to arrest the growth of prostate cancer. Following his father's release from hospital, Jerome started to go home on weekends; the drugs his father took left him weak and haggard. His father was convinced that he would get better. Henry was no raving he-man, but his psyche must have been wounded by the removal of his testes.

His illness couldn't have come at a worse time. The party in power had only just declared that all squatters on the plantations would be given title to the land they were living on. Mrs. Bensie was long dead, but his father had continued to farm her land because her niece, to whom it was bequeathed, lived in England. Henry deposited the money her share of the produce earned in a bank account she had opened for that purpose. With borrowed money his mother and father had also acquired ten acres after young Manchester started selling out the estate.

Comsie hired a couple of labourers to plough the land, dig the banana holes, and do whatever else had to be done. She looked after and milked the two cows they now kept. She got three boys from the village to help her cut, label, package, and arrange the bananas by the side of the road the day before they were graded and shipped, and to harvest and prepare the root tubers and vegetables they grew for sale to the traffickers who bought them for resale in Trinidad. He never understood where Comsie got her energy. She was determined to pay off the land as quickly as possible.

It was then, too, that she told him she had saved the money he had been sending her along with some of their own and had already contracted to build a two-bedroom cement house. "Even if yo father go, we will still manage, cause that house will already pay for. And me and Henry decide that when we go, it will be yos, cause is part of yo money we will buil it with. Wesi will understand. You pay fo his books and buy his uniform and give him spending money when he been in town and you used fo feed him five days a week. and you give him guidance cause o what you done go through. And cause o the help you give him, he done on his way. Is true you only come visit us Christmastime and Easter. But you been like a father to yo brother. And don think he don appreciate it. Since he been bout seven, when you used fo be sending im books, he use to say to me, 'Ma, you think Jerome happy? I think he glad when I come see him.' So me think that is why he use fo spend part o his holiday with you. You remember that time when he been in form III—me think is form III—and you pay his passage fo go pon a school outing to Jamaica, I think he been going to kiss yo bottom foot fo it. He been so happy. The only thing he don like bout you, and everybody gree with him in that, is that you so stiff, and you always talk like a Englishman. You don know how people hate yo fo that!"

Wesi definitely did not talk like an Englishman. During Wesi's first year in high school, they'd debated the subject. "Ah know what you trying fo do, Brother Jerome"—he always called him that even though Jerome had tried to get him to drop it.

"And what am I trying to do?"

"You trying fo get me fo speak like you. I can speak like you, but I keep that for when I'm in school."

"No, you can't. You forget and lapse into shoddy pronunciation and awkward syntax."

"Lissen, me na big nuff fo know all dem big wud what you bussin pon me, but you self gwine admit dat yo writin when you been my age don got nutten over me writin now." Wesi parodied the dialect of the isolated northern villages. "Brother Jerome, you are an Isabellan, but you can't speak the language!" He winked at Jerome. "See you—or yo—Monday morning," and he rushed off to catch a bus to Compton.

His brother was right, and he never afterward attempted to correct him, even though at times he winced at his mixture of dialect and standard English.

But that was Wesi, full of contractions. His desk and notes were always neatly organized. He wrote legibly and artistically. Yet it was rare that his shirt was pushed into his trousers or his tie not askew. He combed his hair, he said, only when he was going to school. He liked the way it looked when it was uncombed. It was clay-coloured, often matted, and felt like steel wool. His skin was pale; he even had freckles; but discounting skin colour and hair texture, anyone could see that they were brothers.

That was Wesi for sure. When he was in form IV—yes, it had to have been form IV—he was the fast bowler for the Expatriates' cricket team. The best team of each of the British islands in the Eastern Caribbean eliminated one another. And the winning team of each division played the winning teams of the others in a series of elimination games. In Jerome's time, it was, like so much in colonial policy, a joke. The only other operative secondary school was Bethel, which didn't have land to expand its building let alone practise cricket. It didn't have a team. (The year before, three other schools had opened; the year following, another three would open, and four others were soon to be constructed.) So, in Jerome's time there, Expatriates was invariably Isabella's team. He had often wondered whether the situation was similar in the islands that Isabella's size: Dominica, St. Lucia, St. Vincent, Grenada.

That Saturday, Expatriates (the name stuck long after it was renamed Hanovertown Secondary School) was competing against the winning team from Dominica. Their school was like the earlier Expatriates: more than three-quarters of the team was either White or Eurafrican, which was strange, for Expatriates was now a good sixty percent Black and twenty-five percent Eurafrican and East Indian—only about fifteen percent White. The coach of the Expatriates team was White, as were two of its players; the wicket keeper was the only Eurafrican on the team, and the only East Indian was the spin bowler. (Of course, the Blacks included a couple of "red men," of which Wesi was one.) Maybe it was because Dominica had not yet got its independence. Wesi dressed hurriedly to go and then looked at him. "You not coming to watch me play?"

He had intended to go. He nodded.

"How come you never…"

"'How come you never…?' What sort of answer am I supposed to make to that non-question?"

"None," Wesi said, passing his hand over the uncombed mass of steel wool, probably debating whether he could get away with not combing it. "Just forget that I spoke."

But he'd never forgotten. He suspected Wesi was quietly worried about his social behaviour. But now he saw that Wesi was afraid of finding out too much.

The national cricket team had wanted Wesi to join, to become their fast bowler, but they practised on Saturday evenings, when Wesi wanted to be home in Compton—probably to screw the village girls. He also cultivated three acres of Miss Bensie's farm and occasionally burned his own coals.

"When do you find time to do all this and get your studies done?" he'd asked Wesi.

Wesi had only smiled.

Two months before Wesi left for Cave Hill, a village girl bore him a son, and three months later, another village girl bore him a daughter. That Christmas, when Wesi returned home, Jerome asked how he, an aspiring scientist, was so unscientific about sex.

Wesi laughed. "Brother Jerome, don't ask me that kinda question. You sound just like Ma. You who they throw outta school for feeling up a White woman bottom. And one from the American South too. You didn even stop to think you mighta get lynched. The feel was the important thing. Brother Jerome, you, more than anybody else, should know 'le coeur a ses raisons que la raison ne connaît point.'"

"But try not to make any more," he begged him, "because it's Ma who helps to take care of them, and she isn't getting any younger." After that he thought when the time came he would tell Wesi everything about himself. His brother was the first person he knew who understood and accepted contradictions, but then he didn't talk seriously with anyone else anymore.

His father's health did improve, but not to the extent where he could resume ploughing or transporting his produce. He had to content himself with overseeing what others did.

The house was finished well before Jerome's his first nervous breakdown. Hetty and Pinchman had seen him sitting on the sidewalk beside the furniture that he had removed from his room. Hetty spoke to him, and he did not answer. Right then he was being commanded to go out and tell the people to start reading and stop spawning—to leave spawning to the fishes and frogs. He ignored her and continued talking to his inspirer. "What all them things here doing here?" Pinchman asked.

"Cleaning out," he told him, "for the incoming inspiration."

Hetty said, "That not coming right now, so we going put the things back inside until later. You look tired. Come sit down in the truck."

He sat next to Hetty while Pinchman took the furniture to his room upstairs. They convinced him to travel back to Compton with them. They dropped him off at his mother's, and Hetty returned to get the doctor.

She was a freckled Scotswoman who was married to a plantation owner. She came within the hour. She questioned him about his feelings, asked him if there was anything troubling him. Sometimes he had to stop speaking to her to answer the voice within him or just to hold on to the sides of his bed with all his strength until the plank-like feeling in his stomach passed, and he had to ask her to repeat the question.

He told her that for about three weeks he'd been sleeping less and less and pacing his room at night. Then there were different voices telling him to do all sorts of things and threatening him if he didn't do them.

"I'll give you an injection that will help you to sleep and will chase away the voices, and I will come back tomorrow to

228

see how you are doing. You are a civil servant. My husband knows about you and your brother. He told me about both of you. I'm putting you on sick leave for a month. I'll be back to see you tomorrow."

She gave him the injection. It did relax him for a while. She left some tablets too, for his mother to give him. He must have slept for a long time, but when he awoke he heard his parents talking in their room. His father was telling his mother that sooner or later Jerome had to break down. "You can't full a pot and set the fire going under it full blast and not expect it for boil over. Nobody can live the way Jerome live. He not interested in women. Everything is book, book. You can't eat book and you can't hug up book. If you don control the fire under the pot, it will dry out and burn up."

His mother was silent.

He guessed his father was right. He had laughed at the idea of sex as a battle—only Yeats's Crazy Jane's statement to the Bishop, which he read years later, had ever equalled that; sometimes he even distorted its meaning when he saw handsome men cohabiting with women with ulcerated legs or twisted bodies, or even that time when everyone was talking about Mrs. Morkham's youngest son, who spent a lot of time visiting a woman, "a sailor pickney," who lived in one of the shacks in Corbeauland; he took her to England, where he married her. Since Jerome had sex with no one, all this aggression was redirected at himself. What was its effect?

During his second year at the Ministry of Communication and Works, Olivia, a "White" girl who spoke dialect and kept her auburn hair cut short, was attracted to him. She was the assistant to the deputy minister's secretary. Whenever she got a chance away from her typing, she came into the general office, where his was one of twelve desks. After repeated visits, the clerks in the office had begun to tease him. Jonas—the half-Indian, half-Black one who often went away from his desk to drink and who talked about the intensity and number of his own and his women's orgasms and who laughed at a pretty Black woman who visited him at the office, saying after she'd left, "You caan find a better fuck than that nowhere, but me caan marry she! Wha me gwine do with a Black wife?"—would say after Olivia left, "But wha fart this! You see how this pretty White woman shoving sheself all over Jerome, and he no making no move! Yo dick caan get hard or is like you don like woman or what?"

A few times he and Olivia had lunch together at a snack bar near the ministry. She occasionally prodded him to take her to the cinema by mentioning the films that were showing. Twice she brought him slices from cakes she'd baked on the weekend. The fellows in the office saw this and teased him to no end about it. He grew to like her, but he didn't desire her.

One Saturday she deliberately missed her bus to the country and asked him to let her stay over that night. He didn't like it, but he didn't say no. They went to the cinema that evening. She wore a pale blue dress that fitted her slim figure quite well and a very pale pink lipstick. She was about five-foot-five. He was five-foot-eleven. He did begin to feel romantic about her after they returned home from the cinema. They'd started kissing from the time they'd entered the stairway. He knew he didn't feel about her the way he felt about Hetty. And he didn't feel about Hetty the way he felt about Errol or even Peter or Philip.

They undressed and got into bed. He didn't switch off the

naked light bulb. They hugged and caressed and he definitely wanted to enter her. But, as he attempted to do so, something happened. He didn't know what it was; there was a blank for some time. When it disappeared, she was kicking on the bed, he was choking her, and he was in the middle of an ejaculation. Confused, he instantly released her. She gasped for breath and tried to get up out of bed.

She hurriedly put on her clothes. As she was leaving, he said to her, "Here's ten dollars to get a cab home."

"Keep it," she said, "for pay a psychiatrist. You is weird."

He'd read about sado-masochism. But it has never been a part of his masturbatory fantasies, so he was at a loss to explain his behaviour. A clue came one day when Olivia introduced a very black woman to him as her aunt.

"How you mean, she's your aunt?" he asked, surprised himself at the way the question blurted out. It was the first time he'd spoken to her after the fiasco. He knew she'd told no one about it because none of his co-workers mentioned it among the silly reasons they gave for her absence in the office.

"My mother's sister."

He lowered his head, for instantly it struck him that his sexual behaviour that night had something to do with his perception that she was White. About nine months later, she went to England as a student nurse. He did apologize to her before she left. He actually cried when she told him that she didn't know her father, not even his name. Her mother had died shortly after giving birth to her in Trinidad. Her aunt had gone to Trinidad and brought her back to Isabella Island and raised her. "I can't help how I look, Jerome; and now that you tell me you choke me that night cause you think I White,

I think I woulda prefer not to know. I woulda prefer to think of you as a weirdo."

His mind pored over it year after year, and it only weakened an already weak sexual attraction to women. The real reason for his sexual behaviour to Olivia varied according to the day the thought came up. Still and all, he resented whiteness as a reference point; sometimes he tried to replace it with greed, the drive to control others, and tribalism, but those terms always gave way to whiteness and blackness, and he wondered when he would stop being a shadow of England and become a person in his own right. It was one of about twenty or so things he had written about in a notebook.

Certainly he could not tell any of this to his father. To Wesi, yes, when he had got up the courage to do so. Traditional people saw things according to the strict norms of nature. They planted during the rainy season, harvested during the dry, paired off for need, not love; if an action worked for their parents, it was good enough for them. Anything out of the norm threatened them.

These thoughts exhausted him and he drifted off to sleep. He had his first complete night's sleep in three weeks. But, within a couple of hours of waking, the symptoms returned: the voices, the plank-like feeling, and the impression that somebody was watching his every move and waiting to harm him. He took one of the tablets before breakfast, and around nine the feelings were still there, though less intense. By four that afternoon, when the doctor arrived, the tablets had ceased to be effective. He told her so. She gave him another injection and left more tablets, telling his mother to give him two tablets half an hour before meals.

The injection left him drowsy all that evening, and he was asleep and awake at intervals. By three the next afternoon he was sure that there was a shadow in the room circling him, and his stomach felt as if he had eaten broken glass. He cried out when it was most intense. He couldn't remain still and he'd begun to drool. When his mother gave him his pills at six o'clock, he was sure she'd decided to poison him because he embarrassed her.

Around ten he had to punch something to break the tension in him. He broke the glass in the window of his room. His mother sent someone over to Pastor O to ask him to phone the doctor. She arrived around eleven and told his mother that he must be hospitalized. Comsie had to call Pongy and Slim to hold him down while the doctor gave him an injection in each hip. By midnight the ambulance was taking him away.

He had no awareness of his arrival at the hospital and did not even know where he was when he saw the strange figure standing over him through a haze.

"Who are you?"

"Nurse Jones."

Then he remembered hazily being taken into the ambulance. His stay at the hospital lasted six weeks. The first three weeks were the most difficult. With drugs they managed to control the plank-like feeling by the end of the first week, but the drugs didn't kill the fear he felt around the strange people who looked after him. And the voices continued to speak to him. At various times Miss Blunt, Mr. Bunyan, Miss Anderson, even old Mr. Manchester. Sometimes they laughed at him. Sometimes it was as if he were going somewhere, and they would just stand in his tracks and stop him. Sometimes they were swallowing him too. Yaw appeared on the scene one time. It was while Bunyan was holding him in a lasso. Yaw clapped.

When he'd begun working, he'd taken out medical insurance. It was a good thing he had, for he shared a room with one other patient, whereas the other patients were in one huge ward that contained some fifty beds. Still, there were iron bars on all the windows. They humiliated him. And the hospital did smell like a barn. There were only three nurses on his ward in the daytime and only one of them was trained. There was a burly orderly among them, and his role was to pin violent patients either to the floor or to the bed while the staff put straitjackets on them or stuck needles in their behinds. He learned after the first week never to complain. Because the staff insulted you whenever you did.

The four patients in private rooms got most of the trained nurse's time. The result was that many of the patients didn't bathe, and when they were in the cafeteria their filthy clothes and body smells—one patient smelled like a cow pen—made him want to vomit. They moved around like ghosts and obeyed the orders of the staff like dogs do their owners. He wanted to get out of there fast, because he knew at one time they had been like him, aware of their dignity, but had given up after they saw no use in having it. So, in his weekly sessions with the psychiatrist, who was Guyanese of East Indian origin, he lied and said that he'd stopped hearing voices, though the nurse had written in his chart that she had seen him gesturing and talking. He didn't answer when the psychiatrist told him what the nurse had written.

Somewhere around the fourth week, he developed a

writing obsession. Most of what he wrote he tore up before rereading. And all of what escaped immediate destruction was destroyed by the time he was discharged, all except a strange letter he had written to W. B. Yeats; it was a letter he could not quite understand, but it intrigued him, so he decided to save it. It went:

Dear Willy Yeats:

What! You're offended I call you Willy? Well never mind that. I have every right. You're public property now, you know? To be leafed through, turned over, chewed, and even spat out. You don't believe me? Ask Auden. You must see him sometimes. Should I spell it with one l or with two ls? Both would be appropriate, you know. You were certainly and most definitely preoccupied with your willy. It seems you hated it too. Well, you were Protestant, you couldn't help it, Wily Willy Puritan Billy Goat Yeats.

Now Wily Billy Willy Yeats, where do you read your correspondence? In the tower? Or on the moon's face? It makes a difference in what I have to tell you.

Now here's something you might relish or add to your relish.

> *In gun mad*
> *Ireland*
> *Willy Yeats gone mad*
> *mad with desire for*
> *Maude Gonne*
> *gone mad*

gun mad
for Maude Gonne.

Improve it and get gonorrhoea in it somewhere. Be grateful you can no longer catch it. You won't from me, never fear.

A mere play upon words, you say. What do you think you were doing with your hammer and gold—beating your hammer with gold? ha-ha-ha. You know, you really got my gorge—no I'm not punning on the name of your wife; bless her, she's dead and gone—exhausted long before by vision—but you live on. You moon-dazed literary pimp! Feeding your blarney to Lady Gregory for cash.

Now that I've cursed you, I have a little secret to tell you. You are my lover for eternity. No till death do us part or any of your monkey business. You and I will be out of nature and we will make passionate love pentametrically, most naturally (Oxymoron? You have a nerve!), and your Manichean soul will outbeatify Byzantine beauty when it is infused with my black light.

Save the acceptance until I see you. And don't breathe a word about it to George. But why am I telling you this? You're too clever to err like this. You held your sanity with verse and won the Nobel doing it. The Oxford says that one of the meanings of willy is basket. Verse kept you from becoming a basket case. You Faust that murdered the devil and ate his liver!

No need to tell you who I am. There's time enough to meet me.

An admirer of W. B.

By the beginning of the sixth week, the voices had gone, but he no longer cared to be discharged. Getting up and not having to do anything, not worrying about balancing books or making decisions about people and situations suited him fine. That same week, Wesi came to see him. He had just come back from his first year at Western Ontario. Wesi talked with him in his room for a long time. He told Wesi everything he thought about the hospital and about freedom from responsibility. Wesi laid him out on that one.

"Brother Jerome, that's for slaves. When you lose yo fighting spirit, you're finished. I don't like to hear you talk like that. When they're going to discharge you?"

"I have no idea, but the psychiatrist is thinking about it."

"When's your next session with him?"

"Next Wednesday."

"What are we going to do with you?" Wesi asked impatiently. "You've refused to learn that the ordinary is ordinary. Don't be like the doctor who runs from his office thinking his patient is a crocodile."

"How's that?"

"How? He'd been examining his skin with a microscope."

It was the first time he'd laughed voluntarily since his admission.

That same evening the psychiatrist made an unscheduled visit to tell him that he thought he was well enough to leave. "How about leaving tomorrow? I've seen your brother. He feels that your family is the best thing for you now."

He went back to work three weeks later, still taking Mellaril but in smaller doses. He was less sure of himself now, and it seemed that he had to calculate the smallest detail of everything he did. Sometimes he caught himself off guard and saw how robotic he was. His co-workers were unspontaneous with him, as if they were afraid that to be natural with him would hurl him back into psychotic darkness. He took a lot longer to finish routine tasks; he later realized that it was because of the pills.

For several years he had been the senior clerk in the office. A lot of the employees who'd entered the ministry after him had moved on to various executive positions, but they hadn't considered him for promotion other than making him the senior clerk, which he had been for fifteen years. Wesi had got after him for not demanding to be promoted. He understood vaguely why he'd been passed over—those who got promoted had relatives who were influential in the governing political party, or they spent a lot of time at the deputy minister's office. He knew they resented him for being different. Sometimes, the accountant, who had been his immediate superior for the last eight years—he was an alcoholic and was himself being passed over for promotion: the party he supported had been out of power for two terms—and the junior office clerks went drinking after work. When the accountant wasn't around, they joked about his incoherence and trembling fingers and showed off their knowledge of terms like delirium tremens, dipsomania, and Korsakoff syndrome. He was uncomfortable with their hypocrisy and loathed their company. Besides, he didn't drink. He never could understand why people would want to dull their senses.

But Wesi had pushed him to seek promotion. "They don't have half your brain. Do something about it." Jerome wrote the Civil Service Promotion Examination and was one of only three passes. But, at the end of the year, when the accountant died and he applied for the position, they passed him over for a political appointee. The deputy minister told him it was completely out of his hands. The minister had made the final decision. "Besides," and he looked Jerome straight in the eyes as he said this, "that job calls for a lot of social know-how and people-management, and we don't think you can do that, at least you don't show it. And there's the other delicate problem."

"What?" he asked him.

"Well, since you insist, I'll tell you. Your nervous break-down."

He left the room with his eyes dim. He didn't even bother to put away the ledgers on his desk. By the time he got to his room the voices had already begun. He packed a suitcase, went to the bus terminal, and boarded a bus straight to the mental asylum, where they admitted him right away. It was exactly ten months since he had been discharged.

14

HE WAS LUCKY THAT TIME. He remained in hospital for only a week. The plank-like feeling never returned, and the voices left after the first couple of days. By the third day he felt like a sponge. He didn't want to do anything, not even to eat. It took the energy of more than a day's work to go to the toilet, and he stayed in bed until his bowel or his bladder could no longer hold out. More than once he thought about defecating and urinating in bed—it was the implications that held him back. He thought about death a lot that week and about the numerous ways he could commit suicide. He debated every aspect of it carefully. There was really nothing he wanted to do with his life. There was nothing left for him to accomplish. He had wanted to see Wesi succeed, and Wesi had. His mother was a survivor. If things got tough with her, the villagers would take care of her; they took care of one another; the Spirituals had taken turns helping her look after his father. True, there was the taboo against suicide and the guilt his parents would be made to carry because of it. The villagers were always using unusual behaviour to justify the way they lived.

"If Jerome did…If…If…," he could hear them saying.

"You don hear how he talk? Want for play he better than we. That is what happen to them when them pretend for be what them is not."

But it wasn't what he thought people would say that prevented him from committing suicide. Why did he let the cruel remarks of the deputy minister knock him into confusion? he'd asked himself accidentally while his mind was set on death. Then he discovered that he had to prove something to that same minister, who'd got his job from arse-licking anyway—in the last election he'd switched parties when he saw signs that the opposition was going to win. He would show him that he, Jerome, would be at his desk when the deputy minister could no longer return to his. *Brother Jerome, that's for slaves. When you lose yo fighting spirit, you're finished. When they're going to discharge you?* This time Wesi was away, but he was going to discharge himself. The memory of Wesi's words was sufficient. So Friday, exactly one week after he had admitted himself, he discharged himself.

The psychiatrist, whom he found to be kind and who came to see him four times that week, just to talk, was becoming something of a friend. Dr. Karmalsingh gave him his home telephone number and told him that in future if he had any problems, he should phone him. That time he spent two weeks convalescing at his parents' home before returning to work.

He was never hospitalized after that, though he suffered three minor breakdowns. And each time he would go home to his mother until he felt sufficiently confident to resume his life. *This constant return to the womb. Home to regain sanity. Baptism. Sleep.* "You don't even want to admit it," he said out loud. "This cave. Our coffins. And finally the earth. Oh well, if we *don't bathe, we stink. If we don't eat, we faint. If we don't renew the ties with the womb, we go mad. Stark, staring mad. In a way, we are all motherfoulers, substituting symbols for the real thing. Something, something branded in our psyches, stencilled in before we make the passage from the womb.*

Dr. Karmalsingh told him that it was because his mind had now added temporary psychosis to its defence mechanisms that he was having these minor breakdowns; it was merely, he said, an extension of the denial mechanism. "What you need is structure. At one point I was going to suggest you get married, but at forty-two that could bring a lot of stress into your life, if you choose the wrong woman, and you never know that ahead of time. Then again, you might not be interested in women." Dr. Karmalsingh observed him silently.

There were known homosexuals in the civil service. The chief technical officer in the works section of the ministry was reputed to be one. But there were also stories about people who had been fired because they'd made their homosexuality known. Isabella was only a hundred and seventy square miles; that sort of information in his chart would be read by all sorts of people. *Now everybody knew who the HIV-positive people were. It was supposed to be confidential information, but confidentiality wasn't in keeping with the way Isabellans lived. In their minds they linked it to trafficking with the devil. "If you ha for hide it, something evil in it." Then again, the swarms of religious fanatics all over the place were engaged in diverse missions related to their religious beliefs. The nurses who belonged to the Church Terrestrial Sanctified would have heard their preacher say that AIDS is God's way of ridding the world of perversion. He wasn't the only preacher to say so either. Some of them would have read in the* Isabellan *where a preacher heard across America and around the world had said that God struck California with an earthquake to punish it for not taking action against the homosexuals in San Francisco. "No God-fearing city would permit the International Gay Games. No God-fearing city would let the demons of Sodom into their gates to practise their abominations."* Even if Dr. Karmalsingh did not write it in his file, what did doctors talk about? When the time came, he would discuss it with Wesi.

But Dr. Karmalsingh struck something when he mentioned structure. It made him think about joining a church and becoming involved in a fellowship of some kind. The thought of having to listen to sermons on Sundays sickened him. They were childish and silly. To hear preachers talking about Joshua commanding the sun to stand still without the faintest notion that it was the Jews' way of consolidating their ethnicity. And the Christian God was definitely a White God—that had to do with White colonial policy, class structure, and rule by force. He could not be a Christian and respect himself.

During the last of the final two recovery stints he spent at home, he spoke to his mother about the Spirituals.

"Talk to yo father," she told him. "He high up in it."

His father was now confined to the village and mostly to the house, sometimes for an entire week to his bed. His cancer was no longer in remission. The doctors hadn't expected him to live so long, and his mother credited his success to the green food she fed him.

"Lotta watercress, lotta dasheen leaf. The ol heads know a lot more than we, and they always used fo say is greens that cure tumours."

243

So, between his walks through the few remaining cane fields and along the coast, he had a lot of time to talk with his father. "If you sure-sure you want to join the Spirituals, I will tell you a few things, but if you not sure, I can't tell you. The only thing I can say right now is that we have a lot of things bout Africa in it, and we see God different from the way other people see him."

He did go to see Pointer Francis, who struck him from the start as a sincere man. He was kind and fatherly in his approach to him and straight off called him son. "Truth is what count, my son."

He'd smiled and wondered whose truth Pointer Francis was talking about. Then he caught himself; skepticism would get him nowhere.

"That's why I'm here."

"If you really looking for it and if the spirit accept you, you will find it." Even the deep lines in Pointer Francis's molasses-brown face held something gentle. His thin neck made Jerome think of pictures he'd seen of Kikuyu herdsmen. Pointer Francis didn't tell him much more about the process of the religion, but he elaborated on how one got called to it and on some of the stumbling blocks one could encounter.

"Like I say, the spirit have fo call you. That American what running the children nursery over the road come to see me all the time, and he been beseeching me to put him through, and I have no way fo make him understand that the spirit got to call him first. 'How I will know when the spirit call me?' he ask me. 'You don will have to ask me that, because you will know and I will know,' I tell him. 'You just got fo be patient and in time the spirit will work its work.' The other day he been back here and he say to me, 'Look like that spirit taking mighty long to work its work.' 'You caan hurry it,' that is what I say to him.

"I will tell you right off, the Spirituals is what save us from total destruction. Young people nowadays look like they know what fo swallow in the White man teachings and what fo spit out. In my time you had to swallow everything in public and yo spitting out was in private. That is why the Spirituals exist. And we had to spit out fo a long time—my parents before me, and their parents before them, all the way back to slavery time. We had to reject the White man. How you can trust a man what make slaves outta his own children? When we see that his God didn punish him fo doing that, we jus had to stay far from that religion. Of course, we had to pretend we believe in his God. So the Spirituals come about fo us to express ourselves to our God.

"We had a way of keeping out the White man spies cause, as you well know, they did make our religion illegal." He became silent.

"Pointer Francis, why did you join the Spirituals?"

"My son, when the spirit call you, how you going to say no? I was a pupil teacher in a Methodist School. And a Sunday was like I didn know anything. When I catch myself I was at Pointer Dublin house.

"Pointer Dublin was right by his door. He said to me, 'You come. I been expecting you. I ha the vision last week, and all week I been expecting you. Is one thing that bothering me: till now we don have people with much book learning, so I ha fo think long and hard before we take you in. I will call a meeting over it. Meantime, you go back home and if the spirit don leave you, come back and see me in a week.' Well, from what I gather, they meet and talk it over, and they agree that since my grandfather did get as far as assistant pointer, that it is probably his spirit that hand down to me. So I was the first educated one sort of to join."

"What kind of rejoicing did you have?" Jerome asked to get him talking again.

"The rejoicing was great. Is what happen after! The day after my rejoicing the Methodist minister bring my dismissal letter. That White man from England, named Reverend Lawrence, tell me that I league myself with a band o devil worshippers and so 'you have made yourself reprehensible to members of the Christian faith. Your example is a bad one, and we have no alternative but to terminate you.' You wouldn believe what was funny bout all that. The principal of the school where I was teaching was a lay preacher in the same Methodist Church. He was a married man with grown children but there was a nineteen-year-old girl with a child for him. And Reverend Lawrence baptize the child his ownself. He never stop him from teaching, and he never stop him from preaching. The same Sunday after he fire me, he tell the church, 'I have been delegated by the leaders to inform you that today we have struck from membership in this congregation the name of Immanuel Francis—for he has chosen to join the Devil's band. We trust that God will have mercy on his soul and bring him back to his flock and that his name will not remain forever struck off from the book of eternal life.' Guess that was the rules he had to operate with, so I don hold anything against him. When they carry him back to England on a stretcher after he had a stroke, I felt sorry fo him, cause he did already spend close to twenty-five years with us. But he wasn like yo frien

Pastor O. Pastor O is one o we now. But Reverend Lawrence always look down on we. Well, that is how it used to be. A lot of people got read out of the churches fo joinin the Spirituals and a lot of people get arrested too fo joining it. But we still here. And our numbers is really growing."

"How did the Spirituals hold on to their secrets?"

Pointer Francis scratched his head and a broad grin covered his face. "You want fo know everything, eh? Well I going tell you a little bit. You see, nobody coulda join us if the spirit didn call them. And if they was false, they get blocked quick and they had to say what blocking them. That is all I can tell you because we have a oath gainst talking too much. You will soon find out fo yoself."

"You think the spirit would call me?"

"Sure, if you is ready. But you should know right now that is one thing fo get called and another fo make the journey. We have trouble no end with educated people like yoself. Most o the time they have fo make it in two separate stages. Although bout two years ago, a woman university graduate make it through in one shot. That was a rejoicing! Trips come from all over the island fo that rejoicing. And the prime minister of Trinidad, a man that have a PhD and used fo be a professor in a university, is one o we. So things looking up. Deputy Pointer Andro is a educated man too. But he make his first journeys in Trinidad and then he come to Isabella Island and like it here. Now he really good to us. I sure you hear bout the farming cooperative what he started. And you know how the government try fo ruin him cause he didn beg them for favours or give any money to they party, and you know they don like people what not beholden to them, cause that way they caan control them.

"Now the colour thing not even a problem. Most of the Spiritual churches near town got two, three, four White people in them, mostly Irish. The pointer up in East Bay is a full-blood White man. But a more African man than he in the ways o the spirit don exist. But the religion ain't change. What change is the different people that join it."

For weeks and weeks after he'd spoken to Pointer Francis, he agonized over whether he should join, whether the spirit would call him, and what was the spirit anyway? Here too, reason did not spare him. He was sure that the spirit called those already disposed to becoming Spirituals. Pointer Francis hadn't told him that he'd grown up in a household where almost everyone was Spirituals. But Henry told him a lot about Pointer Francis. Pointer Francis's mother had joined the Methodist Church because she was the housekeeper at the Methodist Manse long before Reverend Lawrence came, and she was still the housekeeper at the manse after Pointer Francis was put out of the church. Pointer Francis was influenced heavily by his grandpa, who took him to a lot of Spiritualist meetings. Jerome figured out that Pointer Francis had wanted to join the Spirituals anyway. He was sure the spirit was like the dream you had about something you'd thought a lot about during the day. Would the spirit ever call him?

There were other fears too. They began to come after he started going home on weekends to attend their Sunday morning services. They did not jump at these services. The spirit came to them on Sunday evenings, but those finished too late for him to attend and sleep properly and awaken the next morning in time to catch his bus and be at work at 8:30.

His father told him that the brethren at Compton were

generally pleased that he was coming to their services, and that Jerome could expect a call anytime as long as he made up his mind to do it. He knew from his father's "journeys" and other people's that it usually took two to three weeks. His father's were on average ten days, but he knew that his would take the full three weeks. Would he be able to take the stress of it? For thirty years he'd managed to keep the influence of others on his life to a minimum; if the spirit called him, he would have to undergo a three-week seance where he would literally have to hand himself over to Pointer Francis. He had a vague idea what to expect. It was some sort of initiation ceremony that had to involve symbolic burying and resurrection, to fit him with a new identity. He had already read *The Golden Bough*, the *Aeneid*, the *Odyssey*. He knew he'd receive some sort of wisdom, some password kind of philosophy to get around the impasse that his life had become.

But he remembered Pointer Francis's remark "Is one thing fo get called and another one fo make the journey." There was a lot of truth to that. Although it was nearly thirty years since he'd lived at Miss Dellimore's, he vividly remembered Mildred, an insane old woman who lived on the bank above the road about two houses away. She sometimes threw balls of her stool at the people below. People said that she had taken away some woman's husband and had told her neighbours that she'd caught the woman sprinkling grave dirt around her house. In her old age she'd begun hanging around the Spirituals and got a call from the spirit. But on the journey she was blocked, and she confessed to the pointer that she had lied about the woman whose husband she had taken away. The woman was still alive, and the pointer took Mildred to her home around four one morning to ask the woman's forgiveness. The woman gave her forgiveness, but it did not unblock Mildred. There had been no "rejoicing" for her, and she left the mourning house already crazed.

He balanced this fear with the reflection that for close to thirty years his life had been sterile. He had only to look at nature to see that this wasn't normal. For a short while, yes, like the dry season when the trees stopped growing or even in a drought when all their old leaves died. But, when the rainy season came, they grew and grew. The ideal was to work half the time and play half the time. Grow and stop, stop and grow. Work, rest. Rest, work.

He remembered reading somewhere that when the American—or was it the Allied—troops began liberating the concentration camps in Germany, many of the prisoners died from the sudden intake of food because they had been starving for too long.

Wesi was the only person he could talk to about this. He wrote telling him about it. Wesi replied that he shouldn't let fear stop him. "Anything that links you to people who work hard, sweat, and love, hate, quarrel, fight, and make peace again will be good for you."

Bothering him most was his hidden homosexuality. He knew it would block him. His thoughts went, too, beyond the journey. The self-confrontation his insanity had caused created in him a brutal frankness whenever he was dealing with himself. The question was therefore how to feel at ease with the members of the Compton Spiritual Church. Initially, he'd gone home rarely because he was unable to communicate with his parents and the villagers. He had refused then to find a reason for his behaviour. He had started returning often, he knew damn well, because the preservation of his sanity depended on his being around people, whether or not he liked them. He knew, too, that if the time should come that he should be "called," Pointer Francis would be the one he would feel closest to—if only because he could talk and talk and never run out of interesting things to say.

The Sunday morning services were not bad, mainly because it was Pointer Francis who preached. His sermons were a constant reiteration of the duties of the Spirituals to one another. He'd always felt that was what religion should be about or probably *was* about, but the religious bodies simply did not have the courage to say it. It was probably why the Spirituals believed in being possessed by the spirit. It gave them a chance to dance and reaffirm their commitment to the symbiotic practices that were the cornerstones of their religion. In their prayers they mentioned Jehovah and Jesus and read from the Bible, but he wasn't sure how much of this was camouflage—the result of prolonged persecution.

After wrestling with this for some time, he concluded one day that human life wasn't the valuable whatever that religions and politicians and courts held it up to be. And he began to see his place with ants and moths and salmon. Afterward he wondered why this realization had taken him so long. Survival was what all of life was about—with dignity if you could afford it, but mostly without. He merely had to remind himself of this when he began to worry about being called by the spirit or failing the journey. He was ashamed that throughout his life he'd been playing God, judging humanity. What right had he?

At the evening service the Sunday after Christmas, the spirit entered him. He jumped and shouted and talked in tongues, and it did not surprise him when he came out of it. And he knew he was ready. For the first time, he understood the meaning of humility. He could now understand why his father had calmly accepted the removal of his testes and had continued a quiet fight with cancer, rarely ever letting others know that he was in pain.

15

He had to wait until April to begin the journey, the time it took for him to arrange for a month's vacation.

There was a three-day preliminary session during which he slept at his parents' house but rose at dawn, just before the sun touched the mountain tops, and headed to the mourning house. At sunset he returned home. All his meals, which were now meatless, were eaten at the mourning house. Instead of water he drank a tea that Pointer Francis told him used to be Henry's duty to prepare. Now it was Brother Charles's; he used to be Henry's assistant, and he was training two brothers—his successors.

One of the five mothers (Sister Biddows, now Mother Biddows, was one of them) came each day to prepare the meals. He spent those three days receiving instruction from Pointer Francis.

The mourning house was circular with a dome roof and was about forty feet across. Its outside walls were of mud and the roof was thatched with dry sugar cane and palm leaves. It enclosed four rooms. There was an inner circle that was the sacred room, which could be entered by the pointer and the mourner only. Below that was the cellar where the mourning proper took place. The outer circle was divided into three compartments. One was a bathroom, one a kitchen, and the third a small sitting room. The bathroom contained a zinc tub and a slop pail, a jug of water, and a towel. During the first three days he used the outside pit latrine. The pail was to be used during his underground sojourn. The kitchen contained a wooden bench, a platform with three stones that formed a hearth, three large and one small eating calabashes, and two large clay goblets in which water was stored.

The first day, Pointer Francis took him into the sacred room. Pointer Francis lit the candles, about thirty of them, on three carved wooden candelabra. The room had a diameter of about twenty feet and was supported at the centre with a tree-trunk pole. Its floor was pressed earth to which a green colouring had been added, and the mud walls had been sprayed with a beige lime wash. Arranged against the walls were stands with a breadfruit leaf motif carved into them on which stood wooden carvings. There was a dais and two hand-carved stools arranged beside it.

"Look around and think bout the meaning of these things," Pointer Francis told him. "These is our scriptures. I and Deputy Pointer Andro is the only ones that know all the meaning o these things. I train him to take over from me, and he already training somebody to take over from him."

His eyes came to rest on a lovely piece of sculpture depicting a buffalo with a man astride its horns. He examined it intently.

"Ask any questions you want," Pointer Francis told him.

But he was still silent.

"You know the meaning o that?" Pointer Francis asked him, pointing to the buffalo-man Jerome was still looking at.

"I think it means that all human beings are creatures of their passion, but unless they master it, it will destroy them."

"Whew!" Pointer Francis said, shaking his head. "You is the first one to hit that meaning right off. Son, you sure you need this journey?" He winked as he said this.

But there were many answers he did not have as they examined the sculptures one by one. For instance, the carving of the huge calabash with painted human and animal figures and trees. The stand supporting it was in the form of a coiled snake. It did not take him long to figure out that the calabash represented life. He had read too many books on symbolism.

"Why the snake, Pointer Francis?"

"My son, you know the answer. Take another look at the buffalo-man. This piece is here to help explain the meaning o the buffalo-man."

"Does it have anything to do with sex?"

"That is it. You right. You see—lemme see how I can explain it. The snake stand fo sex, and without sex the world can't continue. But we put the world on the snake to show the responsibility that sex carry. Put it this way. Yo father did want yo mother. But he couldn just meet her in the road and take her. She had to want him too, and both o they families had to settle before he could o get her. Then after that you and yo brother born, and he had to take care o the two o you. If he did leave yo mother, all you woulda suffer. That is why we make sure every Spiritual take care o their children, the ones they make befo and the ones they make after the journey. Cause I don ha fo tell you, plenty men breed the young woman them and then say the children not theirs. Well, when they join us they ha for change.

"Before we get further, lemme tell you this: the real name for us is Esosusu, but in here is the only place you is to use it, because it is a sacred word. When you leave here the word you use is Spiritual. Anywhere you go and you meet a Esosusu you will know cause when he shake yo hand he will bow twice. And you all is to embrace when you all find out that you all is Esosusu. And wherever you go and you meet other Esosusu, they will take care of you, and when a Esosusu come to you, you will take care o them. That been part of us befo we leave Africa. Esosusu was who look after one another children when the children or the parents get sold during slavery time. Is a pity the government make us illegal for hundreds o years else more people would o belong to us, and all the fatherless children that everywhere around us woulda have fathers. And all these men around here that treat women like paper plate and banana peel woulda have a little more respect for them."

"You teach this to everybody who begins the journey?"

"Everyone, my son. That is why we only accept them when the spirit call them. Cause this ain't no joke. Is like when you born you can't unborn yoself. And you ha fo follow in the footsteps o humans, sucking the bitter with the sweet."

The entire area of the dais, which was about five feet by four feet, was covered with a painting. It was the last of the icons he had to study. Until he understood its meaning, he could not move on to the second stage. The scene the painting depicted was oriented toward the east. There were two human figures at each end of the drawing. The figure at the western end was monstrous and prostrate and its head was immersed in a pictorial calabash. The calabash alone took up three-quarters of the painting. On its surface were pictures of the moon, the sun, rivers, lakes, animals, trees in all aspects: standing straight, bent by the wind, bare, leaf-covered.

At the eastern end of the calabash was a small opening to which the left foot of an almost standing human figure still clung.

He stared at the painting for a long time, at least an hour before telling Pointer Francis that he was ready to discuss it. "Look at it again for a half hour. Son, what you is looking at there is the centrepiece of Esosusu doctrine. It like this pole here that holding up everything. You move it and everything fall down in a heap."

So he studied the symbols on the dais some more. And then they discussed it. Pointer Francis did most of the talking this time. He told him that the universe is God and God is the universe, that the deformed man at the western end of the dais had not yet understood this. But, after gestation in the womb of the calabash, he would, and so on and so forth.

For the rest of the explanation, Pointer Francis took him walking. They walked into Campden, along the seashore, back through the cane fields, waded through the streams, and all the way to the foothills of the mountains. Pointer Francis hardly ever stopped talking as they walked. He told him a lot, some of it rife with contradiction. But Jerome knew that by the time the spirit called you, you knew that life itself was a contradiction, an incomprehensible paradox.

Looking out at the Atlantic and up at the mountains, Pointer Francis said, "We looking at the different faces o God. All through life we learning to read them. And not abuse them."

At the foothills they looked out over the fields of growing canes below them. "That is abuse of God," Pointer Francis said.

"How?"

"If you was somebody else I would ha to go into a long explanation. Did yo father ever tell you he been to jail?"

"I remember."

"You know what was the cause?"

"They were trying to form a union, and it had something to do with the Spirituals too."

"True. But the greediness o the White man was the real reason. The White man think that God and he own the whole world and all the other people must be his servants. Pastor O and me talk hours and hours bout that. Pointer Dublin and me is who show him the light. After that he go back to America and get all sorts o assistance and come back and buil that child care centre where he use to keep his church." Pointer Francis paused. "You see, is like the buffalo-man. The buffalo is the power inside human beings. And if we let it control us, all we will want to do is control other people just so we can feel we have power, and the mo power we have the mo we will want. And we will destroy people just to get it, and destroy we own self too. Don even talk bout the soul. That is the first thing that get destroy.

"Now that bring me round to something else. We Esosusu love Jesus a lot, but we don want to have anything to do with Christian churches. And the Christian churches don want to have a lot to do with Jesus—the parts they can use to trick people with, yes, but the real Jesus, no.

"Yo father tell me that you use to preach, so you must know the Bible. You remember the story bout the rich man that did want to follow Jesus but couldn part with his money?"

Jerome nodded.

"Well, that is just how people destroy they self. If you love money you can't love God cause you have fo buse God fo get money and you have fo buse yo fellow human beings, and when you busing yo people is the same thing as busing God. That is one reason why we ancestors in Africa never use to low anybody to own land, cause how you will let people own God? When Jesus tell the crowds that been following him every day to stop worrying bout food and clothes and shelter, he been trying to tell them something bout greed. Jesus know what he been doing cause, you see, most people got even mo than they need. Is just that they feel they should have mo. And Jesus know that if you spend all yo time thinking bout food and clothes, you wouldn have time for yo soul. I mean time for think and feel good bout the earth and not worrying bout what other people have and what you ain't have and getting depressed cause you ain't have more than everybody else. You see, like we the Esosusu, Jesus did know that the body wasn the most important thing. How many preachers can tell their congregation what Jesus did mean when he say, 'He that loseth his life shall find it'? I don't think any o them can. Cause the moment yo mind set on how much money going in the collection plate, you can never, never have the understanding and the honesty you need for explain the text. Just look at the buildings called churches. You realize how much tree they cut down and stone they blast and mine they dig just for build and furnish them? And for what? To show off. The spirit o Jesus, if they talking bout the same one that I read bout in the four gospels, will never have anything to do with those churches."

It made Jerome think of a picture he had seen on an almanac. Jesus is wielding a piece of rope, and several buyers and sellers are overturning merchandise and pushing aside and trampling one another to escape from him.

"Jesus been just like we. His first concern was to comfort people. Before he do that he did know he had to conquer the body. That is why he go off in the desert. He had to find out what truth is. Confirmation! Reception! What is that? And the four temptations the Bible talk bout was all the things that was preventing him from overcoming his body. And you see what they was: food and power and fame and money—the same thing White people turn we into slaves for and the same thing the Christian churches let their rulers do to us for."

He paused again. It was a very clear day, blue everywhere in the sky.

"So you see, Jesus set a example. The Christians say that cause he carry the cross we don't have for carry any. We don believe that. When you go down in the cellar tomorrow you going to begin to carry yo own cross. You have to prove that you master yo body and yo mind befo you can become a Esosusu. After that the rest easy."

Pointer Francis began to sing:

I must walk the lonesome valley.
I must walk it for myself.
Nobody else will walk it for me.
I must walk it for myself.

Going into the valley was one thing. Coming out was another, Jerome thought.

"That don mean that when you come out o the valley, you won have problems. As long as we alive we going to have problems and face temptations. It hard to live in this world. Everywhere there is people trying to make a dollar or two off o you. And you ha for fight that. But the Esosusu done gone through one experience and they come out like one body and they have to live like one body. And just like everywhere you have people with long wind and people with shortness o breath, weak people and strong people, so the Esosusu have them too. But like Jesus tell his disciples, them that great among us, that is for say them that strong, ha for help them that weak. And we all strong in something or the other and weak in others. Another way for see it too is for see us like a house. It like a house for the person and it like a house for the whole group. For the person is like this: when you slip you ha to make amends. And you ha to take care o the injuries o the soul like you take care o the injuries o yo body. For instance, if you get a cut and you don tend to it, it will turn into a ulcer, and if you don tend the ulcer, you liable to lose the limb or even die from blood poison. So when cracks start forming in yo soul, you got to mend them. Got to confess the wrongs, beg for fogiveness. And if you ain't got the strength for fight the weakness on yo own, you ask the brethren fo help you."

That would be difficult, Jerome thought. He had never felt comfortable asking aid of others. Humble yourself, he heard himself thinking, and he worried that the doubts he'd vanquished before the spirit visited him might be returning.

"Now for the group. We is all windows and doors and roof and posts. If you don repair the parts of it that need repairing, sooner or later the whole thing will crumble to pieces. It like the schoolteacher woman I tell you bout, Sister Emily, that made the journey in one go. Well, when she home on holidays she get all the Esosusu children and help them with their lessons. And Sister Biddows, who good at that sort o thing too, does give her a helping hand. And when Esosusu parents reap they vegetables they send her some. Sister Gertrude is a first-rate seamstress. She teach all the teenage daughters o the Esosusu how for cut and sew. So they can help themselves. When somebody sick, we take turns looking after them. If they die and leave children, we look after the children and help out the family that take them in."

What would he offer? Would they accept it? He'd never seriously thought that anyone needed anything he had to offer—or, for that matter, of offering anything to anyone outside his family.

"You see, we know that life hard. It like a seine in the water. You need plenty hands to pull it in. Sharing is the way. That is what the ancestors in Africa use to do. That is what we parents did in slavery time. And that is what some of we still doing."

"But, Pointer Francis, we live in a society where people use every trick to rob others. You buy cheaply and sell dear and exploit two sets of people at the same time. How can the Esosusu survive in such a world?"

Pointer Francis took his time replying and broke into a grin. "Ain't the Spirituals done survive until now?"

Jerome nodded.

"We know we paddling against the current. But the good thing bout it is that nobody come to join us that don want to join. And when you conquer greed you know you done conquer a whole lot. That is why some of we members make the journey four, five times in their life, cause each time they come back they is a little stronger."

The sun had already set by the time they got back to the village.

16

AND NOW HERE HE WAS, buried in darkness. He wondered what time it was. He wasn't sleepy, so it was probably still early. He felt very hungry and needed to urinate, so he'd just as well mount the stairs. He ate quickly, made the trip to the toilet, and returned to the cave, where he lay on the ground. The earth was smooth. Once he got tired, he was sure he would fall asleep.

But the hours went, and he began to itch and smell his perspiration. He was in the habit of showering at night. In the capital during the dry season, the water was turned off at the beginning of the day, so he had turned to showering late on evenings. He kept the same habit when he was at his parents' house, now that they had a shower and an indoor toilet.

Small price to pay. He wondered whether ticks and mites weren't crawling over him. He thought he was feeling the sensation of tiny creatures moving over his body. Well, there was no way to check.

There was no way of knowing how long he had been asleep, but it might have been for a long while, for he felt refreshed even though his joints ached from the unaccustomed hardness. His bladder was full, so he mounted the stairs. There was no fresh goblet beside the dais, so it must have been night still. He returned to the cave and tried to sleep again. And did for a little while, until footsteps awoke him.

"Is that you, Pointer Francis?"

"Yes. Just want to know how you getting along."

"Good so far."

"Good. Keep it up."

He heard the footsteps ascending, then the opening and closing of the dais.

He spent most of that day lying on his back, his hands cupping the back of his head, his eyes wide open in the darkness. He ruminated over parts of his life, questioning many of the conclusions he had drawn the day before. But today seemed longer than any other day he had ever experienced. He wished he could read. But he was here to read his soul, he reminded himself. Read what in his soul? Pointer Francis did not tell him. The Bible he had burned? The choking he had given Olivia? Attempting to play with Miss Blunt's bottom to get the approval of his classmates? Secretly enjoying the taunting of Bullock? His non-existent sex life? His contempt for simple, illiterate folk? The shame he felt because of his parents' poverty? Slowly, uncomfortably, he came to realize that the answer was yes.

When he did fall asleep, he dreamt that he was in school and Miss Anderson was the principal and Miss Blunt his class teacher. And he had touched Miss Blunt's bottom and Miss Anderson was about to castrate him with a shaving razor. He awoke to hear the cave re-echoing his screams. The gown he was wearing was drenched in sweat and the ground around him was wet. He felt there was a physical presence in the cave, but nothing made itself known.

He tried to devise a way of keeping time. He could count his respirations: one minute for every sixteen inhalations. But, after the first ninety inhalations, he gave up. There was nothing to do but reflect on his own life. He understood what Macbeth meant by his "Tomorrow and tomorrow" speech, and a few years earlier he had seen a performance of *Waiting for Godot* in which the actors kept forgetting their lines. Now he understood what Beckett was trying to dramatize. But Vladimir could at least talk to Estragon and Pozzo could beat and insult Lucky. *I will endure.* The words had the consoling effect that Pointer Francis said they would. They set him thinking of his father's illness and finally about Bertram, his mother's godson, who used to load and unload a truck until one day it collided with another vehicle and crushed Bertram's spine. Bertram spent the remainder of his life on his back. A catheter voided his bladder. He had seen strings of slime linking the drops trickling into the collection bottle and had concluded that Bertram's semen was mixing with his urine. After a while all of Bertram's buttocks and shoulders became covered with bed sores. Whenever they went to see him after that, he was usually in a daze from the narcotics he was receiving; mercifully they must have made him oblivious of time too. About a month before he died, he smelled like a decaying corpse. *I will endure.*

When later he fell asleep, Miss Anderson returned. She sat with her buttocks on his neck and pinned his arms to the ground with her mango-stump legs. Peter, Sprat, Bunyan, even Mr. Morrison circled him with erect penises and Miss

Anderson gave orders to sodomize him. He thought he'd choke to death. Somewhere in his nightmares he felt himself forcing out the words *I will endure* before he began to reawaken.

How many of these nightmares could he endure before going mad? His mind returned to what Pointer Francis and he had discussed about the temptations of Jesus. He was sure it was myth, but that did not matter: forty days in the desert and lots of nightmares too. And then again Pointer Francis told him that some of the Esosusu make the voyage four, five times. His body felt bruised, as if the nightmare had been a reality. He got up and drank from the goblet. He didn't even bother with the gourd. While he was up he'd better empty his bladder too.

He was a little dizzy going up the stairs, and after he pulled the dais, he was no longer sure which was his right hand. He felt for the scar on his left elbow to be certain which hand was which. On returning, he turned the wrong way and found himself at the back of the dais.

Back in the cave, he drifted in and out of sleep for a long time and felt, each time he was asleep, as if the sun were burning him up and flies were buzzing about and landing on him. After two days of not washing, he could feel his anus blistering from the fecal particles trapped in the hairs. What was the point of complaining? Soldiers, he was sure, underwent worse.

He had now definitely lost track of time. He could not remember what he ate or even when last he ate, and it became so that every time he mounted the stairs, he would feel around to see whether there was a goblet there.

One time, Pointer Francis came down the stairs and was silent. When he heard him ascending, he said, "I'm awake."

"You surviving?"

"Oh yes."

"Well, that is what you have to do."

Before the echoes of the last word had even died, he heard the ascending footsteps. "Don't go," he mouthed as the dais was being pulled into place. He then remembered that once, when he could not have been more than three, his mother had taken him walking along the road between the canes. He had wandered away from her. She had called him but he did not come right away. To punish him, she had hidden behind a clump of grass. "Ma! Ma!" he had called, but she hadn't answered. Only when he began to wail did she get up from behind the grass. "That will teach you to come when I call you," his mother had said. When he caught hold of her dress, he began to thump her on the leg while holding tightly to her. A short while later, she had lifted him up, kissed him, though he tried to turn his face away, and said, "Mama will never let the badman eat Jerome. Mama love Jerome."

There was no point in wailing for Pointer Francis.

And he was no longer three.

For some time after that, he was able to think clearly. It probably had something to do with the brief human contact. When he made his next trip to the kitchen, he accidentally touched the mother who was there to prepare his meals. She said good afternoon. Other than Mother Biddows, he could not recognize them by voice. So he didn't know which one it was. At least he knew it was afternoon. But on which day? He ate and voided and then descended. The high point of his life now seemed to be these trips to the kitchen and the toilet—at least, he told himself chuckling, he didn't wail when he had the urge.

He resumed reflecting on his life—especially his encounter

with Yaw. What would Yaw think of what he was doing now? He'd criticize it because he couldn't identify specific Akan elements in it. He'd called him an Obasafon and had refused to tell him what it meant. It had taken him close to fifteen years to find the meaning of that word. And when he did he was both flattered and insulted. Now he was conquering his Obasafon. Yaw, in a Malawian jail, if he was still alive, could not conquer his. Fear not them that could destroy the body but fear him who could destroy the soul; those weren't the exact words but they were close. It was impossible, he would like to tell Jesus— as impossible as poisoning the pests without poisoning the streams—to have your body destroyed with your soul intact. "Labour is not blossoming where body is bruised to pleasure soul." Yeats was almost right, as was Jesus. But he had seen a lot of bruised bodies and bruised souls, and a lot of brutalized bodies that housed demonic souls, and even bodies brutalized and unbrutalized that never had souls.

His thoughts returned to what Pointer Francis had said about power: "Yes, my son, the earth, the wind, the rain, the sun—these is God. They only have for change their usual pattern and that will be the end o human life. Nothing the White man technology can do to change that. If only they would stop and think bout this, they will stop being so cocksure bout how superior they is, like if something superior bout raping the earth! Imagine going round the world sticking their flag everywhere and saying they discover it when they meet people living there! Then destroying the people, turning into slaves those they don destroy, then poisoning the land!

"And arrogant on top of it! Their God command them to do it! Their God all right! Emptiness! I is nearly eighty years old and I live long enough for know the emptier a man is inside the bigger he want for be outside. The more space he want to take up. My land, your land, this man country, his cattle, and even people. Like if he take pride in seeing how much people mouth he can keep food out of. How much you can eat at a time? You need twenty bedrooms for sleep in? When you in one, how you could be in the other nineteen? You ha for be empty and frighten for think that greed and power is a form of salvation."

A deep sadness filled him, a sadness for the whole human species. Was it worth preserving?

There's something to what you say, Pointer Francis. Just before coming back to Compton to begin the voyage, he listened to a dietitian discussing obesity on the radio. She raised the issue of compulsive eaters and said they were people in many cases whose diet lacked a vital ingredient or whose intestines could not absorb that ingredient but whose body craved it nonetheless, so they ate and ate and ate in a sort of desperate attempt to obtain it.

His mind leap-frogged from topic to topic and must have tired, for he found himself humming a hymn that his mother frequently sang and which in later years he could not stand.

Safe in the arms of Jesus,
Safe on his gentle breast—
There by his love o'ershadowed,
Sweetly my soul shall rest.

He remembered how condescending he had been to the sisters who came to Jesus's bosom seeking solace after the village men had impregnated and abandoned them and their offspring; sisters who sang it at day's end after the daily rounds of hoeing in cane fields under a blistering sun, who sang it to purge themselves of the pain from the abuse they daily endured from the Eurafrican overseers.

He paused in his thoughts and told himself that he was devising games to fight the darkness, to prevent it from swallowing him. Maybe that was part of the test. The pointers did not tell you any more than they had to. Each person's journey is unique, Pointer Francis had said.

He resolved to focus his thoughts on his soul. How can I become a better person? That was one question he could use to keep himself on track. Find another one, he told himself. What can I do to serve my fellow beings? Not bad, he complimented himself. Watch that! Pride. "He that is great among you shall be a servant to all," or something close to that. Maybe that's why intelligent people devised schemes to take people's property and freedom and dignity from them. Cut the sarcasm. What have you done with your brain? Jesus would have told you that you hold it in stewardship. But you are not great.

No one has benefited from your brain.

Wesi has.

That's what you think.

You used Wesi to save yourself.

"Who benefited? Who? Who? he found himself screaming. Then he remembered that, around the time that Wesi was finishing elementary school, he had come to town to spend a week with him. Jerome had gone to the market and paid a lot of money for six mangoes, which were then out of season. It was a special treat for Wesi. He was returning to his room with the mangoes in a plastic bag. As he was about to turn onto his street, he passed the beggar with a huge bandaged ulcer who sat on her wooden crate and leaned on her cane under the overhanging gallery of the hardware store. "Gi me one o them mangoes," she yelled at him. He pretended not to hear her and quickened his pace. Back at his room, when Wesi and he sat down to eat the mangoes, he couldn't bite into his own. Wesi asked him if he was sick. He could not show Wesi that ugly side of him, so he told him yes; and indeed he was, because try as he did, it was as if the mango had metamorphosed into the woman's ulcer. If he'd had any compassion, he would have returned to the spot and given the woman a mango. They could not eat six anyway. He must have been trying to prove something when he bought that many. The unexamined life, someone had told him Plato said, wasn't worth living. He had tried to read Plato but had given up. He couldn't concentrate. He knew his over-analysis of things paralyzed him. Why did he have to analyze everything? Is the intellect a tyrant? Confound the intellect! One had to live, goddammit! The blue fly did not ask why it was blue. It simply buzzed and buzzed until it found a warm, nourishing spot to lay its eggs. Are you a blue fly? Curse the intellect!

After his release from the hospital the second time, he'd had similar reactions and had seen how one-sided such thoughts were. Maybe everything was like the tree of knowledge, a rope to scale the cliffs with in order to continue your journey and to be flayed with after you finished the journey. Mr. Morrison would have said that was a mixed metaphor. Well, life was a mixed metaphor, but it was badly mixed, in proportions undesired. Much thinking hath made thee mad. A little thinking restored thy sanity. Well, thou canst have thy pick.

Later he drifted in and out of sleep and had strange but not nightmarish dreams. His legs were heavy when he next mounted the stairs, and there was a hollow feeling in his chest. There was water at the dais. It must have been a new day. When he returned to the cave, Pointer Francis was waiting for him.

"I come to hear what you done experience so far."

He told pointer Francis every detail of everything he remembered.

Pointer Francis put his hands on his shoulders—he was glad to be touched—and told him, "You doing all right, son. You is on course. If every pilgrim was like you! I like the two questions. Keep on asking them. They will be yo guide." Then he left.

The word *pilgrim* set off an association in his mind with a song his mother but mostly Eunice sang whenever life was grim.

> *Jesus Saviour, pilot me*
> *O'er life's dark tempestuous sea.*
> *Unknown billows o'er me roll.*
> *Jesus Saviour, steer my soul.*

How much you remember that you thought you had forgotten! Eunice used to follow that one with:

> *I am satisfied to know*
> *That with Jesus here below*
> *I can conquer every foe.*

Her breath catching after she had begun to suffer from tuberculosis. He'd already begun to work at the post office

273

when she became confined to bed. His mother told him that the Anglican priest came once a month to give her the body and blood of Christ. He was sure that the neighbours, mostly his mother, gave her food and companionship. He did not know when she died or he would have come home to attend her funeral.

He caught himself, still playing games to avoid the darkness. "The spirit is willing but the flesh is weak." And he couldn't help thinking that there was a point to the belief that the capable should make the sacrifice for the unwilling and the weak. Parasite! Still, few Indians were capable of Ghandi's sacrifice: promotion, power, juggling the games of life even against their own people were more important. So Ghandi achieved the victory for them, paying with his life. And Christians felt that Jesus's blood could cleanse them of every wrong and so went on to commit them, even, they said, to further Jesus's kingdom, as if Jesus had been interested in kingdoms. "The Kingdom of Heaven is within you." They ate a piece of him—even Eunice got pieces of his flesh and vials of his blood: Who would dare accuse the Anglicans of class prejudice?—and were preserved against something or inspired to do something, like Christianizing South America for its gold and exterminating some of its peoples—or nothing, like letting the poor starve to death. Some, like old Mr. Manchester, who had gone to the Anglican church every Sunday and had donated the money to build the church hall that was named after him, did some of everything. People needed their saviours. In Athens—and everywhere in other forms—they used to feed selected victims and then beat them out of the city and either kill them or banish them so they'd carry away all evil with them. It was easier politically to do that than tax the nobles to build the sewers that would have prevented disease. And it was a great occasion for a festival. And, thinking such thoughts, he fell asleep.

He dreamt that he was in a valley with sheer cliffs on all sides, and he was thirsty and hungry and the sun shone fiercely and buzzards hovered overhead noisily. Just as he was wondering how long he'd endure before surrendering to the buzzards, he awoke and didn't know where he was, surprised at the darkness around him.

He soon fell asleep again and this time found himself in a cave with all access barred to the outside world. He awoke standing.

He drank from the goblet and felt the urge to urinate but decided against mounting the stairs.

Later he dreamt that he was in a coffin and was knocking, hoping someone would hear and unscrew the lid. How in this day and age could they bury him alive? Hadn't a doctor come to make sure that he'd died? Well, there was nothing to do about it. Maybe they had already buried him, so in his dream he relaxed into death.

At some point, too, he thought he heard footsteps and opened his eyes, and it was broad daylight and he was in a field of coconuts, such as he had seen on the northwestern part of Isabella Island. A herd of bulls was roaming about. They began to eye him and soon to head toward him. But he could not move, and the bulls got nearer and nearer. Just as he expected to be tossed into the air, caught before falling and tossed again, he opened his eyes, saw the darkness, remembered where he was, and was relieved. But his head was spinning. It was as if the floor of the cave was a spinning top and he was positioned on it. He hoped it was in his head, that it wasn't an earthquake. He was very thirsty and his bladder was full to bursting but he dared not move. Then the spinning left him, and he felt as though he'd metamorphosed into lead, and as he was unable to keep his bladder closed anymore, it began emptying itself. The warmth of the urine puddle in which he was now lying awoke him fully. "Oh God!" he said out loud. "I'm like a little child wetting my bed."

The darkness of the cave was like a weight on him. He had to go upstairs, but he suddenly forgot how to leave. He managed to lift himself up from the floor and sit on the edge of the bed. He tried to remember how to leave the cave. The heat had gone from the urine-soaked gown and now it felt cold and smelled acrid. He must have known how to get out of the cave at one time. He was sure he had left the cave many times before. He stretched out on the bed, stuck his thumb in his mouth, and began to cry. Later his thirst returned and he knew there was water somewhere, but he could not remember where.

There was an intervening blank after which he was absolutely sure he was a baby lying on his mother's lap with a bottle in his mouth. The idea struck him as preposterous, so he attempted unsuccessfully to lift a very heavy hand to feel whether indeed a nursing bottle was in his mouth. His mother had not even lit the lamp.

"You awake?"

It took him some time to connect the voice and Pointer Francis. But he didn't know where he was. He lifted his arms this time and indeed there was a nursing bottle in his mouth. Then he smelled feces, felt the stickiness on his buttocks and between his thighs. He could not speak with the bottle in his mouth. When he could muster the strength to remove the bottle, he found that his throat was parched and speech was painful. "Water," he managed. Pointer Francis lifted his head a little and then arranged him in the bed. He returned with a baby bottle of water.

"Where am I?"

"Making yo journey and doing all right."

He spent a good three minutes putting reality back together again. Then he said, ashamed, "I messed myself."

"Everyone got to."

His head was quite clear now. It seemed a lot of time had elapsed since he was last awake. He wanted to know what day it was, how long since he had been in the cave, but knew the questions were taboo. He even remembered *I will endure.*

"I will be back in a short while," Pointer Francis said.

When he returned, Pointer Francis removed the soiled gown and steadied him on his feet by making him brace his arms against the cave wall. Jerome felt a wet towel wiping him clean. He smelled the soap. He heard him wringing the cloth and rinsing it. Pointer Francis wiped his groin a second time. Jerome felt the sensation of a dry towel moving over him. Pointer Francis put a clean gown on him that still had the wash smell in it. Pointer Francis held his hand and said, "Follow me." He followed. "Move over a little to yo right. Now sit down." His bottom touched a cold surface, and he remembered the two stone seats.

"Stay here until I finish making yo bed."

He heard him stripping the bed. Afterward he felt his nearness. "Come." Pointer Francis helped him get into bed. "I will keep yo company for a little while."

By now his head had cleared enormously. He remembered where he was completely and the nightmares he'd been having. He remembered, too, that he had formulated two questions. But he couldn't remember them.

"How you is now?"

"All right."

"No. You not. You wondering all sorts o things but you too ashamed to ask. You is embarrassed that you mess yoself and wet yo bed. And you embarrass that I ha to come and clean you."

"Yes."

"Well, it nothing to embarrass bout. If it don't happen you can't move on. Is a sign that you done humble yoself. If you can't accept it you will have to repeat it." He paused. "I going to get you some mo soup."

He heard him ascend and shortly afterward descend the stairs.

"This time in a cup."

He sat up in the bed. He drank it. It was bitter but he did not mind.

"I put the pail at the foot of yo bed and yo drinking water is at the head, cause fo a while you will find it hard to climb the stairs."

There followed a silence of about ten minutes.

"What is the password?"

He began to panic.

"Concentrate! Concentrate! It will come. You is not to worry."

There followed another silence, during which he struggled with his memory. He told himself he wouldn't get out of the cave whole without it. Suddenly it was as if his body chose to relax and he heard within himself an echo of his mother's voice. "Some things you can't hurry, no. You just have fo let them finish in their own time. Meekly wait and murmur not."...*I will endure.*

"That is it. Keep a steady course."

He did not even know he'd said the words out loud. A minute or so later, he heard Pointer Francis ascend the stairs.

When he awoke he remembered the pail and the water. He urinated and then drank and went back to sleep.

Olivia was in the room. He was sure he wasn't dreaming. She was there under a spotlight in the darkness. She wagged her finger at him, laughed aloud, and left, taking the spotlight with her.

She hadn't been too long gone when he heard a crash of footsteps coming down the stairs. He opened his eyes and saw his co-workers entering the room. The half-Indian led them. The supercilious deputy postmistress, Marian Myers, was with them.

"He gone back a Africa," the half-Indian one said.

"Cannibal! Cannibal!" Marian began chanting, and the others joined in; they were all laughing.

When they stopped, Bob, who had told the fired workers to eat shit, cleared his throat and spat on him.

He heard himself screaming, "I will endure." They vanished.

But no sooner had they left than he heard the deputy minister's voice. He opened his eyes. It was pitch dark. "All the yams your mother sends you from the country! Never brought me one! Never a hand of ripe bananas. Not a tannia. Not a pineapple. You don't know things cost a lot in Hanovertown! And you wondering why I didn't promote you! Keep on wondering! Keep on wondering! Keep on wondering, wondering, wondering…" His final words echoed.

He heard the voice of the minister. "Yes. And never voted. If you don scratch me back who will scratch yours?"

The room lit up now, and it was the chief technical officer looking at him slyly, as he always did. Then he sucked his teeth aloud.

I will endure, he told himself.

Miss Anderson's elephantine laughter sounded a short distance away, and he tensed in anticipation of violence. The blow landed on his forehead. She was dragging her pumpkin breasts across his face. "You uses fo call them melon," she told him in her singsong town accent. "Now suck them, else I gwine suffocate you with them." Then her full weight was upon him. In a moment she was gone and something hard was being pushed into his mouth. He clenched his teeth but could feel hands trying to pry his jaws apart. "Make him do it," he heard Miss Anderson saying. "He don wan me breasts them so is that he want. Make him do it, Sprat! Come on, squeeze harder! Make the buller do it!" She sounded like an excited schoolgirl enjoying a hair-pulling fight. He could resist no more and his jaws fell apart. He heard Sprat's laughter followed by Miss Anderson's. "Chut, you is too kind-hearted. You shoulda make him do it."

He fell asleep again.

When he awoke, Pointer Francis was sitting on the edge of the bed.

"Come, drink yo broth. Sit up."

Pointer Francis helped him up.

Jerome drank.

"How things going?"

"A living hell!"

"I been waiting to hear you say so. Good. You can't get to heaven without first going through hell. Just keep yo course."

It wasn't long after Pointer Francis left that he saw a ten-dollar bill drift through the air like a leaf falling toward him. It landed on his neck, transformed instantly into a rope, and began to choke him. He pulled and pulled at it until it snapped. But the snapped portion slid out of his hand and became a giant octopus threatening to swallow him, then a bull threatening to charge him—the ten-dollar bill now multiplied and covered them like wallpaper, complete with pictures of Hamilton, everything. Finally it transformed into a mule that took its place beside the bed, still plastered with ten-dollar bills. The mule bared its teeth at him and proceeded to kick him. After a while it stopped kicking but periodically bared its teeth. The mule did not go. And each time he nodded off, it kicked him. He was sure that twelve hours had elapsed during which he did not sleep.

It was a relief to hear Pointer Francis's footsteps. The mule remained in its spotlight, grinning at him, even after Pointer Francis entered the cave. So he told Pointer Francis what happened; the mule listened and nodded. The spotlight and the mule disappeared as soon as he concluded his story.

Pointer Francis told him that somewhere in his past was an American ten-dollar bill that he had done something wrong with.

He told Pointer Francis the story of the ten dollars the sorter had sent him as a Christmas gift the year after he went to

America. He told him, too, why he thought the sorter had sent it, and he told him that he felt it had been wrong to accept it.

"What you do with it?"

"I bought a dictionary."

"You still got the dictionary?"

"Yes, it's at my parents' house."

"What is the title?"

He told him. Immediately Pointer Francis went to his parents' place and returned with the dictionary. "Here," he said, "tear it up." It hurt him to rip up the dictionary. When it was over, Pointer Francis told him, "That not all. When you leave this mourning ground, and you go back to yo job, I want you fo go fo six months and visit the patients in the mental hospital every Sunday."

When Pointer Francis handed him his broth, he pushed it away. "Just a gourd of water," he told him. But no sooner had he swallowed it than his entire body felt constricted and his stomach and intestines began to convulse.

"The pail!" he said, clenching his teeth to keep the second spurt of vomit from dislodging the first. The convulsions came quickly and violently, even after there was nothing left to come out. *I will endure*, he told himself, but the retching did not stop.

Pointer Francis sat with him for what must have been close to two hours, until the stomach convulsions ceased and he fell asleep.

When he awoke, he reflected that it was good that Pointer Francis had not told him what the journey involved, for called or uncalled by the spirit, he would have refused. As soon as he'd uttered the thought, Miss Anderson, Miss Blunt, Mr. Bunyan, the supercilious woman, and the half-Indian descended upon him. Miss Anderson held his head, the others a thigh or an arm each, and they began to bear him away. They carried him to some faraway place, to the edge of a cliff, and hurled him off. He was falling when Pointer Francis's footsteps broke the hallucination.

"How's yo stomach?"

"All right."

"I bring you some ginger tea to settle it."

He drank the tea and felt better. He fell asleep after Pointer Francis left.

He did not know when it began, but he found himself on a platform in the middle of Hanovertown Stadium. What looked like the entire population of Isabella Island was present, more people than he remembered seeing when the Queen had visited. Not far from him on the platform sat his mother, holding his father's hand. He looked to his left and right and directly in front of him and realized that he was in a defendant's box. Above him sat a very black man, with very thick lips, wearing a judge's black robes and a wig. All around were microphones. His mother was crying and his father was staring at the floor.

"What am I doing here?" he asked the judge.

"Silence!" the judge said, pounding his gavel.

"Will Miss Olivia Simmons please take the stand."

Olivia entered the witness box, no longer the young woman he remembered. She told the court and the audience what he'd done to her.

"Does the defendant have anything to say?"

"Nothing," he said, wiping his eyes, ashamed again of his deed.

A woman took the stand next. She said she lived next door to him and was afraid to send her little boy out alone for fear that Jerome might molest him.

"That's a lie!" he screamed, ignoring the furious banging of the judge's gavel. "An abominable lie!"

"I charge the prisoner with contempt of court," he heard the judge say.

He shrugged his shoulders.

Miss Anderson took the stand.

Peter took the stand.

Miss Blunt took the stand.

Mr. Bunyan took the stand.

They all had something to say about having suspected him of being homosexual. But, after being cited for contempt of court, he had stopped listening, aware that he had been pre-sentenced. The sun was pouring down on his head. His box was the only unshaded one.

Occasionally the cries of the people in the stands and on the grass reached him. Some of them were waving their fists at him. "Hang im!" they thundered.

"I repeat for the third time, does the prisoner have anything to say?" he heard the judge asking.

"What?" he replied.

"You've been sentenced to life imprisonment and all you can say is 'What?'" the judge exclaimed, a humorous incredulity in his voice.

"What! What! What!…" buzzed in the cave for hours. It didn't let up until Pointer Francis returned.

He told Pointer Francis the experience.

"I will go and get you yo broth and then we will talk bout yo last vision."

Pointer Francis returned with the cup and Jerome pushed his hand away.

"One mouthful," Pointer Francis told him.

He drank.

"Another one."

He drank.

"See, it not so bad. One more. Only a little bit left in the cup. Finish it off. Good. You swallowed it all."

Pointer Francis and he remained seated at the edge of the bed for what seemed like an hour before Pointer Francis spoke to him again.

"You feeling a little stronger now?"

"Yes."

"Good, because we ha to go to the sacred room. You going to find the climbing hard, cause is days now since you mount these stairs and you ain't been eating, and with all the demons you been wrestling with. Les go. Hol my hand."

He held on to Pointer Francis's hand until they got near the dais and he no longer could. They cleared the dais and Pointer Francis sat him on one of the stools beside it and sat on the other.

"Well, we can't tear this one up."

He was silent.

"I think the meaning o the whole thing clear to you—that you been hiding yo homosexuality on account o all the things people say bout homosexuals. You frighten to let people know that you is that way. I don't blame you. But you ever stop to think the price you pay fo hiding and sacrificing yo life like that?"

He could not believe what he was hearing.

"You ever saw anybody you like?"

"Yes."

"And what?"

"Nothing happened."

He told Pointer Francis about the fellow who had sent the messages and how he'd handled it.

"Before you and me go on, we must clear up a few things. If you sleep with a man, who you hurting?"

"I don't know."

"How you mean you don't know?"

"Nobody, I guess."

"Right. Well, if you don't hurt anybody in doing it, where is the wrong in it?"

He couldn't answer.

"You see what you did with yo life? You put the sex part of yo life pon a trash heap just fo please society. If you did live in the South o the United States, you would o paint yoself white?"

"I get your meaning."

"I want you to promise me when you finish the journey that you will make a effort to find somebody you comfortable with and that cherish and respect you. Don mind what people say. We all come from the earth so we is all children of God. Nothing sinful bout sex. Is a natural thing. You just have for accept the consequence and not use it for hurt people. Sin, my son, is hurting others and hurting the earth.

"Every mortar need a pestle." He fell silent. "And every pestle need a mortar." He was silent again. "Is hard for come up with a proverb that will include you. I guess you is a case of a pestle needing a pestle."

That hurt him.

"The fellow you just talk to me bout, he still around?"

"That's around twenty-seven years ago, Pointer Francis."

"That don't mean he not still around."

"I won't recognize him now if I see him."

"Well anyhow, you think bout what I tell you. I know now that AIDS going round, society even harder on people like you. Never mind that. Just be careful. You don't ha to do everything, if you catch my meaning."

Jerome laughed.

Pointer Francis was silent for a long while after that, after which he led him back to the cave. As he began ascending the steps he called back to him, "Think bout what I tell you and when you clear yo mind bout it, you going to find you able to move on."

His mind was now sharp on account of the walk and the human contact, and panic set in, for it was the first time he had discussed his homosexuality with anyone. How could he go public with it and survive? They called you "buller" because they couldn't get away with pushing a knife or pumping bullets into you, and they hoped that the way they said it would drive you to push the knife or pump the bullet into yourself. He knew that when his cousin Boy-boy had been a teenager, he had arranged to meet a young man in one of the cane fields near Compton. When he got there, there were ten of them. They took turns buggering him; one even used a beer bottle; then they beat him into unconsciousness and left him there. He'd refused to name the young men. But everyone knew who they were because they'd bragged about what they'd done— everything but the buggering. Boy-boy had told Comsie the entire story. Jerome was eight at the time and they hadn't known he was listening. He could see himself reprimanding the junior clerks only to be told that they didn't have to listen to a bullerman.

When they knew you were that way, everyone took liberties with your feelings. He had only known of one exception, and the outcome had shocked a lot of people—Toni Morrison said that Blacks do not stone sinners; maybe not in Ohio, but on Isabella Island they certainly did. Strange how that incident had completely hidden itself in his memory.

Albert Brown was a cashier in one of the cages at the front of the post office. They said he was "so." One morning, before they had gone off to their workstations, a group of them were at the front hallway of the building. For no apparent reason, Brill Jones, a mail sorter, said to Albert, "I hear you does back up man shit."

"Oh yeah, I guess you want me to open you up so yours can flow?"

There was scattered laugher.

"You ain't got no comeback for *that!*" said the senior mail sorter.

"Says who?" asked Brill as the slap he gave Albert resounded.

Tears welled up in Albert's eyes but they did not spill, and a few seconds later he headed for the bathroom, probably to get rid of the blood that had to be in his mouth.

No one, not even Jerome, had reprimanded Brill. The incident had set him to thinking about a remark he'd heard from a fellow who was an arrogant jackass anyway. The jackass had said that he didn't engage in discussions with a certain class of people because they saw everything as a battle, and they couldn't win with words, and when they lost the battle of words they resorted to the battle of fists, which they were surer of winning from long practice.

An hour later, the postmaster had summoned him to his office. Albert and Brill were also there. Brill signalled to him to say nothing. The postmaster asked him what had happened downstairs, and Jerome told him everything.

"Are you sure?" the postmaster asked him. *Perhaps the postmaster would have preferred that he lie and save him from having to take action against Brill.*

"Yes," he told him.

Brill did not show up for work the next day. Within two weeks they heard that he had been dismissed. At the time of the incident, he was on probation for telling a female clerk that he didn't have to "take orders from a cunt."

The sorters and some of the clerks were angry with Albert, saying that he did not know how to take a joke like a man, that he had caused Brill to lose his job, and didn't he know that Brill had a wife and two children to feed? To Jerome they said, "You don know how to see and not see and hear and not hear? Imagine that, losing his job cause he slap a bullerman!" The good thing about it was—he guessed because of the postmaster's action—they said none of it in Albert's presence. They merely refused to speak to him and maintained absolute silence if he wandered near them.

Albert eventually told him that all the sorters and the other two clerks who had been present had told the postmaster that they were vaguely aware of a misunderstanding but had not seen what happened. "You saved me from looking like a fool."

His thoughts returned to his own plight, and he began to imagine scenarios. He began to understand why Boy-boy had emigrated to the US within months of his mother's death and never once returned in seventeen years.

That's what he should have done—emigrated. But he didn't, and at age forty-five he had no intention of doing so. Besides, Wesi told him that the Blacks he'd seen in Toronto were a sad lot. They had hell finding decent apartments, and it was impossible, Wesi said, to walk up Queen Street without a Black somebody offering you crack. And it was as if the police didn't care. They just let them do it. Maybe they wanted them to destroy themselves or they wanted to be able to say, "See, that's what niggers are all about." And Blacks were definitely quite badly off in England. The number of them who lived on the dole was staggering. Even worse off in the US, where they were still battling Jim Crow. Whatever their problems on Isabella, the days of the Manchesters were almost all over. Even the Eurafricans now had to work like everybody else, and now many of them were unemployed because it had been their complexions that got them their managerial positions on the estates, and now that most of the estates were carved up and sold to the peasants, they weren't qualified to do anything else. And they had no money to invest in anything because they had spent it travelling around the world, living lavishly, showing off. Quite something, too, to see how few of their children were getting into the secondary schools.

"I'm supposed to be looking for a solution to my problem," he spoke aloud. "It never fails. I examine every other subject but the one I should be looking at." But he was pleased at how alert his mind was and with Pointer Francis's positive reaction to his sexuality. "Pointer Francis, it's a lot harder than you, full of compassion, make it sound."

17

HE WAS ABLE TO GO TO the kitchen on his own again. He went twice that day but continued to use the pail in the cave. At one point Pointer Francis came down and told him to stay in bed as much as possible because this was the crucial point in the journey. The soup Pointer Francis brought that day was thinner and more bitter.

He slept again and waited and slept again and decided to fast. During his fast, his grandmother appeared. She held his hand, and they were standing on a shore where waves were crashing loudly. "Come," she said. But he was afraid, always afraid of deep water, he remembered.

"Well, you not going to get there if you don walk the water." She stood on a wave, her hand stretched out to him, but as he stepped onto the water he sank and awoke.

First strike, he told himself, before drifting back to sleep.

She reappeared and held him steadily as they skipped over the waves. "You see the land in the distance?"

All he saw was black, angry, swirling water below and ahead of him. But soon he saw the smoke-grey outline of land. They walked onto a rock-strewn beach.

"This is heaven?" he asked her.

"Decide that for yoself."

They walked into the town. It was only slightly bigger than the average Isabellan country town. All the houses were of mud, though, and roofed with thatch. The streets were wide but unpaved, and they teemed with people dressed in African robes made mostly out of the kind of kente cloth Yaw and his compatriots had exhibited in Isabella.

"Are you sure we're in heaven?"

"Don try my patience!" She sounded as choleric as he remembered her being some thirty-five years before. He had forgotten how short-tempered she was.

The people were buying and selling, laughing, and exchanging jokes. In the town square, a musician performed and children and adults—men and women—danced.

His grandmother held his hand and led him up a street to a roofed shed where there were stools, pots of steaming food, and lots of people buying and eating.

"Let's eat," she told him

"I have no money," he said.

An old woman, with facial skin as scaly as a reptile's and bags under her eyes so deep that they folded, but otherwise quite hale, must have heard him, for she turned from one of the pots she was tending. "Come and eat. Everyone is welcome. Those who have give a little in appreciation of the time we spend cooking it, and those who don't have eat just the same, because it's the earth and not we that produce it." She took his arm and he followed her to where her pot was. She put a calabash in his hand and ladled into it a very aromatic soup with large chunks of meat and vegetables.

His grandmother had already been served. He sat on the vacant stool beside her. The food was the most delicious he'd ever tasted. Maybe he was in heaven after all. As if reading his thoughts, the old woman who had served him looked directly into his eyes and smiled. He nodded his compliments, and at that point everyone of the thirty or so men and women in the shed turned to him and gave him a welcoming smile. While they were still looking at him, a youth appeared with a goblet and a cup. He handed him the cup, poured a libation onto the soil, and then filled the cup. "Welcome among us from the uprooted ones across the water. May you learn a lot from us and may you teach us a lot."

"Thank you," he told him. "I come knowing very little and hope to learn a lot." He drank the palm wine.

About half an hour later, holding his arm, his grandmother took him into a courtyard. He figured it was the chief's. There were men and women around the chief. The chief wasn't seated on a stool as he had expected: he circulated among the people. After a while Jerome realized that the men and women were the chief's advisers.

Eventually the chief came over to him. The chief nodded and Jerome attempted to bow low, but the chief caught his head. "No, here we bow low before Nyame only. At one time we didn't even need to until we angered Nyame with our carelessness and wrongdoing. I'm flesh and blood and so are you.

"So you have come to us from across the seas to learn truth?"

"Yes."

"Well, I would like to learn truth myself."

"How's that?"

"Because only the ancestors know truth." He pointed to Jerome's grandmother, who stood by silently. "She knows truth because she is in touch with Nyame. Invoke Nyame and he will inspire you with truth through her. The only truth I possess is granted me through the ancestors. I rely on their wisdom to be chief, to rule justly, to ensure that strife does not plague my chieftaincy, that all are cared for, and that greed and cruelty are kept out of my domains."

"I thought I was coming to heaven," Jerome told him.

"What do you think heaven is?"

"I don't know."

"If you don't know, how will you know when you have found it?"

"I thought I would just know or that somebody would tell me."

"I see."

Jerome studied him carefully. He wore leather sandals and a simple loose garment of brilliantly dyed yellow and indigo cotton threads. If he had met him on the road by himself, he would not have known his station.

"So you have come to Africa looking for heaven? What have you done to help build heaven?"

"Me?"

The chief nodded.

"I, I, I…"

"Well, until you can answer that question, we won't be able to pursue this inquiry. I thought you might have something to teach me. Don't go yet. Walk around the court. Leave and enter as you will. There are no guards to stop you. There's nothing here to steal or to protect. Everything here belongs to everybody." The chief walked off toward one of the mud huts on the compound.

He edged closer to his grandmother.

"Blockhead, where you expect to find heaven on earth? After all the teachings Pointer Francis give you, you still don know what you ha fo do fo build heaven? I should leave you here to find yo way back over the waves by yoself!"

He panicked.

"Don get frighten. I done bring you and I will carry you back, but you should be shamed o yoself."

He and his grandmother wandered around aimlessly; everyone nodded politely to them as if they knew why they had come. Everywhere they went, people offered them palm wine and kola nuts.

When the sun was low, his grandmother took his hand and led him back to the chief's compound, where dinner was about to be served. There were many people there: men and women and children. The pots were on a platform shaded by a baobab tree. The food was plentiful, but none of it was wasted. Before they ate, a flock of birds gathered in the trees. Food was set out a few yards away for them and they descended and ate. The people ate after the birds had eaten. After the people had eaten, the remaining food was transported away.

"Where are they taking the food?"

"To feed the priests, the sculptors, the musicians, and the storytellers them."

"Why?"

"Because they have for eat."

"Don't they get paid?"

"That's part of the payment."

"I don't understand."

"Oh Jerome, you really try my patience sometimes. What fo understand! People work fo buy food, ain't? Well, they have theirs cultivated and cooked fo them."

"Why don't they do it themselves?"

"Because," she screamed at him, "they can't teach the rules and look after the soul o the society and cultivate the lan too."

"Musicians don't look after the people's souls."

"If that is what you think, what can I teach you? The ones you know don do that, but that is one o the main reason they have musicians here."

"The birds, why did they feed them?"

"Because they is the ancestors them."

"I see. How come we don't feed any ancestors?"

"Because we don have no African pride lef. That is why I bring you here, fo discover it all over again."

"I see," he said because he did not know what to say.

"The chief want to talk some more with you," she told him, already pulling him by the arm toward where the chief was standing.

"How do you like what you see?"

"It wasn't what I expected."

"I know," the chief said. "You came to Africa hoping to find all the technology from the West and you are ashamed that you don't find it here. Well, there's a reason for that. If you want to see skyscrapers, you can go to Abidjan, or Dakar, or any other African metropolis. Here, we have plenty of mud to build our houses with. If we cut down the trees, the spirit of the earth will be angered and the rain will not come to wash the earth's body, and all the beautiful sensations that she experiences and that we see as trees and reap as vegetables or as grass to feed our livestock will be withheld.

"But it's more than that. It seems that when we cut down the trees and dig the stones as well as other things out of the earth, it is because we are afflicted by the disease of death."

"Death?"

"Yes. The rooms in those high-rises are used to plan how many trees to cut down and turn into lumber to sell abroad so that the president can buy rifles and equip an army to keep him in power. Other rooms are used to plan the strategies of the military. The armies of Africa do not kill Europeans; they don't burn European farms and houses. Guess whom they kill, whose houses they burn, and whose crops they destroy? Do you know how many millions of acres are used to grow cocoa and peanuts to exchange for guns and bullets while millions of our people starve or suffer and die from kwashiorkor and lack of medicine?

"When the presidents travel overseas, they brag how civilized their countries are by mentioning the number of skyscrapers in their cities, the many planes that land at their airports, and so on and so forth. They never say how many people they have in jail or assassinate every year to stay in power.

"So what happened is that people from all over Africa who saw what the new rulers were doing decided they didn't like the price of this progress that everybody was swallowing everywhere or that was swallowing up everybody everywhere. We were lucky to have the ruler of this region and his people share this philosophy, and so he decided to turn his jurisdiction over for an experiment in living according to the way the ancestors lived. A handful of people came from everywhere in Africa to live among us. And a lot of the people from here left and went to live with those that want progress.

"Two years ago, they made me chief. Every six months the elders meet to review my chieftaincy and decide whether I should stay in office.

"We live according to simple rules. Everything belongs to everybody because everybody works to produce everything. So it is wrong to steal anything. And it is wrong to be be lazy. We must be respectful of the earth, the rivers, and everything that supports life. They do not depend on us; we depend on them. We do not allow people to inflict pain on one another because that leads to hatred, and hatred leads to war and strife, and those things sap a community of its vital strength. We ask residents who can't live according to these guidelines to leave, because there are many societies in Africa and around the world where it is legal and profitable to hurt others and to abuse nature. These are the basic rules. We didn't make them; we got them from the ancestors. It's true that in some societies where they had those rules they didn't obey them, especially in the way they treated women, made slaves of other people, and so on. But, as new people die and pass on to the world of the ancestors, more and more wisdom is added to our collective wisdom, and so we have better rules for our conduct than earlier generations. Even if human nature doesn't change, the ways for managing it can improve. We believe that society must control the individual, because a lot of people, most people it seems, can't control themselves."

That night he was given a hut to sleep in and to use while he sojourned among them. His grandmother was given a hut of her own. He slept comfortably on skins on the floor. When he awoke in the morning, a little boy brought him calabash of freshly tapped palm juice. He drank and was refreshed.

The rest of that day he seemed to travel and travel and travel, his grandmother leading the way. Wherever he went, the people continued to be polite. They were all absorbed in their various duties. Some were dyeing cloth. Others weaving it. Still others preparing the dye. Others stripping the cotton to be woven into skeins. Still others cultivating the cotton. He kept looking around for bosses and nowhere did he see any. Guess those who needed to be bosses and those who needed bosses went to live in another country. He began then to understand the question "What have you done to build heaven?"

Farther inland he came upon a wide river and fishermen. Some were already paddling their boats downstream with their catch. Some were still in the water, pulling their nets. On the shore several men and women were salting and drying and smoking fish. He longed to ask them if they did not sometimes feel like goofing off, if they did not suspect others of goofing off. He would do both, he was sure.

Having faith in others was probably one way they got around it. Ashamed to fail and disappoint others was probably one factor that spurred them on to produce. Communism had tried similar methods and failed. Though it should be said that the communist rulers did not live with the same simplicity as the proletariat. The more he thought about it, the more he became baffled by the presence of the society before him. He had heard that the Hopis of North America demanded altruism of all their members and that they achieved it, but he had never believed it to be true.

"Grandma, did you know before now that heaven was in Africa?"

"No. But if I was born in slavery I would o know. Because in slavery the songs the people sing bout going to heaven was really bout going back to Africa."

"But in those days a lot of people in Africa died from disease."

"You think is cause they was diseased that the White man captured them by the millions and bring them out? You always asking foolish questions. If you get kidnapped from yo country where everybody take care o one another to one where they turn you into mules, beat you from day-clean till night-dark to get you to work fo they benefit, take yo children from you and say they is their property, you won't think the country you get stolen from is heaven?"

"But Grandma, you never lived during slavery!"

"Well, when I born slavery did done abolish on paper but was very living in the way they work us, pay us, beat us, and treat us. My mother come home one day her skin all welt up. The White man boss of Montague estate beat her cause she get back a little late from lunch. That was the reason he give, but the real one is cause she did done hit him one time when he lift up her dress while she bend down weeding cotton."

Such conversations with his grandmother and occasional exchanges with Chief Nfolo and others throughout the chieftaincy confirmed his intimations that people who chose to be governed by Chief Nfolo imposed tremendous discipline on themselves, to instill trust in others and maintain trust in themselves. They had consciously given up progress, knowing that in the long run it was destructive of life. Anything that injured the earth, they said, could not be good for humanity.

He spent what seemed to him like months among them, until one day his grandmother said to him, "You not a ancestor yet."

"What do you mean?"

"I mean you still belong to the world where people hate, rob, and kill one another and do everything to keep you poor and hungry. What you seeing here is the life o the ancestors, and you not a ancestor yet."

"But Grandma, these people are alive."

"True, but I ha to sift through the half billion people o Africa just fo find eighty thousand what capable o this life. Actually, I come ten short of the eighty thousand. They just wasn't there. People like these here ha fo keep they opinions to theyselves, else when they neighbours find out how they is, they find ways fo get rid o them."

"So you created this just for me to see?"

"Yes. So you can see wha people could be if they only make the effort. The ancestors saw you looking for truth and they send me to teach it to you. Now, you see, is time for yo return."

It was as if she had vanished, and when he opened his eyes he was in darkness. It was a while before he readjusted to the cave and stopped confusing the land of reveries with the hard earth beneath him.

18

WHEN HE WAS FINALLY reoriented, he was aware of how thirsty and hungry he was. He got out of the bed to get water and found that he was almost unable to stand. He spilled a lot of water trying to lift the goblet to his mouth. He hoped Pointer Francis would soon descend and bring him some food. He laughed at this thought. He was again very much a part of the real world. He felt exhausted, completely drained, but relieved that the journey had ended and his sanity was still intact.

While he awaited Pointer Francis's coming he reflected on his epiphany. It was so different from the ones he had heard recounted at the canal bridge! He knew his enlightenment, compared to the celestial lights, diamond crowns, streets of gold, and musicians playing harps around God's throne that others talked about when they returned from their journey, would appear quite banal. But no one could doubt that he had made the passage successfully. He'd crossed the water, for one thing, and someone from the spirit world had guided him, and he'd had teachers in that world.

Pointer Francis entered the cave.

"Pointer Francis, I made it! I made it! I made it!" he said, sitting up in bed.

Within seconds he felt Pointer Francis's embrace. "I so happy for you.

"Now you know a little bit bout the truth concealed in the darkness o the human soul and some o the evil too. And you done examined a lot of what you have locked up in yo own soul—good and evil, useful and useless. Drink yo soup now, cause is two days you been on that journey. And you must be weak from that sea crossing. You will tell me bout it afterward."

He drank his soup with Pointer Francis helping him support the cup.

· "Give yoself another half hour," Pointer Francis told him.

"That was wonderful," Pointer Francis said when Jerome had finished recounting his experience.

"You find so, Pointer Francis? Even though I didn't see any shining lights or white robes or hear music in heaven?"

Pointer Francis chuckled. "When people come to me to make the journey, they already have a idea o where they want to go. My job is fo encourage them fo move on, over the boulders, and not fo fall off the edge o the road. Mos pilgrims end up in the heaven the Bible talk bout because that is the only one they know. What important is fo make the journey.

"I like yo heaven. It not no fairy tale. Is just what we could accomplish here on earth if we put aside we greediness and wickedness.

"Tomorrow, I will move you outta the cave and into the sacred room, and you will get yo first bath. That way we going to be able to ease you back into the real world.

"Anything you want fo know before I leave?"

There was a lot he would have liked to talk about, but he said, "It can wait until tomorrow."

The next morning Pointer Francis assisted him up the stairs to the cot that had been prepared for him in the sacred room. He exchanged the black blindfold for a white semi-translucent one.

That morning he had his first bath since descending into the cave. The zinc tub was filled with tea made from scores of herbs that the Esosusu healer had gathered and brewed. Mother Biddows and Deputy Pointer Andro officiated. They added water to the tub until it was almost to the rim. When he stepped out of the water, Deputy Pointer Andro towel-dried him and gave him a fresh robe.

He breakfasted immediately and noted that breakfast was more substantial, even though he could not eat most of it.

After lunch, which included a large portion of fish and several vegetables, Pointer Francis came to the sacred room and removed the blindfold. "You don need this now, as long as you still in here. You done see what it was to help you see. Now we have to ease you back to the world o the living. From now till Sunday you can keep if off when you inside and the windows closed.

"The Esosusu rejoicing going to be on Saturday evening. I will lead you there."

"You mean the one at the canal bridge?"

"No. That one is fo the public, and we holding that one Sunday evening. We have one that is specially fo members. That is when we make you one of us fo life and when you take the pledge fo respect the Esosusu way of life."

"Do I have to give an account of my journey there too?"

"Yes."

"Do I have to tell them everything?"

"No. All yo obstacles and stumbling block is yo own personal business. They say there been a time when every seeker had to tell everything, but that been before my time. And is just as well cause we is all flesh and blood, and whether we is Esosusu or not, we can't resist using a person weak points for make them feel smaller than they already is, even though all o we done do things we don want other people to know bout. All the obstacles you done pass over important fo you only."

At least ten minutes elapsed before he resumed speaking.

"One thing you must remember is you going back to live in the real world, with real people. And people with power can't resist using it, and in the real world the most important thing is to survive.

"Pointer Dublin tell me that a woman come to see him one time cause the estate owner son threaten to take away her job if she didn sleep with him. She had seven children and a sick mother to feed. He tell her to weigh everything, and if she can live with the result she must do what she think she could live with. She choose in favour of feeding her children and her mother. Who could blame her? But you must know why you make yo decision and you must know too that if things been otherwise, yo decision would o been different."

He thought for a while before saying, "I was really under the impression that we had to tell all. I feel, too, that by telling all, it would help me overcome many of the issues I have wrestled with."

"I will let you think bout that some more. Because you just come back from the journey, fresh and clean, you seeing the world a little bit like a little child. Think bout it and I sure you will agree with me that is better to keep those things to yoself.

"Is true that people is always growing, some faster, some slower. But most o the sistren and brethren ain't grown enough for understand why you is how you is and fo accept you as you is. I notice that is only when most people have a son or a daughter or a husband or a wife that is like that they stop ridiculing and start thinking." He paused. "All you have fo do is sum the whole thing up with, 'After many trials and tribulations…'"

The next day he was given another tea bath, and Pointer Francis spent a lot of time with him.

"You feel ready for pick up from where you left off?"

"How will I know that, Pointer Francis?"

Pointer Francis laughed.

"I've been thinking," he told Pointer Francis, "about changes I want to make to my life. I'll go and help to teach at the literacy centre near where I live. There's a sign up outside the building asking for volunteers and I think I could help in that way."

"That is a good start."

Silence grew between them. Not that it bothered him, for he had come to realize that Pointer Francis was a very patient man.

"The hardest part of the change is going to be my sexual life."

"I agree with you."

Again they lapsed into silence.

Pointer Francis broke it this time to tell him, "We going

have the last session tomorrow, excepting if you still have something fo say to me on Sunday," and then he left.

On Saturday morning he didn't get a bath. He would receive one in the afternoon, Deputy Pointer Andro told him.

Pointer Francis took him into the reception room for that day's session. The windows were closed, but there was considerably more light and at first his eyes ached.

"So, the end is drawing near," Pointer Francis said.

He nodded.

"Well, you is not to panic. In all things, let yo conscience be yo guide. Hurt no one. If you do, beg for pardon. When others hurt you, forgive them. When you meet people that delight in evil, keep way from them. Don forget, if you have any problems, I is here. Is true I don know how much longer the rain will wet me and the sun and the wind dry me. And when the earth see fit for receive me, Deputy Pointer Andro is here, and we already training Assistant Deputy Pointer Spring as a backup. I been training them fo accept people with all the faults that nature give us humans, though some that we think is faults is not really faults. The opposite is true too. So I think you will be able fo talk to them. And we careful how we choose the pointers. They have fo be people that slow to condemn, that try fo see the human being struggling fo deliver himself from evil."

Pointer Francis stopped talking and stared intently at him, as though he expected him to say something, but Jerome's mind was blank.

"You must keep cleaning yo soul to prevent evil from building up in it. You must be able to feed the person that already rob you—if you see that he need it. I know the Old Testament tell us that the sins o the fathers get visited on the children, but you mustn have a hand in that. Let every tub sit pon its own bottom.

"You is ready now, my son, to pick up the other journey. This time you know what the present is cause you done face the past."

He nodded.

Pointer Francis left to begin the preparations for that evening's rejoicing.

That afternoon, they soaked him for about thirty minutes in a tea with a gelatinous texture. Deputy Pointer Andro told him the names of thirty odd plants and shrubs that had been boiled to prepare it. He recognized only the prickly pear, the aloe, and the mint. In a second tub there was a thinner tea, like the one he had soaked in the past two days. He stayed about fifteen minutes in this. While he was in it, the first tub was emptied and refilled with clear spring water in which he rinsed.

"In every pore," Deputy Pointer Andro told him, "you must take in a little bit of everything that nature produces." Deputy Pointer Andro dried him and told him to lie flat on a blanket spread on the floor of the bathroom. He and Mother Biddows then massaged every part of his body with perfumed coconut oil. He heard Mother Biddows say, "You hear how he loving it." He realized then that he'd been chuckling.

Afterward they dressed him in white slacks and a white shirt. The brethren had donated the money to buy the fabric, buttons, and thread, and Sister Gertrude had sewn them. Deputy Pointer Andro told him that it was the usual custom.

19

POINTER FRANCIS LED HIM by the arm the short distance to the praise house. Once inside, Pointer Francis removed the mourner's veil. Jerome knew the praise house quite well. Like the mourning house, the praise house was circular and a massive pole at the centre was the mainstay of the entire structure, but the praise house was larger. The outer and inner walls were of mud and washed white with lime. The roof was thatched. The floor was of pressed earth. Rough-hewn benches, made by the Esosusu to fit the circular walls, occupied the front up to the central pole and, beyond the pole, both sides of the building, leaving an empty space in front of the altar.

The Esosusu members—about 150 of them, including his father, who sat in his wheelchair—were already present. About half of them were from Compton; the others came from the neighbouring villages. Other than the five mothers, whose headdresses were lilac, and the pointer and deputy members, who wore purple, black, or blue scarves about their white soutanes according to their rank, they were all dressed in white.

Pointer Francis and Jerome sat at the bottom of the altar on two chairs that had been placed there. Deputy Pointer Andro conducted the ceremony. The congregation sang:

We are glad for the riches of the earth.
We are glad for the riches of the earth.
We treasure them. We treasure them.

We are glad for the sun.
We are glad for the rain.
We are glad. We are glad.

We are glad for our joys.
We are glad for our pains.
We are glad. We are glad.

We are glad for our coming.
We'll be glad when we're going.
We are glad. We are glad.

Glad for the sun; glad for the rain;
Glad for our joys; glad for our pains;
Glad for our coming; glad for our going:
We are glad; we are glad.

The singing ended and the congregation sat down.

"Sisters and brothers," Deputy Pointer Andro stated, "we are gathered here this evening for the important event of deciding whether Jerome Quashee should be joined to the body of the Esosusu. I don't have to remind you how important it is to protect this body from corruption. But at the same time we have to let it grow and repair itself. As you all know, the spirits have to call us, and then the pointer has to direct us on the journey of self-understanding and revelation, and if we come back from that triumphant, then we meet the conditions.

310

"Jerome Quashee—whom we hope to call Brother Jerome Quashee in a short while—was visited by the spirit in this said praise house. Many of you were present when it happened. Pointer Francis guided him on the journey. And now I'm calling on Pointer Francis to give us his report."

Pointer Francis stood. "Sisters and Brothers, I got wonderful news for you all. The pilgrim was excellent. It was a wonderful journey. Only the usual difficulties." He sat.

"I now call on Jerome Quashee to give us an account of his voyage of enlightenment."

He rose and hesitated a little before telling them that, "after many trials and tribulations and much stumbling," he was transported across the water. He gave them a brief account of what he had seen and learned in the land across the water.

They listened attentively. In one of the front seats, a corpulent sister nodded her approval at various times.

As he was about to sit down, Sister Emily, the schoolteacher, dashed from her seat, up the aisle, and to the foot of the altar. She hugged him and said, "Well done, Brother!" At which point the congregation broke into song.

> *Oh well done, Brother!*
> *Good! Well done!*
> *Tell the story!*
> *Well done!*

She clasped him tightly around the waist and began to sway, eventually moving him into the space in front of the altar. The entire congregation assembled there and formed a singing and clapping ring about them. He remained in the centre and various members took turns swaying with him in the ring.

When the singing and dancing ended, they remained where they were. And Deputy Pointer Andro, now standing at the base of the altar, asked, "Does anybody have any objection why Jerome Quashee should not be joined to the body of the Esosusu?"

There was total silence.

"Does the congregation promise to provide Jerome Quashee with the spiritual and bodily support he will need to continue his journey through life until Mother Earth reclaims him?"

"We do," they chorused.

"Jerome Quashee, it is my understanding that Pointer Francis instructed you in all our beliefs and duties to one another?"

"Yes," he said.

"Do you intend to respect and obey them"

"Yes."

Deputy Pointer Andro led him into the aisle. "I now declare Jerome Quashee a living part of the Esosusu body. May he be true to our principles, may his actions keep this body healthy, and may we do all that is in our power to keep him operating properly."

"Amen!" the congregation said.

"Brother Jerome," Deputy Pointer Andro said, thrusting forward his right hand, "with this right hand of fellowship, I declare you a living part of the Esosusu body. I now invite the congregation to do likewise."

He shook Deputy Pointer Andro's hand and one by one he shook the hands of the congregation. The last person to come was his father. They were both crying as they embraced.

Various members began clearing the seats on the right side of the praise house and others slipped out of the building. Soon a large table was set up with pots of stewed goat, rice and peas, and vegetables—including the sacred breadfruit—and buckets of mauby and ginger beer.

They ate and talked and welcomed and encouraged him and shared snippets of their own journeys and their induction ceremonies until late into the evening, when Pointer Francis led him blindfolded back to the sacred room.

Early the next evening, Pointer Francis led him to the canal bridge clearing for the public rejoicing. Because of the blindfold he had no idea until the singing started how many people had come.

They sang and chanted prayers for a while, and then Pointer Francis told them that Brother Jerome Quashee had returned triumphantly "from the voyage to the other side. We Spirituals is proud of him, and I know you is too, cause he spring from the womb of Compton. I now call on our dear Brother Jerome to give you all a reckoning of his enlightenment."

It was easier to speak with the blindfold on and because he had given an identical account the night before. Still he would have liked to see their faces to see how they were reacting. Occasionally, he heard a few amens after repeating the wisdom of Chief Nfolo. When he ended, the thunderous applause he received told him his fears had been unfounded. He was forever underestimating his people.

Pointer Francis removed the blindfold officially and re-stored him to the everyday world. It was like a weight removed, as if his wholeness had been restored.

He was dazed and humbled by the sea of faces around. The people had certainly come to welcome him back. His first impulse was to seek out his mother, who was waving at him from the first line where onlookers encircled the Spirituals. A little farther back he saw an arm raised above the heads of the crowd, waving at him, and wondered whose it was. The light from the Coleman lamps suspended on poles in the ritual space was strong enough for him to see that it was a white person's hand, and he suspected it was Pastor O come to welcome him back. It was a touching gesture.

The rejoicing now took on a joyful atmosphere. They sang—Spirituals and onlookers—and rocked to the spirituals "Michael, Roll the Boat Ashore," "If I Had the Wings of a Dove," "Work on Believers like a Light upon Mount Zion Hill." The spirit came and filled them, and they jumped and danced and shouted.

When he was released from the influence of the spirit, he saw Deputy Pointer Andro and Assistant Deputy Pointer Spring attempting to restrain Pastor O, who was flapping and quivering on the ground under the influence of the spirit that had entered him and drawn him into the Spiritual circle.

When the ceremony ended, Pointer Francis, Deputy Pointer Andro, and Assistant Deputy Pointer Spring accompanied him, along with his mother and father, whom String was pushing in his wheelchair, back to his parents' house. They were all silent. He was full of joy and inner peace. As they got to the door of his parents' house, Pointer Francis said, "Strange thing happen tonight. Fo over fifteen years that American White man been after me to point him but the spirit didn ever go near him. It got him tonight though. That was a powerful possession."

They said goodnight and he entered the house. He was ecstatic, glad for all that had happened. He remained awake for several hours, at first going over in his mind bits and pieces of what he had experienced. But, toward the end, he felt the beginnings of fear. Pointer Francis would not be there to guide him through the life that was to resume tomorrow. Well, we simply learned by going where we had to go. The last thing he remembered before he fell asleep was one of the statements he had written down: "Life is hardly more than a metastasized cancer, the tumours blunting the surgeon's knife: taking care of the pain is probably all, the only thing, that matters." *Old clothes upon sticks to scare birds.*

AFTERWORD

Usually, I become tongue-tied when I'm asked to talk about my writing. This is in some way related to my belief that a published book is the property of its readers, for it's the convergence of the reader's reality and the book's content that constitutes the reading experience. I therefore feel I shouldn't tamper with it. But my publisher has asked me to reflect on *Spirits in the Dark* on its thirtieth birthday, and I'll attempt to do so.

Spirits in the Dark emerged from a series of short stories I began to write in the early nineteen eighties. At the time a couple of questions obsessed me: why weren't Caribbean writers exploring the vast range of complex issues impacting the Caribbean; and, ontologically speaking, who was/is a West Indian.

The stories did not emerge from a conscious desire to write fiction. I had been writing poetry since 1975 and didn't feel any initial compulsion to write fiction. Moreover, in the early 1980s, I was a full-time secondary-school teacher and a part-time PHD student. There shouldn't have been room in my gruelling schedule for the serious contemplation and attention to craft that are prerequisites for creating meaningful fiction. But, beginning in 1981, night after night, the plots of *Spirits in the Dark* and the stories in *How Loud Can the Village Cock Crow?*

took hold of me and kept me awake sometimes until three AM. They demanded to be written down. In 1983, I took a leave of absence to work on my doctorate, but before I could do so, *Spirits in the Dark* held me in its thrall. It was only after writing the first version that I was able to proceed with my doctoral studies.

Intertwined with the foregoing was my luck to be a student at Université de Montréal while the novelist Hugh Hood was a professor in the English Studies Department. I never took a course with him, yet, of all the professors in the department, apart from my dissertation adviser, he was of most help to me. In 1982, in a chance encounter in the English Studies office, we conversed about the use of ritual in Anglophone African literature, and he took the opportunity to ask me if I wrote. I told him yes. "Bring some of it and let me see," he replied, his eyes glowing. Three days later I sat in his office while he read three of my short stories. He said they were good and gave me some advice which today I'm ambivalent about: "Don't send them out. Wait until you have a collection and submit them to a publisher." In 1983, he accepted to read the first version of *Spirits in the Dark.* He felt that it was publishable and offered to talk with Simon Dardick at Véhicule Press about publishing it. I hesitated. He'd told me that the manuscript covered some well-trod ground. I wanted *Spirits in the Dark* to be original. Some months later, he informed me that he would be the guest editor of an upcoming issue of *Rubicon* and suggested that I submit the section that has since appeared in print under the title "From Spirits in the Dark." That issue of *Rubicon* was republished by Véhicule Press in 1984 as the anthology: *Fatal Recurrences: New Fiction in English from Montreal.*

In 1988, Université Laval hired me as a university professor. This was opportune. A professor's flexible schedule gave me more time to write. Even though I hadn't written much fiction or poetry from 1983 on, I'd made notes for a revamping of *Spirits in the Dark* and for *Behind the Face of Winter,* my second novel.

The present incarnation of *Spirits in the Dark* was written over the summer of 1990. My memory (which could be faulty) tells me that I discarded all but fifty or sixty pages of the first version. (That version is in the Austin Clarke Papers at MacMaster University.) The abundance of purple prose in the initial version seemed incongruous to the novel's themes, so I opted for as banal a style as possible (Vicky Unwin, the publisher of Heinemann's Caribbean Writers' Series described it as "bloodless grammatically correct sentences"). I decided too to evaluate key moments of Jerome's early life according to what he knew then and what he knew at age 45. The later reflections appear in italics. I also let the story lead where it would, and it took me on an exploration of the second question mentioned above: Ontologically speaking, who is a West Indian? The research I did for my PHD thesis, which became the book, *From Folklore to Fiction: A Study of Folk Heroes and Rituals in the Black American Novel,* offered me profound insights into African diasporic ways of being. Also, in the interim I'd read three novels that showed me how others used myth and ritual to structure their narratives and imbue them with meaning: Leslie Marmon Silko's *Ceremony,* Toni Cade Bambara's *The Salt Eaters,* and Toni Morrison's *Song of Solomon.* A fourth novel, Earl Lovelace's *Wine of Astonishment,* reassured me that Caribbean beliefs and rituals could yield viable fiction.

Choosing the Spiritual Baptist religion as a locus for the narrative came easily. From about the age of seven I was fascinated by those people who were the poorest members of my village; they worked during the sugar-cane and arrowroot harvests and survived mysteriously in between. From the time of slavery until 1956, the Spiritual Baptist religion had been outlawed. A prerequisite for membership in the religion was the mourning ritual. As I describe it in the novel, the mourning ritual culminated with a celebratory recounting of the "mourner's journey." But not all journeys ended thus. There were transgressions the mourners had to overcome, and if they didn't there was no celebration. This was considered a disgrace and the person could became a pariah.

I had first-hand knowledge of this. When I was about eight, one Sunday around four AM, two women, one wearing blindfold, came to my grandparents' home where I lived then. The blindfolded woman had been my grandfather's mistress during the Great Depression. He'd stopped supporting his wife and children and transferred his resources to her household. "Mrs. Dickson," the blindfolded woman said to my grandmother, "I am on mourning ground and I can't get clearance. I'm here to beg for your forgiveness for all the suffering I caused you." Calling her by name, my grandmother said she'd forgiven her. That woman had no rejoicing. Moreover, she returned from "mourning ground" insane and remained so until her death. Along with the maxim, "Married woman eyewater blight those that cause it," she was mentioned often to caution women who were the mistresses of married men.

Compared to the stories writers tell about the numerous rejections they received, getting *Spirits in the Dark* published was relatively easy. At the time, Anglophone Caribbean writers sent their manuscripts to Heinemann, which had a Caribbean Writers' Series imprint. I'd met the publisher of the series at a conference I attended and told her about the manuscript. She advised me to send it. About a month later she replied that Heinemann couldn't publish it, that they wanted their books to be eligible for inclusion in the Caribbean high school literature curriculum; because of its gay content *Spirits in the Dark* would enrage Caribbean parents, hence they wouldn't publish it. She was right about the antipathy to the novel's gay content. A friend who'd read the manuscript had advised me to remove the same-sex content. In 1991 I sent the manuscript to Penguin UK. They praised it and forwarded it to Penguin Canada. Penguin Canada sent me the reader's report—it was highly favourable—along with their regret that they couldn't publish it because they felt it was imprudent to publish an unknown writer in the midst of a recession. If, however, I didn't find a publisher within a year, they might reconsider their decision. It was then that my mind turned again to Hugh Hood. He read the manuscript, recommended it to House of Anansi, and shortly afterwards I received a contract.

I knew very little about publishing and the book industry anywhere. I bought books and read them; that was it. I was about to find out. I'd learned one thing only from the publication of my first book five years earlier: that before quoting a text, one had not only to secure permission, but also pay a fee and donate a copy of the book to the publisher, all at the author's expense. One good thing that happened was that Anansi convinced Heinemann, whose books, Anansi's parent company, General Publishing, distributed in Canada, to co-publish *Spirits in the*

Dark. The Heinemann UK and the US editions came out a year later, 1994.

Anansi's publisher was very enthusiastic about the book. He told me to keep my fingers warm for the launch that would take place at the Eden Mills Literary Festival in 1993. I enviously watched the long lines of people waiting to have their books signed. I signed five copies that day. The only Canadian review that *Spirits in the Dark* received was in the *Montreal Gazette* and that came only after it was shortlisted for the Hugh MacLennan Fiction Prize. That nomination too earned me two CBC Radio interviews, one local and one national.

The Heinemann edition was favourably reviewed in the *Times Literary Supplement* and in *Sunshine,* a magazine published by the Nation newspaper in Barbados. Heinemann organized a book tour for me in England. Almost instantly I began to receive emails from students who were studying the book in postcolonial literature or in queer studies. Those courses accounted for almost all of the book sales. Eventually critics began to write about it. Although out of print for more than a decade, *Spirits in the Dark* still has a presence in postcolonial and queer-studies syllabi.

Re-reading the entire text for the first time in thirty years, I'm aware that I couldn't have written this novel in my twenties or early thirties. I hadn't yet distilled existence sufficiently to do so. In its subthemes I see the nuclei of all my novels written since. I note too that Comsie is the only one of my mother characters who isn't psychically flawed. Overall, Henry too is a decent, responsible father, the least flawed of my father characters.

I'm often asked about the autobiographical content of my books. Over my objections, one critic, Alan McLeod, insisted that *Spirits in the Dark* is autobiographical. As far as I know, autobiography is present only in the impulse for transcendence that some of my major characters embody. I had seen how colonialism wounded my father, how he in turn wounded his family, and how his children replicated those wounds; but when I turned to fiction, it was mostly to uncover the hidden wounds of the educated Caribbean class. I write fiction to discover, to pull out meaning from the cracks and crevices where it's concealed. My imagination seems to restrict the nuts and bolts of autobiography to poetry.

There are a couple of minor changes in this edition. I've tried to make the Caribbean vernacular more accessible to non-West Indian readers. Here and there I've improved the punctuation and modified the odd sentence. If I were writing this novel today, most of the italicized passages would be in the present tense and unitalicized.

I am deeply grateful to publisher Simon Dardick, and to Dimitri Nasrallah, editor of Esplanade, the fiction imprint at Véhicule Press, for this republication of *Spirits in the Dark*; to fellow writer Kaie Kellough for his thoughtful and appreciative introduction to this edition; and to the professors in Europe, North America, and the Caribbean who've included *Spirits in the Dark* in their courses.

ESPLANADE
Books

A House by the Sea : A novel by Sikeena Karmali
A Short Journey by Car : Stories by Liam Durcan
Seventeen Tomatoes : Tales from Kashmir : Stories by Jaspreet Singh
Garbage Head : A novel by Christopher Willard
The Rent Collector : A novel by B. Glen Rotchin
Dead Man's Float : A novel by Nicholas Maes
Optique : Stories by Clayton Bailey
Out of Cleveland : Stories by Lolette Kuby
Pardon Our Monsters : Stories by Andrew Hood
Chef : A novel by Jaspreet Singh
Orfeo : A novel by Hans-Jürgen Greif
[Translated from the French by Fred A. Reed]
Anna's Shadow : A novel by David Manicom
Sundre : A novel by Christopher Willard
Animals : A novel by Don LePan
Writing Personals : A novel by Lolette Kuby
Niko : A novel by Dimitri Nasrallah
Stopping for Strangers : Stories by Daniel Griffin
The Love Monster : A novel by Missy Marston
A Message for the Emperor : A novel by Mark Frutkin
New Tab : A novel by Guillaume Morissette
Swing in the House : Stories by Anita Anand
Breathing Lessons : A novel by Andy Sinclair
Ex-Yu : Stories by Josip Novakovich
The Goddess of Fireflies : A novel by Geneviève Pettersen
[Translated from the French by Neil Smith]
All That Sang : A novella by Lydia Perović
Hungary-Hollywood Express : A novel by Éric Plamondon
[Translated from the French by Dimitri Nasrallah]
English is Not a Magic Language : A novel by Jacques Poulin
[Translated from the French by Sheila Fischman]

Tumbleweed : Stories by Josip Novakovich
A Three-Tiered Pastel Dream : Stories by Lesley Trites
Sun of a Distant Land : A novel by David Bouchet
[Translated from the French by Claire Holden Rothman]
The Original Face : A novel by Guillaume Morissette
The Bleeds : A novel by Dimitri Nasrallah
Nirliit : A novel by Juliana Léveillé-Trudel
[Translated from the French by Anita Anand]
The Deserters : A novel by Pamela Mulloy
Mayonnaise : A novel by Éric Plamondon
[Translated from the French by Dimitri Nasrallah]
The Teardown : A novel by David Homel
Apple S : A novel by Éric Plamondon
[Translated from the French by Dimitri Nasrallah]
Aphelia : A novel by Mikella Nicol
[Translated from the French by Lesley Trites]
Dominoes at the Crossroads : Stories by Kaie Kellough
Swallowed : A novel by Réjean Ducharme
[Translated from the French by Madeleine Stratford]
Book of Wings : A novel by Tawhida Tanya Evanson
The Geography of Pluto : A novel by Christopher DiRaddo
The Family Way : A novel by Christopher DiRaddo
Fear the Mirror : Stories by Cora Siré
Open Your Heart : A novel by Alexie Morin
[Translated from the French by Aimee Wall]
Hotline : A novel by Dimitri Nasrallah
Prophetess : A novel by Baharan Baniahmadi
A House Without Spirits : A novel by David Homel
Dandelion Daughter : A novel by Gabrielle Boulianne-Tremblay
[Translated from the French by Eli Tareq El Bechelany-Lynch]
Because : A novel by Andrew Steinmetz
Spirits in the Dark : A novel by H. Nigel Thomas